8/20

Hayner PLD/Large Print
Overdues .10/day. Max fine cost of
item. Lost or damaged item: additional
$5 service charge.

ENAMORED

Center Point
Large Print

Also by J. S. Scott and available from
Center Point Large Print:

Entangled
Ensnared

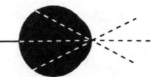

ENAMORED

THE ACCIDENTAL BILLIONAIRES

BOOK THREE

J. S. SCOTT

CENTER POINT LARGE PRINT
THORNDIKE, MAINE

This Center Point Large Print edition
is published in the year 2020 by arrangement with
Amazon Publishing, www.apub.com.

The text of this Large Print edition is unabridged.
In other aspects, this book may vary
from the original edition.
Printed in the United States of America
on permanent paper.
Set in 16-point Times New Roman type.

ISBN: 978-1-64358-553-6

The Library of Congress has cataloged this record
under Library of Congress Control Number: 2019956936

As I'm finishing this book, I'm coming up on the second anniversary of my sister's death. It's merely two days away, and I still miss her as much as I did right after her sudden departure from this world.

So this book is for my sister, Beth. I miss you, Sissy, and I hope you're somewhere watching when this title is released.

All my love,
Jan

CHAPTER 1
Seth

"Just turn that damn property into a wildlife refuge, Seth," my sister Jade said as she stopped directly in front of my desk. It was hard *not* to notice the displeasure on her face as she continued, "The birds on your land are *endangered*. They don't need to lose their new nesting site."

"Hello, and nice to see you, too, little sister," I said drily. *Damn!* Didn't I deserve *some kind* of greeting before she started to rip me a new asshole? She'd just bulldozed her way into my office, and *immediately* proceeded to talk about a subject I really *didn't* want to discuss. I had no desire to talk about my beachfront-property acquisition. Truth be told, I'd been hoping she'd *never* hear about the property I'd purchased or discover that endangered birds had taken up residence there right after I'd bought it.

Obviously . . . she heard.

Jade just kept glaring at me, which told me that she wasn't about to be deterred from her apparent mission.

I knew *that* look. I'd helped raise my little sister, so I was well aware of how stubborn she could be when it came to wildlife preservation.

This time I'm absolutely going to say no to my younger sister.

Regardless of Jade's outrage, I'd be damned if I was going to lose millions of dollars because some birds had decided to use the prime coastal land I'd purchased as their new nesting site.

Jade wasn't the first person to object to me building a resort on that beachfront location. Some tree-hugger female attorney was also trying to make my life miserable over starting construction on that property, because it had become the nesting spot for a colony of threatened feathered creatures. I'd fought a legal battle with Riley Montgomery *all summer*—a battle I *intended to win.*

After months of legal bullshit, I really didn't want to argue with my little sister about it, too.

I leaned back in my office chair, determined not to let Jade talk me out of the property I'd spent a small fortune on. "The birds are gone," I told her irritably.

Okay, they *might* come back *next* nesting season, but I didn't see how that was *my* problem. I'd waited until the damn birds had laid eggs, nurtured their young, and finally vacated the property just last month. Now that summer was over, and my sister's feathered friends had flown off to a warmer climate for the winter, I wanted to move ahead with the resort I planned on building on the beach.

The construction had already been delayed long

enough. In fact, I thought I should get some kind of award for my patience. Sinclair Properties was a pretty new company, and the deal would mean further growth for my fledgling corporation.

Jade crossed her arms over her chest. "The majority of the species *will* come back next year," she argued.

Okay, I wasn't *completely* heartless. Well, *not really*. But this was the *first year* the endangered species had found their way to this beach. So they could very easily find another spot next year, right?

"Not if I can help it," I grumbled. I was hoping I could finally get the building permit that had been on hold for months. Once my project *was* completely in motion, I had a feeling the birds would avoid the site in the future.

Riley Montgomery, the pain-in-the-ass attorney who seemed to have a thing about saving endangered birds, had apparently made my wildlife-conservationist sister into her ally.

How else would Jade have found out about the situation? I sure as hell hadn't told Eli, her husband. And my brother Aiden was sworn to secrecy about the bird thing.

Obviously, this new *friendship*—or whatever the hell it was—between Jade and Riley had happened recently, because my sister hadn't mentioned the bird situation . . . until she'd come busting into my office today.

"So Riley got to you?" I guessed.

"I heard about this from her, yes. I wish I had heard about it from *you*."

"Couldn't," I informed her. "I knew we'd end up fighting just like this."

"What in the hell is wrong with you, Seth? You haven't always been this callous. In fact, you *used to be* a really nice guy." Jade let out a huff of frustration.

Yeah, well, I didn't *use to be* one of the richest men in the world, either. When I'd been poor, it hadn't mattered if I had a heart.

Now, I was a businessman with a company to grow, and I *had* to be ruthless. It was *necessary* in my business.

I'd recently discovered I was pretty damn good at being a dick when it came to business.

I was a property developer, and Sinclair Properties was quickly becoming a force to be reckoned with in commercial real estate. I couldn't afford to be a damn bleeding heart.

I ignored my sister's question. "I'm not giving up that property, Jade," I said tersely. "It's a prime building lot right on the beach. There aren't many of those spots available anymore."

The small city of Citrus Beach was growing rapidly. With its proximity to San Diego, it was bound to happen sooner or later. The area was becoming the place to be when one wanted to hit the beach.

"So your stupid resort is more important than killing off an entire species?"

I shot her a disgusted look, something I rarely did with my younger sister. Then again, Jade was usually a lot more even-tempered. She only got this tenacious when it came to killing off endangered species. "They can go nest somewhere else next season."

"They came *here* because they probably lost their previous spot to some jerk who didn't care that they were about to become extinct."

Okay, *that* hurt a little. I was used to my younger siblings looking up to me as a somewhat paternal figure. Me, and my brothers Aiden and Noah, had been the only parent figures my three younger siblings had ever really had. Jade had certainly never referred to me as a *jerk*. She used to idolize me.

Guess those days are gone.

Of course, Jade was no longer a kid. Hadn't been for a long time. There actually weren't *that many* years between us. Jade was highly educated, with a doctorate in wildlife conservation, and was now married to a very powerful billionaire, a guy who also just happened to be my mentor and silent partner, Eli Stone.

At least she hadn't mentioned this to . . .

"I'm going to talk to Eli," she threatened, immediately nullifying my previous thought.

So much for *not* using her husband as a weapon.

Just when I'd been thinking that she wasn't going to throw Eli in my face, she . . . did.

Truth was, I *needed* Eli's advice. Often. That's what happens when a guy goes from being a construction worker to a billionaire in a matter of minutes.

Up until the current moment, Eli and I had worked well together. My brother-in-law had his own business to run in San Diego, but he always made time to help me out.

I wasn't seasoned enough yet to go it on my own. Problem was, Eli adored Jade and worshipped the ground that my little sister walked on. If Jade even hinted that she wanted something, Eli would find a way to get it for her.

My property doesn't stand a chance if Eli gets involved.

I shrugged. "Do what you have to do. I've already argued this with the tree hugger a million times."

"Riley is not a *tree hugger*," Jade said defensively. "She's a highly respected attorney who champions endangered wildlife."

I lifted a brow. "Which means *she is* a tree hugger."

"Then so am I," she said, sounding indignant. "And I'm not ashamed of trying to protect *any* endangered species, nor am I about to apologize because I care about the environment."

I raked a hand through my hair in frustration.

"There's nothing wrong with that, Jade. But giving up a deal this lucrative would be crazy."

"It's not crazy," she said in a softer tone. "It would be the right thing to do. And I really don't want to be forced to put my husband at odds with my own brother. I know you two are close. Honestly, if you give up the land and make it a wildlife refuge, you'd never even miss the money. If you want, I'll buy it from you."

"Not happening," I said brusquely.

Not that my billionaire sister and my billionaire brother-in-law couldn't afford to drop what for them would be a minuscule amount of funds on some land. *That* wasn't the point. My issue was that I could never take a dime from Jade, and she probably knew it.

"Then I guess I'll just encourage Riley to keep fighting this through legal channels," Jade said in a snippy voice I'd never heard come out of her mouth before.

"When in the hell did you two get so chummy?" I asked unhappily.

Jade frowned. "She didn't come *to me,* if that's what you're thinking. I actually sought *her* out after I read an interview with her in the *Citrus Beach News.* I was having a hard time believing that the brother *I knew* was going to put a stupid piece of land over an endangered species. My plan was to tell her off about making you a villain, initially."

I smirked. I'd read the damn article in the local paper last week. Riley Montgomery hadn't exactly painted me as a benevolent business owner. "And then?"

"Then I saw all the legal paperwork and realized you really were being a jerk."

"So you decided to come here to talk me into giving the whole project up?"

She chewed on her bottom lip, a habit she'd had since she was a child. "I'd hoped I could. Money has never been all that important to you, really."

My sister was *wrong*. Maybe I'd never dreamed of being as rich as I was now, but I'd damn well wished I'd had more funds when my brothers and I had been busting our asses earlier in life to raise our younger siblings. We'd barely been able to keep food on the table.

"It isn't all about the money," I told her irritably. "Sinclair Properties is still growing, and it can't take that kind of hit."

She frowned. "But *you* can. You'd never even miss the money."

"That's not the point." She was right. My personal accounts kept growing larger every single day because I had invested my billions of dollars well.

"You're being deliberately pigheaded," Jade accused.

"Guilty," I answered, trying to be nonchalant.

My secretary knocked on the open door. "Mr.

Sinclair? Your two o'clock meeting is on the phone."

"I have to take this," I said to my sister abruptly.

Jesus! I needed to get my little sister gone before I caved in and gave her the damn property. I'd always been a sucker for both of my younger sisters. They rarely asked for anything, but when they did, I was screwed. It was difficult to be hard-nosed when I knew this land meant so much to Jade. Especially when I could easily afford to give it up.

Logically, I wasn't really sure why I *hadn't* already capitulated a long time ago, why I'd dug my heels in so hard about the whole situation.

Donating the land would be a very tiny drop in the bucket for me, personally.

Jade sighed. "At least tell me you'll think about it."

I nodded sharply. "I'll think about it."

My sister turned on her heel and left my office without even saying good-bye.

I released a long breath of relief, feeling guilty because I hadn't let Jade have exactly what she wanted.

My brain balked at the idea of simply blowing off the building site, maybe because I knew Sinclair Properties could use that location.

Bullshit! Be honest. This isn't even about the business. I know exactly why I'm being a stubborn asshole.

15

Yeah, I *did* want to build Sinclair Properties into a billion-dollar corporation, and I was well on my way to doing that.

However, what was making me hold on to my obstinance had very little to do with *money*.

And *very much* to do with the stubborn redheaded hellcat attorney who was doing everything possible to keep me from building my beachside resort.

Over the months, I'd found myself enjoying the email sparring that we'd been doing at least a few times a week.

Little by little, it had turned just a bit more . . . personal. At least for me. Not that Riley had become any more *pleasant;* she was a major challenge. I had to wonder if *that* was why I enjoyed our exchanges so damn much.

She was highly intelligent.

Ornery.

Stubborn.

And so damn beautiful that just thinking about her made my dick hard.

I'd only met her once in person. *One time.* And she'd made one hell of an impression on me.

For some reason, she'd plopped her gorgeous ass down across from me at a local coffeehouse, chasing away a woman who had only been throwing herself at me because I was now a billionaire.

Somehow, Riley had sensed my discomfort

that day, my hesitation to be rude to any female, even though I'd known the woman had only been interested in me because of my brand-new ultrawealthy status. Although we didn't know each other, Riley had intervened, pretending to be my girlfriend to make the clingy female go away.

When I'd been a construction worker, not a single female had been interested in a *relationship*. Sure, they'd have a *one-nighter* with me if I'd wanted that. But they'd leave the next day, moving on to greener pastures. And I mean *green*—like in . . . money. They'd all wanted a lot more of it than I'd had back then.

Now, I couldn't get away from the female sex. It seemed like every single one of the women who approached me was now interested in a long-term relationship with a *billionaire*.

Riley Montgomery had been completely . . . different.

She hadn't wanted *anything*.

In fact, she'd helped me out.

Her actions had been purely selfless.

Until we'd realized each other's identities.

It had pretty much gone to hell *after that*.

I clicked on the space bar of my computer, bringing up the latest email I'd gotten from Riley.

I'd been getting ready to answer it when Jade had barged into my office.

Okay, maybe I *was* being an asshole, but

17

if I gave up the land without a fight, Riley Montgomery would have no reason to ever contact me again.

And *that* would be a damn shame.

I grinned, knowing I'd reply to her missive right after my two o'clock appointment.

I picked up the call to get my meeting underway, still wondering what I'd say to Riley.

CHAPTER 2
Riley

Dear Ms. Montgomery:

First, although I'd very much like to kiss your ass as you suggested, I could think of several other places I'd love to put my mouth on first if I could get you naked.

Second, my sister Jade visited my office today. Apparently, she's become one of your allies. If you think she'll help your cause, believe me, she won't.

Third, the birds you worried so much about are now gone, which means I can proceed and get my building permit.

Like I've mentioned before, I'd be more than happy to discuss this situation in person. Let me know when your schedule permits a face-to-face meeting.

Also, in response to your question about whether or not I'm capable of reading, I can, but I often don't. Since I was raising my younger siblings during my adolescence and most of my adulthood, I've had very little time for books.

Sincerely,
Seth Sinclair
CEO
Sinclair Properties, Inc.

"Jackass!" I growled out loud as I slammed my fist on my desk, something I did nearly *every time* I got an email from Sinclair.

Refusing to think about the inappropriate communication I'd just received from the most annoying, irritating, cold-blooded male I'd ever had the misfortune of meeting, I rose from my seat in my home office.

"Tea. I need a cup of tea," I mumbled as I made my way to the kitchen.

Honestly, my blood was *still* boiling from reading his email. But what really pissed me off was the fact that I knew my face was still pink from his suggestive comments.

I can't let him get to me.

I was a professional. I shouldn't be blushing like a ridiculous teenage girl just because some jackass was throwing suggestive comments out by email.

How does he manage to turn every insult into something sexual?

I shoved a mug underneath my coffeemaker to get hot water for my tea.

Okay, maybe not *every* hateful comment I wrote to him became a sexual innuendo. Lately, he'd made it a point to write something about himself at the end of each communication, being deliberately obtuse about the true meaning of my words.

Can't you read well, Mr. Sinclair?

That had been my original jab.

He'd turned it into an answer that had *nothing to do* with my put-down.

I frowned as I dropped the bag of tea into my mug.

Seth Sinclair was presumptuous. I didn't *want* to get to know him.

Then why does the fact that he gave up everything to take care of his younger siblings leave me with more questions I really want to ask?

Occasionally, when he was nice to me, I dropped a tidbit or two about myself, too. In between contemptuous remarks, of course.

I added a small amount of milk to my tea, and a ton of sugar. Just the way I liked it. I leaned my hip against the kitchen counter and took a sip.

Ahhh . . . bliss. Not as good as the chai mocha lattes that I drank way too much of from the Coffee Shack. But any strong, hot, sweetened tea would do in a pinch. It helped calm the desire to slug Sinclair for his current email.

For months, I'd managed to be professional

with Seth Sinclair. I wasn't even sure how my emails to him had become personally insulting—with some tiny fact about myself mixed in at the very end.

Maybe because *he'd* started it.

Well, not the *insults,* because he never really seemed to lose his temper and write something insulting, but the dropping of a little bit of personal information in each email.

So, he isn't a reader.

That was understandable if every moment of his day had been filled with working, sleeping, or taking care of his family, I supposed.

I kept sipping at my tea, telling myself that I *didn't* give a damn about *his life.*

All I wanted was for him to cease his plans to build on land that would probably see the return of the least tern birds again the following year.

Their situation was *critical*.

As a serious environmental and wildlife-conservation attorney, achieving my goal of protecting their habitat was my primary mission.

However, I was disappointed with myself that I'd lost my cool more than once while I was defending the birds.

I hadn't *ever* resorted to personal insults while I was in a legal battle, until I'd met Seth Sinclair. The cheap shots I'd directed at him weren't the way I did business at all.

It wasn't professional, and I was generally a

powerhouse at my job. In fact, I was downright anal about always keeping a very distant demeanor when dealing with the opposition.

But just this once . . . I *was* failing to keep things strictly business.

Dammit!

Maybe I *should* have met with Seth Sinclair in person. But I'd avoided it so far.

Months ago, we'd met up by chance in a coffee shop. I'd discovered that *one* encounter with him had been *more than enough*. I'd been mildly attracted to him, which was also something I'd never experienced in business. And shouldn't.

I smirked as I wondered how he would feel when he found out I'd actually purchased Jade's small cottage on the beach.

I hadn't *meant* to buy it, but when I'd met with Seth's sister, I'd fallen in love with this cozy home near the sand. And when I'd found out it was for sale, I'd jumped at the chance to own it.

My phone suddenly blasted a vintage rock-and-roll song, and I picked it up from the counter.

"Hello, Mother," I said unenthusiastically.

"Margaret," she said in her usual cold tone. "I've been trying to reach you for days."

I rolled my eyes.

Margaret Riley Montgomery was my legal name, but I'd gone by Riley since I was a child. Even though I'd asked my mother a million times to use my middle name, she'd ignored me.

For the most part, I'd given up.

"I've been busy," I told her.

"Too busy to speak with your mother?" she chastised. "I was calling about an event. Eli Stone is holding a fund-raiser. I think you should come."

That was the problem. My only parent was *always* calling about some haughty party that I almost always tried to avoid. I'd been my mother's disappointing child, but things had gotten even worse since I'd put my education to work preserving endangered species, and she never let me forget it.

"Let me guess . . . there's some insanely rich man you want me to meet?" I asked drily.

She still thinks if I'm attached to a highly successful male that it will give me a bigger social advantage?

I let go of a quiet sigh. It wasn't like I didn't know that she disapproved of the fact that I hadn't used my Harvard Law School education to be upwardly mobile in the corporate world. In fact, I was used to her pointing out every single mistake I made.

Including the fact that I was nearly thirty, *still* single, and not searching for a guy to validate me.

"I'm already planning on attending," I finally answered. "I'm acquainted with Jade Stone."

The fund-raiser was being hosted by Jade's

philanthropist husband, Eli Stone, and would benefit Jade's research lab in San Diego. For that reason alone, I'd decided to attend.

"You are coming?" my mother asked. "Well, of course, you and Jade are both interested in rare animals. But since Jade is attached to a man like Eli Stone, she's able to indulge in whatever *hobbies* she wants."

"It's not her *hobby,* Mother. She has her own research lab in San Diego now. She's *Dr. Stone.* And the work she's doing to preserve the DNA of nearly extinct species is groundbreaking and important."

"Personally, I think her career choice was unfortunate," my mother answered loftily. "She's obviously a smart woman. There were so many other career paths she could have followed."

Just like me.

"Maybe she likes what she does," I argued, although I knew it was fruitless to even bother.

My mother was never going to understand that some people followed their own hearts and their own dreams.

For her, there was only upward social mobility, something I'd never cared about. *At all. Ever.*

"Like your father always said, there's room for diversion *after* success," she answered in a snobby voice I'd always hated. "Look at your brothers. They've all used their connections to become more successful over the last year.

25

Hostesses everywhere are just dying to have them attend one of their events. Granted, they didn't start out making good decisions, but they're fully focused on their business now."

I shuddered. God, I hated it when she parroted my deceased father.

And yes, all of my three older brothers *were* billionaires. But it had nothing to do with their social connections. They hated social functions as much as I did. Maybe even more. And their achievements had come at a high emotional cost.

"I'll be there," I confirmed, wanting more than anything to get off the telephone with my mother. I'd learned to tolerate her criticism, but all of her little barbed comments still made me feel small.

"What gown are you wearing?" she questioned. "Surely you aren't coming in your usual . . . attire."

Since my normal clothing included sturdy jeans and a few power suits for when I had to appear in court or at meetings, she knew damn well I wasn't wearing either one of those to a social affair.

"I'll let you know when I decide," I mumbled, knowing I'd have to purchase something new, since I hadn't attended an affair with the San Diego elite in some time.

Once, I'd tried to be the only daughter my mother wanted, but I'd given up on that when I'd broken an engagement that my mother had found highly suitable.

"If you're looking for something new, you aren't going to find it *there*," my mother sniffed. *One more of my failures, in her mind.* I'd left San Diego for good once my engagement had ended. Then I'd taken up residence in Citrus Beach. I'd found more peace and contentment *here* than I'd ever known. Yeah, maybe I *didn't* have a home in Carmel Valley, Del Mar, or Coronado Island, but I'd never needed that to be happy. In fact, I knew I'd be absolutely miserable if I did.

"I do have a car," I answered. "I can travel anywhere I want to go, Mom."

"Please don't call me by that ridiculous nickname, Margaret," she said icily.

"I forgot," I muttered. The only title matriarch Carol Montgomery would tolerate was *Mother.*

"Wear something nice to this affair, Margaret," my mother suggested harshly. "There will be some very eligible men there. Since you foolishly threw away an excellent choice, it would be nice if you could attract another one. You're not getting any younger, you know."

I had no plans of trying to attract any *man*. "I'll try to find something appropriate," I snapped back.

I ended up rushing her off the phone, just like I always did. Even though I'd set out to find my independence, my mother could still make me feel like a disobedient child. As of yet, I hadn't been able to completely shake off those uncomfortable feelings every time I spoke to her.

After draining my mug of tea, I went back to work, reminding myself that I *was* a more useful member of society than most of the women who were in my mother's circle. Even if I didn't always *feel* like one.

CHAPTER 3
Seth

Dear Mr. Sinclair:

First, I'm going to completely disregard your vulgar comment about my derriere. I will admit that I started it by throwing out a highly unnecessary, derogatory suggestion.

Second, I never intended to involve your sister in this fight. The last thing I want to do is cause strife within your family. But did you really think she wouldn't learn about it? She is a crusader for all things involving wildlife conservation.

Third, the least terns will come back to nest on that property next spring. And I'll do everything possible to make sure they have a place to return to so they can reproduce.

Also, I really don't think we need to meet in person. We can communicate just fine through court documents or email.

Really, it's a shame you don't get time to read. When I was younger, it was my only escape.

Sincerely,
Riley Montgomery
Law Office of Riley Montgomery

I grinned as I took a slug of my coffee and looked at the response I'd gotten from Riley Montgomery.

Was she getting just a little bit . . . nicer?

Yep! I was pretty sure that was the case.

Not once had she called me an asshole or asked me to kiss her ass. So that was a definite improvement.

In fact, there wasn't a single personal insult in the entire email.

To be fair, her early correspondence had been *civil*. Only recently, after I'd been a total dick about her birds, had she started throwing out obscenities.

Now it looked like she was back to being professional again.

Except for the comment she'd made at the end. It left me curious. Why had she *needed* to use reading as an escape?

I lifted my head and continued to drain my coffee. The coffee shop was almost empty, which was the only reason I'd grabbed a table and pulled out my laptop.

The Coffee Shack had been a permanent fixture in Citrus Beach for as long as I could remember. Admittedly, the selection had gotten larger, but otherwise, the place hadn't changed all that much.

I leaned back in my chair, surveying the small city from the big picture window next to me. Since the summer crowds had thinned out, it wasn't as busy downtown. But unlike some beach communities, we had plenty of permanent residents, so there were a lot of people running around on the sidewalks, hurrying to complete their day so they could go home.

Strangely, I'd picked the *exact same* table where I'd met Riley Montgomery for the first and only time.

She doesn't want to meet me in person again.

That particular fact had been made pretty clear in her email.

What I really wanted to know was . . . why?

Maybe because I've been a complete asshole about her birds?

I frowned at the idea that she didn't really *like* me, but it wasn't like I didn't already know *that*. It just . . . bugged the hell out of me that she considered me her *enemy*.

I watched a couple of construction workers come into the establishment. Followed by several other customers.

Hell, I should be heading back to the office. The late-afternoon crowd is starting to come in.

It wasn't that I didn't like swimming with the sharks in the corporate world, but I *wasn't* used to a sedentary lifestyle cooped up in an office all day.

I glanced at the grubby men in orange vests who were ordering their coffee, knowing I had

31

more in common with *them* than I did with all the other suits I saw on a daily basis.

But I wasn't one of *them* anymore, the guys who busted their asses physically every single day to make a living.

In some ways, I really missed the comradery I'd had in construction with all of my fellow builders. I'd been part of a team. Yeah, it had been tough, exhausting work sometimes, but I'd liked getting my hands dirty, and most of all, I'd loved being outdoors as much as possible.

It was my restlessness in the office that had drawn me outdoors. The walk to the Coffee Shack had helped some. It usually did, which was why I was here pretty often, working in a coffee shop.

I'll get used to being in an office.

Eventually.

Having my own company had *always* been my dream. I guess I'd just never figured I'd be a player in international commercial real estate. Not even in my wildest dreams.

I could see the top of my office building in the distance. Then, my eyes drifted from my high-rise building, and back to the construction workers who had gotten themselves a table.

Where was I? *Who* was I? Somewhere in between the two worlds now?

Not a manual laborer, but not exactly comfortable in a fancy office in a suit all the time, either.

I wasn't part of a construction team, but then, I didn't exactly blend in with the old-money social scene, either.

I shook my head slightly. Hell, I didn't know where the hell I *should* be. When a guy suddenly went from busting his ass to put food on the table to a billionaire with unlimited resources, it was more than a little mind boggling. Not that I was complaining. I *liked* being filthy rich. What guy *wouldn't?* But I wasn't the type to be happy with a very *large* trust fund, even if I could easily never work another day in my entire life and not put a dent into my inheritance.

I wasn't built that way.

Never had been.

Never would be.

I *needed* to work. And I was pretty damn driven to be successful now that I'd been given the opportunity of a lifetime to do whatever I wanted.

"Mr. Sinclair!" an excited young voice called from the cash register. The woman waved like she knew me.

I didn't respond to the pretty blonde. I didn't even know the female.

Shit! I should have left before the place started to get busy.

The woman was with a couple of friends, and they were all eyeing me like a potential target they wanted to bull's-eye.

I had to wonder whether the females were even drinking age yet.

But it seemed like I was sought out by every single woman in the city above the age of eighteen these days.

My gut hurt as I watched them elbow each other, knowing they were going to invade my table within moments.

Fuck!

I was almost into my midthirties. Did they really think I'd want to get busy with a female who was barely an adult?

Disgusted, I started to put away my laptop as the young women made a beeline for my table.

I was just wondering whether or not I should stand up and make a break for it when a familiar face dropped into the chair across from me.

"They're getting younger," my new companion observed in a familiar voice.

I relaxed and kept my ass planted on the seat.

I wasn't about to lose my chance to chat with Riley Montgomery face-to-face.

In fact, the current situation definitely brought a sense of déjà vu.

The beautiful redhead across the table from me had rescued me just like this once before. Only the woman trying to get my attention back then had been a little bit older last time.

Same place.

Same circumstances.

Same woman who had sat down and pretended to be a love interest to scare away the woman who had been throwing herself at me.

I grinned. "We really need to stop meeting like this."

Riley Montgomery rolled her eyes. "If you'd stop sitting in my favorite coffee shop attracting superficial women, maybe we could."

I scowled as the gaggle of young women reached our table.

Riley put up a hand. "Scram, ladies. Mr. Sinclair doesn't do jailbait."

The pretty blonde glared at Riley. "I'm twenty."

I watched as Riley held her ground and gave the younger female what I had to admit was a pretty intimidating stare. "He's taken. Back off."

The almost-teenager finally let out an indignant *huff* and moved away with her friends in tow.

There was no denying that Riley staking her claim had gotten my cock harder than it had been in a long time.

She was pretty damn hot when she was defending her territory, even if it was only pretend. My dick didn't seem to recognize the difference.

She wasn't dressed for business today. Riley Montgomery looked way more approachable than she had last time we'd met. Casual was a good look on her. I hadn't gotten more than a glimpse of her blue jeans, but the light sweater she was wearing that fell off one shoulder made my eyes drop to her breasts, trying to figure out if she was wearing a bra. Today, her fiery hair was pulled back in a messy bun, with loose tendrils framing the creamy skin of her face.

Jesus! She was breathtaking. I was having a hard time *not* staring like a horny teenager.

"Eyes on my face, please," she ground out, sounding extremely unhappy.

Okay. Yeah. I *had* still been focused on her breasts. I looked up as requested, and it was like a sucker punch to my gut when I met her eyes. They were hazel, but in the low light of the coffee shop, they almost looked green. The gold flecks I could see dancing around in her irises were pretty damn mesmerizing.

However, it was the sharp intelligence I could see in her steadfast gaze that *really* drew me in.

Riley Montgomery was *the whole package*.

Physically stunning.

Sexy . . . without trying to be.

Kind . . . well, at least she was when it came to endangered animals.

And way too intelligent for a guy like me who had barely graduated from high school.

Something told me that there was a plethora of emotions behind those beautiful eyes, even though she was still shooting me an admonishing look. One that would probably make a lesser man cringe.

36

Maybe I wasn't college educated, but I was stubborn. And not the least bit intimidated by the gorgeous, redheaded vixen. No matter how fierce she looked sometimes.

"Sorry, not sorry," I said with a grin. "It's a little bit hard not to get distracted."

She crossed her arms over her chest. I was pretty sure she was trying to make it look like she was angry, but I sensed a slight vulnerability there, too. So I was nearly repentant about getting caught leering at her chest.

Almost. But *not quite.*

"You really should stop sitting in this place," she grumbled. "Unless you like the attention from all the single women in the city."

I shook my head. "I think you know that I don't."

The distance between her brows narrowed, and the little crinkle that formed on her forehead when she was thinking was pretty damn adorable.

"Then why do you hang out here?"

I shrugged. "I get tired of sitting in my office staring at the same four walls. I work on the top floor of a high-rise, so there's little communication with anyone except my secretary. Don't get me wrong, I love Edie. And I don't mind hearing about how cute her grandkids are, but sometimes I want to connect with the rest of the world. Sometimes I really miss doing physical work for a living."

She tilted her head. "What kind of physical work?"

"Construction. Before I started buying sites and *arranging* to build on them, I was one of those guys busting my ass to build them for rich people."

She nodded slowly. "I've heard your rags-to-riches story. I have no doubt the entire country has heard about it."

I frowned. "None of us exactly wore rags," I said defensively. "My brothers and I made sure our younger siblings had the basics."

Her mouth curved into a small smile, and I immediately discovered that I loved seeing those full, plump lips tilted upward.

"So, what you're saying is that you're getting soft from all those hours in an office?" she asked curiously.

I was far from *soft*. In fact, my dick was so hard that it was getting uncomfortable. But I wasn't about to mention *that* right at the moment. "I still work out to blow off steam, but it's not the same as being physically active all day."

We were interrupted by the manager of the coffee shop as he set her paper cup in front of her. "Here you go, Riley. Sorry for the wait."

The man was younger than her, probably midtwenties, but the adoration in his eyes as he glanced down at Riley made me want to punch the guy in the face.

It got even worse as she tilted her head up and graced the manager with a full-on smile that made her face light up. "No problem," she answered graciously. "It's getting busy."

"It is," I growled as I shot the manager my most intimidating expression. "So maybe you should get back to work?"

It wasn't a suggestion. If the bastard didn't stop ogling Riley, I'd make him go away crying like a child.

It didn't matter that I'd been doing exactly what he was doing just moments ago.

Thankfully, he nodded his head and walked away.

"Interesting that you rate personal delivery of your coffee," I observed.

"I'm a good customer," she shot back. "And it's not coffee."

"So am I." *But nobody comes and delivers my drink to my table.* "What in the hell are you drinking? I didn't know they did anything *but* coffee."

"Chai mocha latte," she answered right before she took her first sip.

I watched, fascinated, as her eyes closed for an instant as she sampled her drink.

Damned if her enjoyment didn't mimic a pleasurable sexual experience.

"Good?" I asked in a husky voice.

She opened her eyes and swallowed. "Orgasmic,"

she acknowledged. "I'm pretty addicted to tea. Nobody makes better chai than this place."

I held up my nearly empty extra-large cup. "Plenty of sugar and cream in mine." I'd ordered the mocha latte. "Yours, too?"

She blew off the unhealthiness of all the additives. "Cream and extra sugar. Doesn't matter. I stay in shape, and it's not like I'm trying to impress some guy with a skinny body."

Hell, she didn't need to be thin. She certainly wasn't overweight, and her lush curves were hot enough to inspire any man's wet dreams.

I smirked. I loved the fact that she didn't give a damn about what anyone else thought about her.

And she didn't have to.

She was fucking perfect.

The fact that she probably didn't have a man in her life at the moment made her even more irresistible.

"Question?" I ventured.

"Shoot," she replied.

"Why did you need to escape your childhood with books?"

She looked taken aback, and there was a brief flash of pain on her face, one so fleeting that most other people probably wouldn't even have noticed it. After that, her expression grew stubborn, and I knew I *wasn't* going to get my answer.

CHAPTER 4
Riley

I wasn't about to answer his question.

Maybe we *were* being cordial. But I knew better than to give the opposition anything about myself that would hand them a weak spot to poke at when I was in a court fight.

"I've always liked to read," I answered vaguely. Then, I quickly got off the subject. "So, have you changed your mind about building the resort?"

There! I'd turned things back to business. It was far better that way.

He shot me a smile that said he knew *exactly* what I was doing. But he answered, "No."

I felt my irritation rising. "Mr. Sinclair, don't you care about the fact that those birds won't have a nesting place to come back to?"

Maybe it was useless to try to pull some sympathy for the poor least terns from a man with a heart that only beat for business. However, I felt like appealing to his better nature—if he had one—might work better than insults.

"Seth," he insisted smoothly. "And I'll call you Riley."

The last thing I should be agreeing to was

anything that allowed for any kind of intimacy between us.

He was the enemy.

My adversary.

I wasn't sure why I nodded. "Seth."

I wanted to slug him when he shot me a satisfied smile. "Riley, it isn't that I don't care. Not exactly. But sometimes a man has to choose business over sentiment."

I flinched like he'd hit me. I knew *all about* men who chose business over humanity.

"What's the matter?" he asked, sounding concerned.

"Nothing," I said snippily.

"Your reaction just now wasn't *nothing*."

Dammit! He'd seen my startled expression.

What in the hell am I doing?

I was *Riley Fucking Montgomery*.

One of the best damn environmental attorneys in the country.

Harvard Law graduate.

Summa cum laude, for God's sake.

I usually didn't crumble under any kind of hostility or resistance, much less blink an eye when a defendant said something I didn't like.

I thrived on it.

"I have no idea what you're talking about," I answered in my chilly lawyer's voice.

I silently beat myself up for letting Seth Sinclair get even a tidbit of a personal reaction from me.

He finished putting away his laptop with a thoughtful look. "How badly do you want that property, Riley?"

I desperately wanted my own computer to hide behind, but I hadn't planned on working. I'd just wanted my chai fix to take home to my office.

I shot him a lethal glance. "Very badly." Like he didn't already know that? I was pretty sure I'd made myself perfectly clear.

"I might be open to doing a trade," he mused.

"For what?" I was confused. I didn't own any prime building lots.

His mysterious gray eyes pinned me to my chair. "Your services."

"You could have *any* big corporate attorney at your fingertips," I scoffed. "I only do conservation and environmental cases now. Certainly not something *you're* interested in."

"No," he agreed. "But my little sister is, and the last thing I want is to make her unhappy. Not to mention the fact that her husband, Eli Stone, is an investor in Sinclair Properties, and a rather important advisor."

My stomach dropped. I could certainly fight dirty when I needed to, but I didn't break up families over a case. *At all. Ever.*

"I honestly didn't mean to cause a problem," I confessed. "I like Jade, and from what little she's told me about her family history, I know she adores every one of her siblings."

He nodded. "We're all close. My father was mostly out of the picture, and my mother died when we were young. My oldest brother, Noah, took custody of all of us when he was barely eighteen. Noah, Aiden, and I went to work to keep food on the table and our younger siblings safe."

I lifted a brow. "Exactly how many Sinclair siblings are there?"

"Including me, there are six of us. But as you probably already know, we have other half-siblings on the East Coast."

I *did* know that. His other family on the East Coast were old money, well known among the elite. I'd gotten the gist of the story about the impoverished Sinclairs in California turning into billionaires almost overnight once they were discovered by their wealthy half-siblings. It was hard to stay ignorant when the news story had been in almost every paper and on just about every major television channel. The news had been all about how the now-deceased patriarch of the family had been a bigamist leading a double life.

However, I hadn't known that Seth had really never had parents and had helped raise his younger siblings. The media had never mentioned that their life had been *that tough*.

"You were so young to have that kind of responsibility," I said, momentarily forgetting that Seth was the enemy. "You must be really proud of Jade. It must have been a struggle to help her through that much higher education."

He shot me a genuine smile. "Proud of all of them," Seth said gruffly. "They all worked hard. My youngest sibling, Owen, is done with medical school and is nearly done with his residency. And Jade's twin, Brooke, is living on the East Coast now. She's a financial consultant. She married a self-made millionaire."

"She married down," I teased, surprising myself because I'd dropped my defenses.

He shrugged. "We didn't give a shit whether she married someone with money or not. She's happy. And Liam treats my sister like a queen. That's all that matters."

His words touched me more than I was willing to let on. Seth wasn't *completely* motivated by the money he'd inherited. Obviously, all he'd wanted was for his siblings to be *happy*.

"You and your older brothers sacrificed your own education to give your younger siblings a hand up in life?" I contemplated aloud.

"Noah managed to get his degree. And I'm not sure that Aiden would have gone to college. He was into commercial fishing, and he liked it. But I think he's a hell of a lot happier now that he can build his own fishing empire."

I listened as Seth explained how he and Aiden were silent partners in each other's businesses.

That both of them had decided to do what they wanted to do, but were still supporting each other in their companies.

"Noah is into technology," he further explained. "There isn't a one of us who cares much about tech, but we still support his ambitions."

I blinked hard when he stopped talking.

No matter how a person looked at it, the Sinclair family would be remarkable even if they *hadn't* come into a fortune. "What about you?" I questioned. "Did you give up the chance for a higher education?"

"Maybe. But it was well worth the trade-off," he said nonchalantly. "Plus, I'm getting a crash course in business from Eli Stone. I doubt there's a better businessman out there to learn from."

I felt my heart wrench just a little. It was incredible how willing Seth had been to help his siblings at the expense of his own possible career choices.

Honestly, he *was* right about Eli Stone. I didn't know Eli well personally, but he was a business legend. He could probably teach Seth more than he'd ever learn by getting an MBA.

"That's an amazing story," I said with a sigh.

So much for my assumption that Seth was *completely* coldhearted.

"I come from a pretty incredible family," he said casually. "What about you?"

"I was able to afford my Harvard Law degree.

Not a single member of my family had to suffer to get me educated," I answered carefully. "So, tell me about your proposed trade deal for the property. I understand why you don't want to cause friction with Jade and Eli. What's the answer?"

I really didn't want to talk about *my* family, so the sooner we moved away from that line of discussion the better.

"You said you'd trade for my services," I prompted. "But I don't have much to offer to a man like you."

He studied me for a moment, which made me uncomfortable.

I didn't want anyone to know me better.

A man like Seth would *never* understand me.

"You have a hell of a lot to offer *any* guy," he considered.

"Not exactly true," I disagreed. "I was engaged once, but I was never enough for Nolan Easton," I muttered, instantly wishing the name hadn't left my mouth.

For some odd reason, Seth was easy to talk to, but I needed to guard my words a hell of a lot better.

He whistled softly. "Nolan Easton? Head of Easton Investment Firms? The *very wealthy* Nolan Easton?"

"Yes," I said tightly.

"Even so, I can't believe he dumped you," Seth answered.

"He didn't," I admitted. "I finally broke it off. He didn't know how to keep his dick in his pants, and I didn't want to spend my entire life being who he wanted me to be." I coughed nervously. "Now can we get back to the business at hand?"

"Not yet," he insisted. "I'm still trying to get why any guy would want to change a single thing about you. Not that I exactly love your line of work *right now,* but you're passionate about it. You're beautiful. You're smart. You seem to know exactly what you want. Considering our circumstances, I can't say I've seen your sense of humor, but I'm assuming you have one of those, too. What the hell else did he want?"

I ignored his question. "I have three older brothers," I shared. "I have to have a sense of humor or they'd drive me crazy."

He rested his arms on the table and leaned forward. "You didn't answer my question, Riley. What else did he want?" His voice was low and persuasive.

"It's not important. My engagement has been over for a while, and I'm happy. I finally found my own home here in Citrus Beach, and I'm pretty content with being alone. It's a lot nicer here than San Diego. Quieter."

It was a hell of a lot better than being with a man who made me feel like I was less than nothing.

"When exactly did you move here? And where are you living now?"

48

"Almost two years ago," I ground out, growing impatient to get back to business. It wasn't wise to dump a lot about my personal life to a defendant—no matter how good a listener he might be. "I had a condo, but I recently purchased your sister's cottage. I've settled there now. She and Eli have the bigger home next door, so I already knew I'd have good neighbors."

"I'm right down the beach from there," Seth said, sounding surprised. "I've never seen you."

"Like I said. It's recent. I just moved in."

I was squirming in my chair. I didn't care for the feeling of being interrogated. I was usually the one *asking* the questions.

He shot me a playful grin that made my heart trip. "Welcome to the neighborhood," he said jokingly.

"Thanks," I said uncomfortably. "Now tell me what you want from me to leave that piece of property alone."

He took his time answering, and the silence seemed to stretch out forever.

I gulped down the last of my tea while I waited for him to answer.

Was he playing with me?

Or did he actually have some kind of proposition?

Probably the former—since I really didn't have much to offer him in the way of services. I could guarantee that Eli Stone had set Seth up with his gaggle of business attorneys. Why in the hell would he need an environmental attorney?

"If you're playing with me, this encounter ends right now," I said tersely.

"I'm not," he said emphatically. "I'm just wondering how to explain what I want."

"If it's acceptable, I'll write up the contract today," I offered.

"It's not exactly the contract I'm thinking about," he said thoughtfully.

God, I was jittery, and I wasn't used to feeling that way. I was pretty certain that it wasn't the extra-large chai I'd just consumed, either.

It was *him.*

Maybe it was the way he studied me.

Or the way his steely gray eyes never left my face.

I couldn't *read* him, and that completely pissed me off. As an attorney, I'd gotten very good at judging exactly where a defendant's mind might be, and what their motives were.

"Just name your terms," I said irritably. "I'll work out the details."

I forced myself to meet his eyes in what I *thought* would be a battle of wills, and then was sorry that I had even glanced his direction.

My breath hitched as I fell into a stormy gaze that *wouldn't* let me go.

I was stunned at the possessive way he eyed me.

I was confused about the emotions I saw there. And I was mesmerized by the carnal desire that flared up in his steely irises like a bolt of lightning as he held me still with a single look, unable to rip myself away from his fixed stare that was holding me in place.

Heat exploded between my thighs, and I knew I was blushing like a damn teenage girl with her first major crush. My brain was begging my body not to react, but my stupid body wasn't listening.

His voice was hoarse and beguiling when he finally said, "I need a woman, Riley. And that woman has to be *you*."

CHAPTER 5
Riley

Dear Mr. Sinclair:
After careful consideration of your offer,
I feel I have to decline . . .

"Dammit!" I cursed with disgust as I took my hands off the keyboard of my laptop.

I'd been *trying* to write this simple email all damn day, but I hadn't been able to *complete* it.

It would really be *relatively* easy to get the sanctuary for the least terns. Just what I wanted.

Problem was, it would come with a *personal* price.

I hadn't accepted Seth's offer outright. I couldn't. I'd told him I needed time to think about his proposition.

However, I *knew* myself, and I couldn't just let go of the opportunity to get what I'd been fighting to achieve for months now. The least-tern situation was critical, and there were so few locations where they could safely nest anymore. The fact that they'd turned up in Citrus Beach was nothing short of a miracle. How could I blow off an opportunity to give the critically endangered species a safe place to reproduce?

I was almost relieved when I heard the doorbell ring. I needed some kind of distraction.

"Jade!" I exclaimed as I opened the door. "You're home."

Eli and Jade spent a lot of time in San Diego, and I generally didn't see them around their house next door until the weekend.

She laughed as she walked in the door. "Weird, right? It's strange to be here on a Monday. But Eli wanted to stay to go over some stuff with Seth. And the research facility can function without me once in a while. I have plenty of competent scientists there to carry on in my absence."

I cringed a little inside as I asked cautiously, "Eli isn't planning to confront Seth about the sanctuary, right?"

I really, really wanted to avoid family conflict for them. It was obvious that Seth adored Jade.

She shook her head as she plopped down at the table near the sliding-glass doors. "No. Not since you told me that Seth made you an offer. I'm dying to find out if the terms can be worked out."

I'd been stewing about Seth's proposition for days. I'd just texted Jade last night about the possibility of working out a deal with her brother. But I hadn't counted on her showing up *today* to discuss it.

I went into the kitchen and started making some tea. "Do you want coffee or anything?"

Jade held up her hand. "No. I'm good. Eli

already took me to Maya's Bistro this morning for one of Skye's amazing croissant breakfast sandwiches. I had tons of coffee."

I knew Jade's sister-in-law, Aiden's wife, had done a complete overhaul on her café. I'd been wanting to get in there since it reopened right at the end of the summer. "How's business for her?"

Jade beamed. "Excellent. It's so adorable now that it's been completely remodeled, and the food is nice and trendy. But delicious. I can only imagine what a success it will be in the summer."

"I'm glad," I answered sincerely as I added cream and sugar to my tea. "I'd love to get there soon."

She nodded. "You should. Her sandwiches are all a work of art."

I took a seat across from her at the table. "Okay, so about Seth's proposed deal . . ."

"Tell me. Can we save the property?" she asked breathlessly.

I shot her a small smile. Jade was so passionate about preserving species. Her cutting-edge work in her laboratories with DNA was way above my head, but her vision was always very clear. "We can. But the deal is pretty . . . unconventional."

"What does he want?" Jade asked.

"Me," I answered flatly.

Jade's eyes became round and befuddled. "I don't understand."

I sighed. "I don't exactly understand it well myself. But according to your brother, if he's losing millions on this property, he wants to find more big investors, and wheel and deal for other potential real estate to build the resort on. Which means he has to mingle with some of the San Diego elite. He's had plenty of invitations to exclusive parties and fund-raisers, but he put a halt to attending them once he realized that he was getting mobbed by ambitious women or their mothers. He wants me to accompany him for a few months as his fake girlfriend. It would give him more opportunity to talk with some potential investors and real-estate moguls."

"Seriously?" Jade croaked.

I nodded. "He was completely serious."

"Oh, Riley," she said softly. "That puts you in a pretty uncomfortable situation, doesn't it? There's a good chance you'll end up face-to-face with your ex-fiancé, right?"

Yep, there is, and Jade doesn't know all the reasons why I want to stay out of that crowd, either.

I took a sip of my tea before I answered, "It would be awkward. But if it makes you feel any better, I don't think Seth realizes it. I've been trying to figure out a way to refuse him all morning, but I just can't, Jade. It's too important to keep that property intact for me to just throw the opportunity to do that away. And honestly, your brother *would be* giving away millions for just a couple of months of my time."

She tilted her head. "You like him," she accused.

I rolled my eyes. "I think *like* is a little too strong a word. He's *tolerable* when he isn't being a jerk."

Admittedly, he *had* been pretty pleasant when we'd met several days ago in the Coffee Shack. Until he'd dropped that damn bomb on me about masquerading as his girlfriend.

"Seth is actually a pretty nice guy, and I'm not just saying that because he's my brother," Jade said. "Maybe he *has* been a lot more guarded since he went to work in the corporate world, but he's done some things for my whole family that none of us could ever repay. He would always go without, just to give Owen, Brooke, and me something as simple as an ice cream or some kind of treat. And I don't think there was a single day that he resented it. All he ever wanted was to see us smile. He started working in construction when he was sixteen just to help Noah. And then Aiden started to work as a fisherman as soon as he was old enough to work. None of my brothers ever wanted us to feel deprived. They gave us all a childhood when they'd actually not had one themselves."

I had no idea why her words made me blink back tears.

Or maybe I *did* know, but I didn't want to reconcile the "business" Seth with the man who had always put his family first.

"You have an amazing family," I said reverently.

She asked softly, "Don't you? You said you love your brothers."

I'd never shared all that much about my family with Jade. "I do. Except when they're trying to steer me away from men that they think aren't good enough for me."

Jade snorted. "I think that's just a protective-older-brother thing. My three older ones grilled Eli so hard that I'm surprised that he hung around."

I smirked. I'd seen the way Jade and Eli looked at each other. I certainly wasn't shocked that her husband had taken the inquisition in stride. If Jade asked Eli to go jump off the nearest bridge, he'd do it without asking any questions. And vice versa. The two of them were so in love that it was almost nauseating. But it was sweet, too. I guess maybe I just couldn't relate because my personal experience with men was far from stellar. "He loves you," I said simply.

Jade's face softened. "I love him, too. It's a little strange to have a guy who loves me as much as Eli does. I've never had a guy who just accepted me exactly as I am. Science geek and all. Honestly, there has *never* really been a guy like him in my life before. He was worth waiting for, though."

I smiled at the dumbfounded look on her face.

It was like Jade was still trying to figure out how she'd ended up with Eli. Even though it was obvious to everyone else. Granted, they were both so different on the surface, but the two of them just . . . fit.

"So enough about me and Eli," she said sternly. "What are you going to do about Seth? And why in the world did he pick you as a possible fake girlfriend? Oh, wait! Maybe I know. You're totally unimpressed with him, right?"

"I kind of rescued him twice," I explained. "Women were pestering him at the Coffee Shack, and I sort of gave them the impression that Seth and I were together to make them go away."

Jade's face suddenly went dark. "That makes me so angry," she said vehemently. "I've seen it. Not a single one of those females would have had him for a serious relationship before he had money."

"Why? I know he's your brother, but he *is* hot." *Smoking hot,* but I wasn't going to tell Seth's little sister that his muscular, totally ripped body, dark hair, and enigmatic ashen eyes were enough to make a woman want to toss her panties aside in mere seconds.

"I didn't say they wouldn't *screw* him," she said, disgust dripping from her voice. "But he was always broke. A manual laborer who got sweaty for a living and had younger siblings to support."

"But that's actually admirable," I argued.

"Most women wouldn't see it that way, Riley. He wasn't a good boyfriend or marriage prospect."

For an instant, the way he'd been treated pissed *me* off, too. "*Some* women would give anything to have a guy who was that loyal, that responsible, and that dedicated to his family," I answered.

"Not many," she said unhappily. "And my brothers know that from experience. Which is why Seth is probably so eager for a diversion. What are you going to do?"

"I don't know," I told her honestly. "He wants me to start out by being his escort for your benefit in San Diego. I have to decide, since it's coming up this weekend. Really, he's not asking for all that much to obtain that property. I kind of suspect he would have given in to you eventually, Jade. He knows it's important to you. But I'm not sure I want to take the risk that he'd just turn it over to you. The last thing I really want is to cause family issues for you and Eli."

Jade bit at her lip. "But I don't want you to do anything that you don't want to do."

I smirked. "I have to admit that I don't mind chasing women away from your brother, because I suspect they're just after a rich guy. But I'd rather not have to go back into that crowd in San Diego. I'm happy here."

"Then don't," Jade encouraged. "We'll figure

something else out. I don't belong in that world, either. I only do it to raise funds. And Eli is so comfortable with it that it makes it easy to bear."

"So much of it is so damn trivial," I complained. "It's all one big game to see who can outdo who. But I can handle it, I guess. I've had plenty of experience adopting the facade."

Jade shot me a dubious look. "Are you sure?"

I nodded firmly. I'd made up my mind during my conversation with Jade. "Positive. And it won't be so bad since you and Eli are going to be there this weekend."

"Do we need to go clothes shopping?" Jade asked teasingly.

"Seriously, we might," I replied. "I pretty much traded in my formal gowns for power suits and jeans."

"Seth cleans up well," Jade answered with a grin. "All of my brothers look good in a tux."

"He looks pretty good in a custom suit, too," I blurted out without censoring my words.

"I knew it," Jade said excitedly. "You're attracted to him."

I lifted a brow. "Like a praying mantis is attracted to a mate," I grumbled. "But don't forget that the female rips the head off the male once they've gotten it on."

Jade busted out laughing. "He's not so bad," she said once she'd recovered. "If you get to know the real Seth, you might actually like him.

Like every single one of my brothers, he's a pain in the ass at times, but they all have some redeeming qualities."

"I'll have to take your word on that one," I mumbled. "I've been doing battle with him for months, and he hasn't budged until now."

"Oh, I never said he isn't *stubborn*," she answered with humor in her tone.

"And that's a good quality?"

"Actually, I think it's a quality you both *share*. You are on the other side of the argument."

"I'm an attorney," I reminded her. "I get paid to be argumentative."

Jade smiled as she stood up. "Thank you, Riley. But please know that if this ends up painful for you in any way, it stops. I know how much you dislike being in a fishbowl. We can resolve this a different way."

"I'm good," I told her with a falsely cheerful tone. "I just need to lay some ground rules, and everything will be fine. In a few months, that property will be safely in our hands so it can become a protected breeding ground for the least terns."

We said our good-byes, and I headed back to my office.

This time, I had absolutely no problem writing back to Seth.

If we were going to do this masquerade, I was going to do it on *my terms*, with very little room for negotiation.

CHAPTER 6
Seth

Dear Mr. Sinclair:

After careful consideration, I've decided to accept your offer, but you'll need to take it with the following terms:

GROUND RULES

Rule #1—I will dress appropriately, but under no circumstances will you get to dictate what I wear to each function.

Rule #2—You're not allowed to ask me to dance with any male at the event, even if it will benefit your business.

Rule #3—You'll hold your criticism of anything you dislike about my behavior, unless and until there are no other parties present. We discuss things alone.

Rule #4—NO SEX. AT ALL. EVER.

Rule #5—YOU WILL NOT PUT YOUR HAND ON MY ASS UNDER ANY CIRCUMSTANCES.

Rule #6—You have to be respectful at all times.

If you can agree to these terms, you

can send me a list of events you'll be attending, and I'll draw up the contract.

Riley

"Is she fucking serious?" I grumbled aloud as I sat in my office alone on Tuesday.

Okay, maybe I *did* have a little bit of a problem with rules four and five. I was going to be tempted to stroke that shapely ass, and I definitely wanted to have sex with her.

But the rest of the rules were complete bullshit.

If I had Riley by my side, I'd *never* disrespect her. And it annoyed the hell out of me that she'd even have to put that in her ground rules.

Never, in my entire life, had I disrespected *any* female. Hell, I had *sisters*. I wouldn't want any male to ever treat either one of them with anything but the utmost courtesy.

I stared at the other requests, wondering who in the hell would want her to dance with another guy. I sure as hell *wouldn't*.

It wasn't my nature to be a control freak, so the other stuff didn't make sense, either. Like I'd ever censor what she wore? Riley could come with me naked if she wanted to.

Wait! Scratch that!

I didn't want any other guys to see her nude. Just the thought of it made my gut ache. But did she really think I cared whether she wore whatever the hell she *wanted* to wear?

What the fuck did she mean that I couldn't *criticize* her? What asshole would do that when they had a woman like Riley at their side?

Truth was, I'd feel damn lucky to be with her, even if it *was* only an act.

"Son of a bitch!" I said in a gravelly voice as I picked up my cell and punched in her number.

Luckily, we'd traded contact information before she'd left the Coffee Shack so we could have a discussion after she'd had time to think about my offer.

Honestly, I probably would have caved in and *not* built the resort because of Jade. At some point in time, I knew I'd give it up because it would hurt my little sister if I built a high-rise and scared her beloved birds away.

As much as I didn't want to admit it, I was a sucker for my little sister's sad face.

The idea of getting Riley to go with me to various social gatherings had simply been a way to make sure I kept seeing the stubborn, gorgeous redhead who I couldn't get off my mind.

Yeah, it would be nice to have a date for every function I wanted to attend. It would make them easier to deal with. But I wasn't going to bullshit myself into thinking that was the *only* reason I wanted to make a bargain with her.

Truth was, I didn't just want a *date*. I wanted *her*. And if I just gave up the property, we'd never have a reason to meet up again. For me, that was completely . . . unacceptable.

"Law Office of Riley Montgomery," she chirped when she picked up the phone.

"What in the fuck was that email all about, Riley?" I rumbled, without messing with a general greeting.

"Seth?" she said, her tone cautious.

I hated myself for loving the sound of my name coming from her lips. "How many other guys do you set ground rules with? What in the hell did you mean by writing that bullshit email?"

"I don't know what you mean," she said in her lawyer voice. "I wanted to lay down some general terms. If you don't agree, there's no point looking at further negotiations."

"Cut the crap with me, Riley," I barked. "Did somebody really do this shit to you in the past?"

"I-I don't understand," she said in an unusually vulnerable tone.

Fuck! Her hesitation made my damn chest ache. Someone *had* treated her like shit. "Let me make myself perfectly clear to you, then. Rules one, two, three, and six should be completely unnecessary, and I doubt you would have included them if you weren't afraid they might happen. I'll grant you that four and five might need to be *mentioned,* because it won't be easy to keep my hands off your beautiful ass when nobody is looking. And I think you already know that I'd like to get you into my bed, but not unless you want that, too. It's not going to be negotiated in a fucking contract."

There was total silence from her end of the phone until she finally murmured, "Y-you're okay with the terms?"

Dammit! There it was again. That hesitation. That uncertainty. I tried to tamp down my indignation a notch. "What I'm saying is that I would *never* disrespect you under *any* circumstances. I don't give a damn what you wear or what you say, and it would be a cold day in hell before I'd ask you to get close to some pervert just because it would help my company. Jesus Christ, Riley. What guy would do that shit?"

"Some would," she replied.

I was relieved to hear her go back to her normal argumentative tone.

"Some? Like your ex-fiancé?"

"He wasn't exactly tactful," she replied drily.

"Must have been a dick," I observed.

"Which is why we're no longer engaged," she replied grimly.

Well, at least she'd kicked the bastard to the curb. But that fact didn't keep my fist from clenching on my desk.

I had two little sisters who my brothers and I had taught to be themselves, to be unique. None of us would have ever wanted to mold them into what we wanted them to be.

Sure, we'd scrutinized every *love interest* they'd ever had, but only because we wanted to make sure any guy they dated was safe, and good enough for Brooke and Jade.

Protective? *Yes.*

Control freaks? *Hell, no.*

"If it makes you feel better to write those terms in there, go for it." I was never going to need to be "contracted" to treat Riley with respect, but knowing her history, I wasn't as affronted as I'd been when I called her. "But you could leave out numbers four and five."

"Not. Happening," she answered rigidly. "I don't like men groping my ass in public."

"How about in private?" I asked hopefully.

"Neither. Seth, none of this is *real.* It's supposed to be a ruse to help you."

She was right. But admitting that didn't exactly make me happy. "Fine. Write the contract," I said in a businesslike tone.

I noticed that she hadn't mentioned *number four,* and a guy could hope.

If both parties agreed, contract terms *could* be changed.

If not, I'd just have to be content with spending more time with her. Riley was worth a hell of lot more than just a quick screw.

I wouldn't deny that I hoped I could persuade her to change her mind about number four. Eventually.

It had been so long since I'd wanted a female this damn badly. Hell, maybe my cock had *never* been as hard for *any* woman as it was for Riley.

"Anything else? On your side, I mean?" It sounded like she was taking notes, because the sound of a keyboard was clicking away.

"Signs of affection are a must," I said thoughtfully. "If we're supposed to be dating, it will be expected."

Maybe I couldn't fuck her or grope her ass, but I refused to not be allowed to touch her in any way. That was too much to ask when we were going to spend so much time pretending to date.

There was silence at the end of her phone until she finally asked, "What kind of affection?"

Hell, she sounded nervous, which wasn't a good sign at all. "Simple stuff," I said vaguely. "But no butt grabbing."

"All right," she snapped. "I'll touch you. And you can touch me. Casually."

My cock twitched, liking the possibility of touching this particular female in almost any way possible. "I'll pick you up Saturday night. Six thirty?"

The fund-raiser was starting at seven thirty, but it would take us a while to get into San Diego.

"I can drive myself," she said hesitantly.

"Nope. Hard terms. You always go with me. My girlfriend wouldn't be driving herself. We'd be together."

68

"Okay," she murmured, still tapping away at her keyboard.

Oh, hell, she sounded uncertain, and that was a part of Riley I *definitely* didn't know. And didn't like.

Generally, the woman was confident to the point of orneriness. And I was starting to like her stubbornness. Most of the time.

"Anything else?" she asked briskly.

"Relax," I told her in a soothing voice. "I'm not going to embarrass you. Maybe I was a blue-collar guy, but I know how to be cordial and appropriate in public. Unless somebody really pisses me off."

She let out a startled laugh. "I'm not worried about you. I'm more nervous about me."

Okay. She didn't mingle with this crowd. Apparently, the thought made her edgy. "Be whoever you want to be, Riley. Don't worry about not fitting in. You have nothing to prove to anybody." I hesitated before I asked, "Do you need anything for these events? I'll pick up the tab for whatever you need."

"Like what?" She sounded confused.

"Clothes, shoes, anything. Weapons of self-defense so nobody grabs your ass? I don't want you picking up the bill for stuff that you're only going to use to go with me."

I didn't really know her financial situation, but I hardly thought that environmental attorneys made

69

a ton of money. I knew for a fact that she was doing the work on this property deal pro bono.

"I'll manage," she said hastily. "I'll pass on the weapons for self-defense. I'm hardly going to shoot someone for pinching my ass."

"I might," I grumbled under my breath.

"What was that?"

"Nothing," I said in a louder voice.

"Can I ask you something?" The sound of tapping on her keyboard suddenly stopped.

"Anything. Shoot."

"Are you really ready to mingle with this crowd? They aren't exactly your average party-goers."

Was she worried about whether or not I'd be accepted because I was new money? Or a previously broke construction worker? "I'm not going so I can be inserted into their circle, Riley. I don't give a damn whether any of them *like* me. It's business. I've already gone to a couple of events with Eli, which is how I know I need a date to go with me. I already know that the majority of the elites are snobs. They go to events to see and be seen, not for the charity itself. Even Eli won't associate with most of them outside of a social gathering, and he grew up with that crowd. We can treat it like a game to be played, something we don't take seriously."

She let out a breath of what sounded like relief. "I can do that."

"Do you want to have dinner tomorrow night? Just so we can go over the contract?"

"No need," she said abruptly. "I can send it to your office."

I grinned. *That* was the Riley I recognized.

Stubborn.

Independent.

And totally evasive.

"Okay, send it over," I agreed, hoping like hell she'd forget all about number four when she wrote the official contract.

CHAPTER 7
Riley

When Saturday night arrived, I stood in front of my mirror, knowing my mother *definitely* wouldn't like my choice of apparel. She never had.

My new cocktail dress was a deep forest green, a hue that always complemented my flaming-red hair. I'd kept it tame. But the hem *did* end above my knees. However, I'd opted for three-quarter-length sleeves because it was getting cooler.

Is the neckline too low?

I shook my head. Rationally, I was aware that the style wasn't *scandalous*. Yeah, the V down the front flirted with my breasts, but it showed absolutely nothing.

I eyed the strappy silver heels I was wearing, knowing my mother would have dictated black for formal wear. But I loved sparkly shoes, and I had a complete adoration for . . . color. Lots of color. I'd gotten tired of wearing basic black when I'd barely been out of my teen years.

Unfortunately, neither my mother nor Nolan had ever encouraged my style choices.

That color is appallingly inappropriate.

Your heels should be black.

Your hair is messy.

Etc., etc., etc.

I smiled at my reflection.

Fortunately, I didn't need approval from either one of them anymore.

I'd swept my hair up with a large, beautiful silver hair clip, but curly tendrils still framed my face.

Maybe my makeup had required a little heavier hand than usual, but it was far from plastered on.

I sighed and picked up a tiny silver purse and got my black cashmere dress coat out of my closet.

In spite of my pep talk, I was *still* feeling edgy.

I'd promised myself I'd never go back, but here I was, ready to attend my first of many fundraisers and social events with my mother's crowd *again*.

Think about the property. It's a means to an end. And Seth will be there with me.

I frowned as I made my way out to the kitchen. Why did it matter if Seth Sinclair was at my side?

Strangely, it *did* matter. Ever since he'd let me know that he didn't give a damn what other people thought about him, I'd felt a lot more relaxed.

He was my escort, and if he didn't give a damn, I didn't have to, either.

There was a purpose behind this whole facade, this game to be played.

And if I could just keep thinking *that way,* everything would be fine.

Honestly, I *could* be an asset to Seth.

I knew who had the deepest pockets among the elite, and who just *acted* like they did.

It wouldn't hurt to be able to point out a few of the nicer attendees who might make good investors for him. Or the guys who were the most honest in their real-estate dealings.

I set my purse and coat on the counter and pulled out a mug, desperate for a cup of tea since I was a complete addict. I hadn't had one since this morning.

I wonder if Seth really thinks I'm a struggling attorney?

Since he'd offered to pay for my clothes, he obviously thought I might be short on funds for some reason.

His suggestion had been rather *sweet,* something I didn't exactly expect from Seth Sinclair. But completely unnecessary.

My mind drifted back to his comments earlier in the week about my ground rules. I'd been surprised that he'd sounded irate about some of the terms. Like I'd *insulted* him.

Maybe I did.

Most people with new money wanted to fit in, and were overly obsessed with being just like others in the ultrarich circle.

Not that I'd ever tell *him,* but I'd been ecstatic

when he'd said he didn't give a damn what I wore, how I acted, and that he'd never want me to make nice with a guy on the dance floor to further his business.

It would be a cold day in hell before I'd ask you to get close to some pervert just because it would help my company.

Funny, but I could still hear his angry growl in my head.

I snickered as I placed my mug under the coffeemaker.

His proclamation was certainly one that I'd never heard from my ex. And Seth's words had somehow made me feel . . . free.

The doorbell rang, disrupting my thoughts.

I glanced at the kitchen clock, realizing that it was later than I thought.

I looked longingly at my mug that was just waiting for me to dispense some hot water for tea.

No time. But later . . .

I hurried to the front entrance, my heels clicking on the wood floor right before I opened the door.

All of the air was sucked out of my lungs as I saw Seth Sinclair on my doorstep.

To say he *cleaned up good* was an understatement.

He was heart-stopping gorgeous in a tux. And he appeared like he was perfectly comfortable in his formal wear.

My heart skittered as I simply gaped at him like an idiot.

He stepped past me, inviting himself in.

I shook myself and closed the door, savoring the musky scent of male and probably a very subtle aftershave that wafted through the air around us.

Stop salivating, for God's sake. This is not real. Not a date. At all. Ever.

"Hi," I said belatedly as I turned to face him.

"Hello, gorgeous," he said huskily. "You look stunning, Riley."

A shiver of pleasure slithered up my spine. "So do you," I said honestly.

"I come bearing gifts," he said with a grin as he held up a large paper cup. "One extra-large chai mocha latte to go."

He remembered.

I had no idea why I was touched that he recalled exactly what I liked from the Coffee Shack.

"You're a lifesaver," I said gratefully as I took it from his hand. "I haven't had any tea since this morning."

"Then you're definitely deprived," he teased.

"I am, actually. I'm an addict," I confessed.

"Ready?" he asked as he continued to stare at me.

I nodded firmly. "Let me grab my coat and purse."

I hurried to the kitchen to retrieve the items

from the counter and then rushed back to the door.

Before I could reach for the door handle, Seth moved in closer and put his hands on the wood, trapping me between his arms without really touching me.

"Did I tell you how damn proud I'll be to have a woman like you as my date, Riley, even though it's a ruse?" he asked hoarsely.

My breath hitched as I tilted my head up to look at him. His expression was unfathomable, and almost . . . harsh. His square jaw looked tight, and his eyes deadly serious.

For some odd reason, the compliment meant so much. "I-I'm really glad that I'll be able to scare all the women away from you," I blurted out, feeling mesmerized by the intensity that flowed between us.

Heat seeped between my thighs, and my nipples were as hard as diamonds as my body responded to Seth's raw masculinity and the naked desire I could see in his stormy eyes.

When his mouth came down to steal mine, I let out a gasp of relief against his lips.

My heart cantered out of control as Seth's embrace completely consumed me.

I wanted to throw my arms around his neck and beckon him to do so much more, but I was still clutching my jacket, purse, and tea.

Only our lips met, and it was almost erotic

because it was the only place our bodies were actually touching. All of the wanting was confined to just one place.

His tantalizing scent wrapped me in a blanket of desire that I didn't want to escape.

The kiss was over way before I wanted it to end.

"We shouldn't have done that," I whispered as he lifted his head.

Because now I felt too much.

Needed too much.

And my whole damn body ached for him.

He put a gentle hand to my face and traced my lips with his thumb. "Relax, Riley. It was just a kiss. I think we needed to get it over with and done. Expressions of affection, remember? Do you feel more comfortable now?"

Oh, God, no!

I *didn't* feel the slightest bit at ease.

My body was clamoring for satisfaction. To the point where I wanted to climb up his smoking-hot body and beg him to fuck me until I couldn't walk straight anymore.

"Is that why you kissed me?" I asked in a breathy voice that sounded nothing like my own.

He shook his head as he stepped back. "No. But it sounded like a good excuse."

"It was a mistake, Seth. One that we *can't* repeat," I said icily.

My head was getting clearer. My brains had

momentarily scrambled from that kiss, but I knew getting involved with Seth Sinclair would be a mistake. One I wasn't willing to make.

"It wasn't a *mistake,* Riley. We're attracted to each other. Sooner or later, we're both going to act on that chemistry."

Not a chance in hell. Kissing him was a mistake. Sleeping with him would be a monumental disaster.

"We'd better go," I prompted, eager to shake off the embrace we'd shared.

My heart rate had slowed, but it was still skipping an occasional beat as I stepped back from Seth to give myself a break from the intense emotions he drew from me.

"It's going to happen, Riley," he warned.

"It isn't," I replied firmly. "Number four in the contract, remember?"

"And I think I told you that my sex life is not *ever* going to be dependent on a goddamn contract." He sounded irritable.

"You signed it."

"I did it knowing that terms are easily changed."

"I refuse to negotiate," I said emphatically.

"We'll see," he answered vaguely.

As I locked the door after we'd stepped outside, I knew I was going to have to be more careful. Being seduced by a guy like Seth wasn't part of my future plans.

At all. Ever.

CHAPTER 8
Seth

I'd seen a glimpse of the real, passionate Riley Montgomery earlier in the evening, but she hadn't revealed even a flash of that same vulnerability in the hours after she'd shared that mind-blowing kiss with me.

Everything was all about the business at hand for her.

Getting her property by playing the game.

And it annoyed the hell out of me.

I wanted to *know* her, find out why she was so adamantly against pursuing anything except a business arrangement.

But Riley remained a mystery to me, even though we'd spent most of the evening together.

"You might want to approach Mr. Rutledge," Riley whispered next to my ear, and then nodded her head at an older man sitting by himself at a small, linen-covered table. "Insanely rich, and known to be an honest, straightforward business-man."

I turned my head to look at her, and *that* was a goddamn mistake.

My cock hadn't deflated once the entire night, and every time I glanced at her, it was full staff all over again.

Dancing with her had been torture, but one I'd been more than happy to endure just to have her lush body within my grasp.

As expected, there were more than enough snobs at this gathering, but since it was being hosted by Eli and Jade, a lot of them seemed to be on their best behavior. It was like every person here realized that if they stepped out of line, they'd never be invited to another Eli Stone event. And they were right. My brother-in-law had no tolerance for malicious fools.

Riley and I had eaten and danced, and then I'd watched her work the room with absolutely no hesitation.

"You've done your homework," I told her.

I'd already approached several people she'd obviously researched, and she'd been right about every single one of them. I'd picked up several new, eager prospective investors, and learned about several properties for sale. Now, I was starting to itch to get out of the overindulgent atmosphere.

I could only play the game for so long.

The crowd wasn't overly loud. The orchestra was playing, but it was fairly sedate. Simply background noise—until you were actually on the dance floor. People seemed to group together to chat—or gossip. I wasn't sure which one, since Riley and I had spent a lot of time circulating, and very little standing still in any particular gathering for any amount of time.

Riley had done so well at scoping out the crowd that I hadn't needed Eli's help when he'd offered it a short while ago.

I looked around the room. I had to admit that it still seemed surreal that I was even *among* these people. Not that I'd ever aspired to spend an evening with a bunch of snobs, but the fact that I was wealthy enough to *be here* was pretty unbelievable.

Being at the fund-raiser reminded me that sometimes I still *felt* like a fraud.

Going from incredibly poor to super rich was still something almost unreal to me, but I knew as long as I never forgot where I came from, I could see all this as just a game.

I still preferred having a beer over champagne.

I still considered a good day of fishing the best way to spend a day.

I still liked to get outside and active, although more often than not, that was accomplished by indulging in a long run that would work up a decent sweat.

Granted, I was getting used to being brutal in the business world, but all in all, the money hadn't really changed me and my siblings that much. It just made shit easier to accomplish.

"Do you want another drink?" I asked Riley.

She shook her head as she smiled up at me. "No, thanks. Two is my limit. Although I wish I had access to a decent cup of tea."

Her smile hit me like a kick to my gut. She looked so elegant, and so damn beautiful that I couldn't think straight.

There wasn't another woman at the event who could even *compare* to Riley. And every time another bastard even *looked her way,* I wanted to beat the crap out of him.

My protective instincts were probably why the three men who were presently pointing in Riley's direction and checking her out stopped me in my tracks.

Instantly, I forgot all about my reasons for being at this gathering. My complete attention was focused on a potential threat.

"Are you going to talk to Mr. Rutledge?" Riley asked curiously.

"Not yet," I replied, my eyes glued to the three guys who were now coming our way.

Dark hair. Blond hair. And the other guy is somewhere in between.

That was about the *only* observation I had time for before the man with the dark hair wrapped his arms around Riley from behind.

"Hey, gorgeous," the man said as he draped his beefy arms around Riley's shoulders. "How about a dance?"

Fuck! I saw red in an instant. "How about you take your goddamn hands off her before I break both of them," I growled, moving forward to loosen his grip on Riley. I stepped between him and the woman I considered mine, at least for tonight.

"She doesn't belong to you, man," the guy said casually, but his eyes were deadly and dark.

"She does right now," I barked. "If you want me to prove it, we can take this outside."

I'd make damn sure he was in no shape to find his way back inside the building.

I'd been in my share of brawls over the years, and I didn't mind getting my hands dirty. The asshole had *touched* Riley without her permission, which meant I wanted his head.

Right. Fucking. Now.

I reached out to grab the guy's jacket and haul him outside, but Riley suddenly pushed between the two of us. "No, Seth. Don't."

I glared at her because she'd put herself in harm's way, but she stared back at me with a pleading look I couldn't fucking ignore.

"He was mauling you, Riley," I informed her irritably. "Give me one damn good reason why I *shouldn't* take his head off."

"Because he's my brother," she said firmly as she waved at the two guys next to the dark-haired man I'd wanted to pound into the ground seconds ago. "*All three of them* are my brothers."

It took a moment for her words to soak through my anger.

Son of a bitch!

Riley *did* have brothers. She'd mentioned it. But I hadn't expected them to be *here*.

She quickly made the introductions. "Seth, this is Hudson, Jaxton, and Cooper. My older brothers."

Hudson, the asshole I'd nearly punched, shot me a shit-eating grin, and then held out his hand. "Hudson Montgomery," he said gruffly. "Glad you're so diligent about protecting my little sister."

I shook reluctantly because I was still a little irrational. "Seth Sinclair."

Once I'd shaken the hand of Cooper, the *blond,* and Jaxton, the *somewhere-in-between,* I was a little bit calmer.

I watched as Riley enthusiastically hugged each one of them as she said, "I didn't know you were going to be here."

Hudson shrugged. "We like Eli and Jade."

As the siblings continued to chat, I was wracking my brain.

Hudson Montgomery.

Jaxton Montgomery.

Cooper Montgomery.

Montgomery Mining Company.

The lightbulb finally went off.

They were *those* Montgomery brothers.

I frowned as I looked at *Riley Montgomery.*

Montgomery Mining was the biggest operation of its kind in the whole damn world. Had been for decades.

Obviously, Riley was part of that dynasty, along with her three brothers.

Why in the fuck am I just learning about this right now?

"Montgomery Mining?" I asked aloud. "You three head the company, right?"

Hudson nodded. "We do. And I'm assuming that you're one of the lost Sinclairs."

Shit! I really hated it when people referred to our family that way.

"We've never exactly been *lost,*" I said in a gravelly voice. "*I've* always known my exact location."

"No insult intended," Cooper spoke up. "All of us admire your whole family. Jade is an incredible woman. She's told us about how you guys all killed yourself to get her an education. And Eli is a friend."

Jaxton added, "Being a lost Sinclair isn't a put-down, Seth. It's actually a compliment, considering how hard you all worked to help each other out. None of you needed money to succeed. But if some family was going to be found and inherit a fortune, you all deserved it."

"I'm not sure how many people in *this room* could manage success without money," Hudson mused.

Maybe I had overreacted. I *was* a little touchy about my father being a bigamist, which made me and my siblings *bastard Sinclairs.*

I relaxed and actually found myself enjoying the banter with the brothers as we made casual conversation.

There wasn't a single thing about any of the Montgomery brothers that was pretentious, even though they were filthy rich. Yeah, they *were* in the required formal wear, but they looked even more uncomfortable than I was with the company around us.

Am I the only one who notices how damn badly they want to get the hell out of this atmosphere?

I could sense that they were kind of kindred spirits, so I chalked up my awareness to like-mindedness.

I was eager to end the evening, and they obviously wanted the same damn thing.

"So what's your relationship with our sister?" Hudson asked bluntly.

"We're friends," Riley answered swiftly.

Friends, my ass. But I let her get away with the proclamation. For now.

Hudson lifted a brow. "That didn't look like a *friend* reaction a few minutes ago. Seth and I were moments from exchanging blows. And doesn't he own the property that you were trying to acquire for endangered birds? I thought you two were doing battle, not chumming around."

"Seth is giving the property up," Riley said as she beamed at her brother. "It's going to become a wildlife sanctuary."

"That right?" Hudson looked at me.

I shrugged. "I'm not quite sure I'd get away with building on that site, since Jade is my little sister." I sure as hell wasn't going to tell Hudson about the agreement I had with *his* younger sister so she could acquire that land.

Jaxton laughed. "Probably not. It sucks that you lost that opportunity. Citrus Beach is growing."

"There will be others." In that moment, I knew I was showing my weakness for my family, but I didn't give a damn. There were limits to what I'd do to be hard-nosed. And making my sister sad just happened to not be one of them.

Maybe I *had* manipulated my way into Riley's life by holding out on forking over the prime building lot, but I wasn't a complete asshole. Giving over that property had been inevitable. I just wasn't willing to do it easily. Not when I had the chance to use it to spend time with a belligerent, beautiful attorney who had caught my interest from the very first time I'd met her.

"You can take the hit," Cooper added. "It might not feel good, but Eli has told me about some of the stuff that you have in the works for Sinclair Properties."

I'd never miss the money, so it was no big deal to me. Sure, it would have given my business a bigger boost. However, Sinclair Properties didn't really need that much of a climb to keep growing, and there were plenty of other lucrative deals to make up for the loss.

"If you're interested in investors, I don't think any of us would mind coming in," Cooper said enthusiastically.

I certainly wasn't going to give up the opportunity to get the Montgomery brothers as investors. We quickly made plans to meet up and discuss the possibility.

I was *definitely* interested. Besides the fact that the Montgomery brothers had an endless amount of cash to push into Sinclair Properties, they'd also have endless knowledge they could share with me.

They'd be doubly valuable, but I still tried not to show them how eager I was to get them into the business.

Honestly, if I had the Montgomery brothers, I really didn't need a lot more backing for Sinclair Properties to explode.

Before we parted ways, I hesitated. I wanted to ask them one more thing. "Aren't you guys treasure hunters?"

If my memories were correct, the three brothers traveled the world to look for lost artifacts.

I was a guy, so of course I was interested in their adventures. My brothers and I had always dreamed of hunting for hidden treasures, probably because we'd been so damn poor. I was eager to hear about their searches that had actually brought success.

"The main industry for Montgomery is mining diamonds and precious gems. The treasure hunting is more like . . . a hobby," Hudson answered.

"It's something we all like to do," Cooper explained. "But our mining operations have to take priority. Montgomery has been around for generations. It's our legacy."

I lifted a brow as I stared into Riley's beautiful eyes. "Is it your legacy, too?"

She shook her head, but didn't speak. I suspected there was more to her story. I wanted to know what it was, but now wasn't the time to push her.

As Riley was hugging her brothers good-bye, Hudson pulled me to the side. "I don't buy the *friends* bullshit. If you hurt her, I'll kill you," he said in a dangerous tone.

I nodded my head sharply. "Understood. I have two younger sisters."

I got Hudson's message loud and clear, but it sure as hell didn't feel quite as good on *this side* as it did when *I* was the protective big brother. I'd felt the same way about Eli when it had been obvious that Jade was crazy about him. Noah, Aiden, and I had grilled the hell out of him, and pretty much threatened him the same way Hudson was doing to *me* now.

Note to self: apologize to Eli for being an asshole back when he was first dating my little sister.

I retrieved Riley's jacket and tugged her toward the exit once we'd ended the discussion with her brothers.

I was determined to find out exactly why my date hadn't leveled with me about her connections, or her past.

I handed the valet the ticket for my vehicle and then turned to Riley. "When were you going to tell me that you're completely familiar with this world? Hell, you must have *grown up* in it. Montgomery is a giant, and you were raised filthy rich, right? No fucking wonder you knew every person at the party. I thought you were nervous about going into a world you aren't completely comfortable with, but you're actually *one of them,* aren't you? Why in the fuck didn't you tell me that?"

CHAPTER 9
Riley

I wasn't sure why I nearly flinched at Seth's accusation.

Really, I didn't owe him an explanation. "Why does it matter?" I responded in a clipped voice. "Is it really necessary for you to know my background to fulfill my side of our contract?"

The brief flash of disappointment in his eyes nearly made me apologize.

Almost.

Then I quickly remembered that all of this *was* a contract. A deal we'd made so I could get the property turned into a protected area.

In reality, there was nothing personal about this facade. *At all.*

His steely gaze felt like he could see right through me, but I knew he couldn't. Thank God. There were far too many things I didn't want him to see. That I didn't want *anybody* to recognize.

Deep inside, I was damaged. I didn't want to reveal that to anyone who could use it against me.

"That's a whole lot of bullshit," Seth ground out. "You could have warned me, Riley."

Sometimes I found it intriguing that he could

switch between a blue-collar man who used to do manual labor, and a coldhearted billionaire businessman. It shouldn't have been surprising, since he really was *both* of those things. It was fascinating to watch the chameleonlike behavior firsthand.

Was he still unsure of which one he *should* be? Or was it a tactic to catch people off guard?

The problem was, because he could change in the blink of an eye, he kept me off balance.

Remember that all of this is business. It's not real.

I didn't *need* to know him or figure out his entire personality. I just had to fulfill my end of the deal.

"Margaret!" I heard the sharp tone of my mother's voice as she approached us.

Dammit!

I'd managed to avoid her all night because she'd been busy socializing every time I'd seen her.

I was so damn close to making an escape, but she'd caught me.

Seth was staring curiously as Carol Montgomery stopped in front of us. "Margaret?" he said in a low voice next to my ear.

"Later," I said in a whisper that only he could hear.

"Were you going to leave before you spoke to me?" my mother questioned in the pretentiously cordial but snippy tone I'd come to hate over the years.

"You were busy," I muttered, hating myself for feeling like the unsatisfactory daughter, even though I was an educated adult female now.

As usual, the woman who had borne me looked immaculate. Her black evening gown was paired with black shoes, and I already knew the outfit was custom tailored to skim down her slim body perfectly.

Carol Montgomery was a beautiful woman, even though she was in her sixties. She hadn't needed the plethora of plastic surgeries or Botox she got on a regular basis, but growing older was never something my mother would do gracefully. Her hair was dyed in her usual choice of color, a dark brown. God forbid she should show any of the bright-red hair color that was natural for her.

"Introductions, Margaret," she said like a strict teacher talking to an unruly student.

I sent her a plastic smile. "Of course," I replied, falling into my social role with more ease than I would have liked. "Seth, this is my mother, Carol Montgomery. Mother, this is Seth Sinclair."

"Charmed," she purred as she shook Seth's hand, and then turned back to me. "Margaret, have you gained weight?"

I cringed, but I guess I never should have expected my mother to act any differently than she ever had. "A few pounds."

More like five or ten, but who was counting— except my mother.

"And that dress, Margaret?" she said. "It certainly isn't becoming on a curvy woman. Not to mention that the color is garish. Perhaps you should rethink those shoes, too."

God, I knew she would hate the silver shoes.

"I like the color of my dress." I finally found my rebellious streak.

She made a tutting sound before she said, "It's not your style, dear. It's so much better when you cover your legs."

"I love this dress," I mumbled.

"I see you've gone back to your natural hair color." She sounded incredibly disgruntled.

Like it was a disgrace to be a natural redhead?

I shot her a fake smile. "Why not? I inherited it from you."

"She's an absolutely stunning redhead," Seth interrupted. "And she looks drop-dead gorgeous tonight in that dress. Just for the record, some men like curvy women instead of skeletons. Your daughter takes my breath away. Riley is unique, which is incredibly appealing, take my word on that."

My parent stared at Seth like he was an insect, but my heart skipped a beat.

No one *ever* disagreed with my mother, and I found myself surprised and a little bit touched to have some kind of backup. It was a novel experience. One that made me just a little bit more comfortable with myself again.

"Then you're obviously . . . different, Mr. Sinclair," my mother replied in a tone that said she wasn't giving him a compliment.

Seth shot her a cheeky grin. "I'd rather be different than ordinary."

"How . . . charming," she replied unhappily.

My mother was in a position she definitely didn't like to be placed in. She didn't want to snub Seth because he was so wealthy, not to mention the fact that he was the brother of the woman who had married Eli Stone, but she didn't like his offhand attitude, either. Carol Montgomery was used to people deferring to her, and she liked it that way.

I spotted Seth's black Range Rover stopping in front of the venue as it was delivered by the valet. I let out a sigh of relief. "We have to go, Mother. I hope you enjoy the rest of your evening," I said politely.

I didn't touch her or hug her. She would have been mortified.

"Nice to meet you, Carol," Seth said with a nod before he went to open the car door for me.

My parent shot a dubious look at his vehicle. Thank God she didn't comment on that.

In her mind, a man should drive a car that screamed *expensive* and *luxurious*.

Seth's . . . didn't.

It was obvious she didn't approve of an SUV or any vehicle that didn't cost as much as some people's homes.

I happily hopped into the sporty SUV and relaxed against the plush material of the passenger seat. Unlike my mother, I happened to love the comfortable vehicle.

For the average person, it was plenty pricey. The vehicle suited the man who was getting behind the wheel.

I let out an audible sigh as he smoothly got underway for our journey back to Citrus Beach.

"Are you going to explain what just happened?" he finally asked huskily as he took the on-ramp to the freeway.

"What do you mean?" I questioned evasively. I was glad it was dark, so I didn't have to be under his sharp, assessing gaze.

"You can start by telling me who Margaret is," he suggested.

"Me," I told him. "My real name is Margaret Riley Montgomery. But I've been going by Riley since I was a kid. My brothers always hated the name Margaret, and I wasn't exactly fond of it myself. My mother is the only one who calls me that, other than my ex. And my father. But he's deceased now. He died ten years ago of a stroke."

"I'm sorry," Seth said huskily. "I know how hard it is to lose a parent."

"Thanks," I said stiffly.

His voice was warm and genuinely sympathetic, which made me remember that he'd lost his only real parent at a very young age.

"So now you can tell me why your mom is a walking self-esteem destroyer," he insisted.

"She's never my *mom*," I corrected. "She only answers to *Mother*, and I don't remember a time when she wasn't critical."

"That's not just critical, Riley. It's downright abusive. You look gorgeous tonight, and that dress? We won't go into how elegantly sexy it is. Or how damn much I love every curve of your body. What parent ever implies that her daughter doesn't look fucking perfect?"

"Mine," I said with a sigh. "She's firmly entrenched in her world, Seth. She doesn't believe in even dipping a toe into anything that might cause gossip about her."

"So it's not a game for her," he concluded. "But she can't seriously believe that what those people think really matters enough to hurt you."

"She doesn't hurt me anymore," I replied. "I'm used to it."

"Do you really believe that?" he asked low and softly, his irate tone suddenly morphing into one of sympathy.

"Of course. I'm a grown adult."

"It matters, Riley. No matter how old you get. My father was a bigamist. We were his throwaway family. Granted, we didn't know that until we were all grown up, but he was our sperm donor. So it was a slap in the face to all of us. It hurt. Maybe not as much as your mother hurts you, because she raised you. But I'm not falling for the excuse that you're used to getting mentally beat up all the time. She's your mother. The one person who should love you unconditionally."

"That's easy for you to say," I answered defensively. "My family has never been like yours. Everything in mine *was* conditional. And *nothing* was ever good enough. It's been that way as long as I can remember."

"Your brothers seem to love you that way," he observed.

I squirmed in the passenger seat. Talking about my family at all wasn't something I normally would do. "I love them the same way. But we didn't really grow up together. My father wanted all of them in boarding school. So they were rarely at home."

"Jesus!" Seth exploded. "Is that even a thing anymore?"

"Boarding school?"

"Yes."

I nodded even though he couldn't see me. "For rich people it is."

"What about you?" he asked irritably. "Did they send you away, too?"

"No." Admittedly, there were many times I wished I'd gone off *somewhere else* as a child, but I'd stayed in our home.

99

"I don't understand your world," Seth grumbled.

"It's not my world anymore," I said flatly. "And it's really hard to know there's any other way when you grow up in the thick of it. Everything was normalized because it was all I knew. Maybe I didn't go to boarding school, but I was isolated in private schools with students just like me. It wasn't until I got to Harvard that I realized some people actually do love their children—no matter what."

"Why do I still think that you're not okay, even though you don't circulate in that crowd anymore?" Seth asked.

"It's a process," I replied uncomfortably. I hated that he could *see me,* even though I'd done every single thing I could to hide my insecurities. "I've been doing a lot better since I went my own way."

"I guess I get why you were engaged to a rich guy," he mused.

"It couldn't be anything less than a leader in society. I think I got engaged to Nolan to please my mother. I was still looking for her approval back then. According to her, he was absolutely perfect in every way."

"Was he?" Seth asked gruffly.

"No. He wasn't. But those things aren't discussed in polite society, unfortunately. *Money* talks in that world. And he definitely has a lot of *that*. Enough to keep anyone from calling him out. Things get whispered about, but never said out loud."

"So what happened to you two?"

"I broke the golden rule," I explained. "Not only did I say something out loud, but I screamed it during a very exclusive ball."

"He cheated on you?" he guessed.

I took a deep breath. "Not only was he unfaithful, but he did it by sleeping with a fifteen-year-old girl."

I swallowed hard. The dead silence in the vehicle seemed to stretch on and on.

CHAPTER 10
Riley

"Are you fucking kidding me?" Seth roared, breaking the long silence with a vengeance.

I was relieved that, for the very first time, someone other than my brothers and I was infuriated by Nolan's disgusting behavior.

"I wish I was," I confessed. "I caught him with the girl at the ball. In a bedroom. With her clothes half off. She wasn't fighting it. Her mother thought Nolan would be a good catch if her daughter could steal him away from me. I grabbed her and hauled her out of the bedroom and back to the ballroom. Her name is Penny, and she told me everything. I vented with Nolan near the ballroom floor, which is highly frowned upon."

"The bastard should be in jail," Seth growled.

"Her parents refused to press charges. They still hoped she'd eventually marry Nolan."

"He's probably old enough to be her father," Seth answered, sounding disgusted.

"Twenty years older than her," I confirmed.

"What happened to their relationship?"

I smiled into the darkness. "I convinced her that she needed to be a teenager instead of trying to catch a daddy husband. She comes to visit me in Citrus Beach as much as possible. Penny will be off to Harvard next year. She's smart, Seth. Yeah, she's still a little confused, but I think she's getting her head on straight."

"With your help?" he said with admiration in his voice.

"Maybe," I answered. "I couldn't be mad at her. She was still a child."

"You're an amazing woman, Riley Montgomery," he said hoarsely.

"Not so much," I argued. "It was the right thing to do."

"He's an idiot." Seth still sounded pissed off. "He had *you,* for fuck's sake. What else could a guy want? So you chucked him and coaxed his prey away, too?"

"I did. The whole incident was the catalyst that made me finally make a clean break. I didn't think I'd ever go back."

"Why didn't you tell me about all of this, Riley? I never would have forced you back into a situation that had bad memories for you." His voice was full of regret.

"So are you going to let me out of the contract?" I asked hopefully.

He was silent for a few minutes before he answered. "Not completely. But no more fancy events. If your brothers decide to come on board, I don't want to take on anybody else."

"They will." I knew my brothers well enough to recognize when they were interested in a particular deal. "They want in. And you won't find better men to be involved. They're all honest, sometimes to a fault. They could help you just as much as Eli does."

"That's what I'm hoping." His voice was thoughtful. "So there's no need to keep playing the game. Honestly, all the pompous, pumped-up shit isn't for me. I'll do it when I have to, but I'd rather not make a habit of it."

"Like Eli does? He circulates, but mostly for charity, I think."

"I'm willing to do it for a cause, too. So yeah, I'll support the charities, but I wouldn't go to have a good time, or rub elbows with the rich and famous. I've discovered they aren't very good company, for the most part."

I smiled. "There are exceptions. People like my brothers and Eli."

"I sensed that your siblings weren't all that thrilled about being there, either."

"They hate it," I informed him. "They'd rather be out on an adventure than stuck in the middle of a crowd in formal wear. I think they came because they like Jade."

"Good reason." There was a smile in his voice.

I wasn't sure I was exactly envious, but it was nice to see a family that wasn't as screwed up as mine. The Sinclairs had been through hell, yet they'd come out fine on the other side. The elder siblings had obviously been good parent figures for the younger ones, and I was equally sure that the three oldest men had supported each other in their common goal of keeping the family together.

What family fought that hard to stay together?

"So what do we do now?" I wanted to know how I could fulfill my contract. Not because I had to, but because I wanted to do it. Seth *was* making a sacrifice, and I wanted to do something for him in return.

"We just date." He sounded firm in his solution.

"What?" I must have misheard him.

"I said, *'We date.'* Dinner, movies, the Coffee Shack, and other things we both want to do. That's the normal stuff, right?"

I was dumbfounded. "We can't just . . . date. For no reason."

"Why not? We like each other, we're attracted to each other, and I see no reason why we can't do fun stuff instead of work."

I had plenty of arguments on why that wasn't a good idea. "I don't date. I haven't since Nolan and I broke up. I don't need a man in my life. Honestly, I prefer to be alone."

It was quiet for a moment before he spoke. "Considering your history with your engagement, I get that. But I'm not asking you to change who you are, Riley. I also get that you don't *need* a man. I'm assuming that you're wealthy in your own right."

"I am. My brothers bought me out of Montgomery Mining because they knew it wasn't what I wanted. But even if I wasn't rich, I'd feel the same way. I have an education. I can support myself." I didn't mean to be defensive, but I was sick of feeling like I was nothing if I wasn't attached to an eligible male.

No matter how strangely attractive Seth's offer to just date might seem.

"I'm not exactly a playboy, Riley," he said ruefully. "Truthfully, I've never really dated much at all. When I was younger, I didn't have time, and very few women wanted to date a construction worker with dependent siblings. Now, it's hard to escape from the women who wouldn't have dated me before I became a billionaire."

My heart squeezed. Obviously, there were a lot of stupid women in and around Citrus Beach. "Any guy who is as devoted to family and those responsibilities would be a great guy to date, no matter what his occupation."

"Glad you feel that way. So do we have a deal?"

"I didn't mean me. Any *other* woman."

"What in the hell are you afraid of, Riley?" His voice was low and persuasive.

In spite of my external strong shell I'd created,

106

I was terrified of a lot of things, and Seth Sinclair was probably the most dangerous of them all. "I'm not afraid," I lied. "I just don't really see the point. I'm not going to sleep with you, Seth."

"I must have missed the part where I asked you to," he answered, sounding frustrated. "I'm just asking you to go out with me, have some fun. We can get to the sex part later."

Have some fun?

I really had no idea how to indulge in happy diversions. Growing up, it took all I had to stay relatively sane. "I'm not sure I know how to do that."

"Have sex? No worries. I'll teach you."

He spoke in such a nonthreatening way that I released a short laugh. "I don't know how to have fun. Not really. I never did kid things when I was younger. And life at Harvard was all-consuming. I studied because I wanted to be independent. Then, I stupidly got myself engaged to a man my mother wanted me to marry, because there was a part of me that still wanted to make her see me as a daughter she could be proud of. Nolan wasn't exactly a barrel of fun. He had no other interests except being seen by the elite and screwing underage girls."

"Jesus. Maybe our family was poor, but we had all the cheap fun we could have for our younger siblings," Seth explained. "My brothers and I loved just about every water fight, bike ride, and

107

beach day we got with our family. We made our own fun."

I briefly thought about how idyllic it might have been for Owen, Brooke, and Jade to be raised by their elder brothers. If nothing else, they had definitely known that they were safe and loved.

"Why can't we just separate and call it good now?" I felt my spirit balk, but it would be the reasonable solution. "It's not like there's a future for us. It would be wasted time."

"Not a single minute of being with you would ever be insignificant, Riley," he argued.

I was glad it was dark. I felt my eyes get watery, and I blinked back the tears.

I'd never had a guy who just wanted to . . . be with me. Without conditions. Without rules of conduct. Without . . . criticism.

"Why me?" I'd wanted to ask him that question for some time. Deep inside, I knew that Seth wasn't out to date every female he met. Or get them into bed. He wasn't a flirt. There wasn't a single moment in the evening where he had even eyed another female, which was so much different from being with Nolan. My ex-fiancé had never seemed like he cared much about being with me. I'd been more of an object than a partner.

"Why you?" he repeated. "Maybe I just like women who argue with me," he said with a chuckle.

It was an interesting answer, because I'd *never* argued with Nolan. *At all. Ever.* I'd accepted whatever he'd thrown at me.

However, I *was* a different woman than I'd been back then. "I'm likely to do that a lot," I warned him, feeling myself caving in.

Would it really hurt to spend some time with Seth? That was what I'd agreed to in the first place. And it could be done in a far less stressful atmosphere.

Maybe the truth was I honestly *wanted* to spend time with him, too, even though I knew I was probably flirting with the danger of becoming attached to him.

He was protective.

He was funny.

He loved, and was loved, without apology.

God knew the man was attractive, which could become an issue.

Am I really ready to be myself with a man?

I wasn't sure, but I *felt* ready to poke my head out of the shell I'd built around me.

"Same terms," I said before I could stop myself. "No sex. No ass grabbing—"

"No criticizing," he finished. "I think you know by now that I won't do that, Riley. At least I hope you do."

"Then I guess you have a date. Same days and times we already agreed on?"

His laughter boomed through the vehicle. "Do

we really need to plan *everything?* These are dates, not business commitments."

I frowned. "I suppose not. But I want to make sure I have the appropriate attire for whatever we're doing."

This whole *dating* thing had me rattled, and I already felt like it was out of control. Planning made things more normal for me.

Seth didn't say anything as he exited the freeway and drove to my house.

In fact, he didn't comment on what I'd said until we got to my door.

When I put my key in the door, he grabbed my arm gently and turned me around to face him. "I'm going to say this one last time, and then I hope I never have to say it again. But if I have to say it a million times, that's okay, too. I like you exactly the way you are, Riley. I don't care what you do, what you wear, or how you want to express yourself. I really just want to be with you. Do you get that?"

A lump formed in my throat as I saw the truth in his turbulent gaze.

"No. I actually don't get it." My voice sounded strange as I tried to speak. Probably because the lump in my throat was actually my heart. "I'm used to conditions. I think I'm more comfortable knowing what somebody wants."

He reached out a gentle hand and tipped my chin up. "No, you aren't. You just aren't used to being spontaneous. You're afraid of losing control because you don't trust very many people. But I'm willing to wait until you *do* trust me. I'm not going to hurt you, Riley."

He might!

It just wouldn't happen in the way he imagined. What if I did come to trust him?

What if I got used to being with a guy who didn't want anything from me except . . . my company?

I knew he was getting ready to kiss me. I could feel the tension between us. It was thick enough to cut with a sharp knife. I was disturbed by how badly I wanted to be intimately connected with him. My body was shivering with anticipation, my senses filled with his masculine, alluring scent. I wanted to get *closer* to him. I was drawn by an inexplicable source.

What in the hell am I doing?

I turned away, breaking our contact, and fumbled with the lock on the door. "Same terms. Two months. Nothing else after that. Since it's your contract, you can pick where we go and what we do."

"You'll be consulted," he said, sounding amused.

"Fine."

Sweet Jesus! I need to get away from him before I tear his clothes off.

"You can run away, Riley, but I guarantee that I'll catch you," Seth said in a husky voice behind me.

Not tonight you won't.

By the time I stepped inside the house, my heart was racing.

"Good night, Seth," I said in a breathless voice.

"Good night, gorgeous," he answered, his eyes scanning me covetously before he walked back to his car.

I flipped on the lights and leaned heavily against the door I'd just hastily closed.

I was breathing hard, wondering why I wasn't completely relieved that I'd escaped so easily.

CHAPTER 11
Seth

"She'll either make me happy or she'll end up killing me," I told my brothers Aiden and Noah as we sat at Noah's kitchen table drinking coffee the next morning.

I'd just finished spilling my guts to my elder and slightly younger brothers about the situation I'd gotten myself into with Riley.

It wasn't unusual for Aiden and me to meet up several times a week, but we normally had to come over to Noah's place to pull him *physically* out of his home office.

When we were younger, my eldest brother had been around for all of us, even though Noah had worked like crazy to keep our family together. But lately, we didn't see much of him. He was always busy developing some new app, a career choice that he'd taken on when we'd all come into money. Before that, he'd worked for various companies to put his computer-science education to work.

I looked at the exhaustion that clearly showed on Noah's face.

None of us liked the way that Noah seemed more overworked now than he had been *before* the inheritance.

Not to say that Aiden didn't work hard at his goal of building a fishing empire, but his daughter, Maya, and his wife, Skye, were his priorities. Unlike Noah, Aiden had a life outside his career ambitions.

I didn't want to remember that I'd nearly ruined Aiden's life by doing something stupid when we were younger, but at least he was happy *now*.

Unfortunately, Noah . . . wasn't. My eldest brother might say he was doing what he wanted to do, but I had a hard time believing it. It was like he was trying to avoid some kind of hidden demons by immersing himself in work.

For about the millionth time since our inheritance, I had to wonder exactly what Noah was trying to evade in the world outside his work.

"I honestly think she's smart to avoid the life she used to lead," Aiden observed. "I met her once when she was with Jade. She didn't seem like the snotty type."

"Haven't met her," Noah grumbled. "But I can't help but think *anybody* is better off not being with a superficial, rich crowd."

I smirked at Noah. "I hate to tell you, man, but you're one of those rich guys now."

He shrugged. "Maybe I'm rich, but I don't fit into *that* group."

"None of us do," Aiden commented. "And most likely we never will. Thank fuck. I'm pretty damn happy the way I am right now. I have

114

everything I want, but it has nothing to do with material stuff."

"I almost fucked that up for you," I told him regretfully.

"I'm over all that," Aiden said sincerely. "I *was* pissed, but even then, I knew your heart was in the right place."

It was the first time my younger brother had told me that he'd completely forgiven what I'd done when we were younger to screw up his relationship with Skye back then. It was a relief for me that he no longer held a grudge, and it made my heart feel a little lighter.

"Now let's figure out how to make sure you're happy, Seth," Aiden added. "Are you sure you want to pursue this with Riley if she has no inclination to date or find a relationship?"

"I think she wants to," I mused. "I think she's just scared. Apparently, she had a pretty bad experience with her ex."

The only thing I hadn't told my brothers about was Riley's private pain over Nolan Easton's choice of cheating partners. She'd been so broken up about her ex sleeping with a child in her underage teen years that I knew it was incredibly personal to her, so I'd skirted around the details.

Noah took a slug of his coffee like he desperately needed it before he said, "I think you have to give her credit for breaking her relationship off with him. And for wanting a different kind of life."

"I do," I admitted. "It's one of the things I really like about her. She's unique and trying so damn hard to find her individuality, even though it's pretty damn clear to me that she's already her own person. Maybe she just needs to learn to let go, laugh, have a good time without everyone around her judging her for it."

Noah eyed me suspiciously. "This is about a hell of a lot more than having fun, Seth, and you know it."

Shit! Sometimes I really hated that Noah knew me better than most other brothers would. From an early age, he'd felt responsible for all of us, even though Aiden and I were only a few years behind him in age. I wasn't going to go as far as saying he was exactly a father figure. At least not for me or Aiden. We were too close in age. But he definitely considered *himself* the patriarch of the family.

"She's thrown in a no-sex rule," I admitted unhappily. "And I'm not allowed to put my hand on her ass."

I frowned as Aiden let out an evil laugh.

"So you're going to date, you're attracted to her, but you can't touch her?" Aiden snorted. "That sounds like self-inflicted torture, man."

I pushed my empty coffee mug aside and crossed my arms over my chest. "Don't sound so damn amused," I grumbled. "I'm pretty sure Skye didn't give in to touching at the very beginning, either."

Bastard! Aiden was obviously enjoying all this.

"She didn't," Aiden confirmed. "But at least I knew I had a future with her if I could convince her that we belonged together, which I did. And we were always going to have Maya connecting the two of us. But Riley has already told you she's not interested in anything long term."

I lifted a brow. "Maybe I'm not, either," I said defensively.

Noah butted in. "You are, and that's what concerns me. I don't want to see you get destroyed by this woman. You've never really dated, Seth. Why her? Why not somebody who could make you happy in the future?"

I shrugged. "There's no such thing as guaranteed happiness when you start dating anyone, and there isn't another woman I want to date. They're pretty much after the money now. Hell, women who didn't even see me before I inherited are suddenly finding me fucking irresistible. I think I'd rather be with Riley. At least I know she's not after the dollar signs."

Aiden shot me an assessing look. "She doesn't need to be, since she's wealthy herself. Is that the attraction?"

I shook my head. "No. I've been attracted to her ever since she rescued me the very first time in the Coffee Shack. And I had no idea she was rich at the time."

"You're screwed," Noah informed me.

"I think I can convince her that not every guy is a major control freak," I informed my brothers. "Okay, yeah, I'll admit that I want to protect her from some of the bad things she's experienced in her life, but I'm sure as hell not going to criticize her for being exactly who she wants to be. It wasn't just her fiancé who messed with her head. Her mother is a piece of work, too. I don't think Riley has ever had anyone who actually supported her."

"Maybe you should go for it," Aiden said thoughtfully. "If you're that attracted to her, it might be worth it."

"I'm not so sure about that," Noah said skeptically. "Most women are basically trouble. Some worse than others, I suppose. But I'm not so sure *any* woman is worth the hassle."

Aiden shot a disappointed look at Noah. "Some are worth it," he argued.

I could tell my younger brother was defending his own marriage to the woman who had held his heart for his entire adult life.

Noah gave Aiden an apologetic look. "I didn't mean Skye. She's a rare exception. And you wouldn't have Maya if she'd never existed."

I smirked. Noah adored Aiden's daughter, just like every single person in our family did.

Aiden let out a bark of laughter as he looked at Noah. "You adore my wife because she drops you off dinner all the damn time. She's so damn sweet that she worries about your workaholic ass."

"I didn't ask her to do that," Noah said gruffly.

"She does it because she sees you as family, and she worries about the fact that you rarely come out of your office."

"Like I said, she's an exception," Noah said grudgingly. "But Riley is a complete unknown."

"I care about her," I said. "Yeah, I'm attracted to her. But I actually *like her,* too. She's pretty damn gutsy."

I was still thinking about how Riley had wrenched Easton's child prey away from him, and taught Penny to value herself.

Problem was, who had ever been there for *Riley?* Nobody had rescued *her.* She'd had to figure shit out on her own.

Maybe she was close to her brothers, but by her own admission, she'd rarely seen them growing up.

"Just be careful," Noah insisted. "From everything you've told us, this could have a very unhappy ending if you get too attached."

"It's just dating," I asserted. "It's not like I'm ready to propose or something."

"I have to add my warning, too," Aiden said regretfully. "I'm starting to think that when a Sinclair finds the right person, that's pretty much the end of the road. There isn't anybody else, ever. I fell in love with Skye a decade or so ago, and I never forgot her. Jade fell in deep with Eli in a short period of time, and there had never been anyone else for her. Same with Brooke and Liam. And from what I understand, all our half-siblings were the same damn way. I think we're loyal once we fall for someone, even if we don't want to be after they're gone."

I scowled at Aiden. I didn't want to think about Riley *ever* walking away from me. But Aiden might have a point about a Sinclair only having one shot once they fell hard for someone. "Wasn't I the one who told you not to judge Skye until you knew the whole truth?" I asked him.

"I'm not telling you *not* to date her," Aiden considered. "I'm just adding my advice to use caution. You're pigheaded, so I have no doubt you can sway her opinions on men if she ends up feeling the same way you do. But like you said, there's no guarantee."

"I don't think you should date her," Noah said glumly. "Better to avoid a possible disaster."

I glared at my eldest brother. "So do you plan on being single your entire life?"

"Yes," Noah responded immediately. "I've raised my siblings already, and I have zero desire to have any more kids around. I'm done. So why bother with marriage? But this isn't about me, Seth. It's about you."

Aiden shot me a grin, and I was pretty sure we were thinking the same damn thing . . . We both hoped that Noah would fall hard for a woman someday, so he'd deviate from his workaholic tendencies. Fuck knew my oldest brother deserved his own life and happiness now that all of his siblings were grown adults.

"I'll be fine," I assured Noah. "Hell, I could use some leisure time myself. You're right about the fact that I've barely dated. Maybe I need to hone my skills. Unlike you, I'd like to have a female companion."

I had to wonder whether Noah had even made the time over the years to get laid.

It was hard to imagine that he *hadn't*.

"Maybe you and Riley could come over for a barbecue," Aiden suggested. "Now that she's bought Jade's old place, we're almost right next door."

I threw him a grateful look. Our homes were all close together, and right on the beach. It was a short walk from house to house.

Aiden was obviously on board with the whole idea now, even if Noah wasn't.

"I'd probably come," Noah mumbled. "I'd like to check this girl out for myself."

Okay, I was shocked. Noah rarely got out of the house unless one of us was getting married or having a major event in our lives. That's why Aiden and I showed up at *his* place.

"Thanks. Let me know what works for you guys, and I'll ask Riley." I gave Noah a warning look. "Just don't be a dick," I warned.

He raised an eyebrow. "When am I ever anything other than discreet?"

I could mention several times that he *wasn't*. Like when he'd been right there with Aiden and me when we'd grilled the hell out of Eli and Liam. Instead of pointing out those occurrences, I let the comment slide.

Honestly, if I thought that Noah was headed for trouble, I'd probably discourage him from doing it, too. We'd fought growing up, but our strongest inclination was always to protect each other.

Aiden stood. "Much as I'd like to continue this conversation, I have a meeting with a prospective captain."

"I have to go, too." I hadn't been in the office yet, and I had a meeting later that morning.

"I've been waiting to get back to work," Noah said predictably.

When is he not waiting to get back to his office?

When Noah and I rose from the table, Aiden gave me a brotherly slap on the back. "Good luck," he said, sounding genuinely supportive. "If you need any advice or somebody to listen, call me. You were there for me."

"I suppose I'm available, too," Noah rumbled. "But I have no damn idea how to charm a female."

I grinned. I had no doubt that Noah was clueless, but I appreciated the fact that he was willing to leave his office if I needed him.

"I'll call you," Aiden informed me right before he walked out the door.

I wasn't far behind him.

Although I'd appreciated my brothers' advice, I'd already known what I was going to do *before* I'd spilled my guts to my siblings.

Now it was time to set things in motion before Riley changed her mind.

It was way past time for her to date a guy who was going to appreciate her.

And I knew there was no better man for the job than me.

CHAPTER 12
Riley

What in the hell had I been thinking?

That thought rolled over and over inside my head as I sat at my desk the morning after I'd made the stupid agreement with Seth to go on regular dates.

I'd been trying to work on an important case all morning, and I was failing miserably at keeping my thoughts off Seth.

Honestly, I knew *why* I'd gone along with his idea.

Other than Nolan, I'd never really dated. I'd had a brief relationship in college with a guy who had been my first, but we'd separated soon after that. I was curious to know what it would be like to go out with someone who really liked me and wouldn't be so damn judgmental. Going to events with my ex had felt like I was always walking on eggshells. Every moment, I was waiting for the other shoe to drop and squash the life out of me completely.

With Seth, I might not have to be worried about being uncomfortable. The only real anxiety I felt when we were together was over the sexual tension that seemed to sizzle around both of us.

It was uncomfortable, but in a far *different* way.

I can handle this thing with Seth. I have to stop stressing over it.

I wasn't getting any work done, and that wasn't *at all* like me.

I heard my phone ping, signaling that I had a text. Generally, I ignored my cell when I was working, so I surprised myself when I reached out and picked up the phone.

Seth: The Coffee Shack? I want to get out of the office and take a walk, and I need some late morning caffeine to function. No pressure, but I'll be there if you need a chai as bad as I need a coffee right now.

I smiled. We were both addicts when it came to our caffeine, so we had at least one thing in common.

I shouldn't go. I have work to do. And he is giving me the choice.

Seth hadn't ordered me to be there. He'd just thrown out the tantalizing invitation to join him if I wanted to go.

I can't go.

I won't go.

It's not exactly a request for one of our promised . . . dates.

"Maybe that's the problem," I mumbled aloud. "It almost feels like he was just inviting . . . a friend."

Strangely, it was for *that very reason* that I was tempted to go.

I sighed. I really hadn't had the opportunity to make that many friends since I'd moved to Citrus Beach. I knew people *casually,* but I didn't really hang out with anybody.

Before I'd moved here, there wasn't a single person in my mother's crowd who I'd trusted enough to share anything personal with, and really, I'd never had much in common with anybody within that group.

Friends had never been in large supply in my life, and I suddenly wished I had some.

Or at least . . . one.

Recklessly, I typed out a reply.

Riley: Fifteen minutes. I have to drive.

My beach house was too far away to walk to the downtown area.

Seth: Want the usual? I'll order for you since I'm already on my way.

He'd order for me? Why did it feel so weird for someone to do that? Maybe because nobody ever had.

I was pretty damn accustomed to being treated like a nonperson for the most part. Knowing my needs mattered to somebody was a pretty strange experience for me.

I typed back to him as I stood up.

Riley: Yes, please. I'd never change up my order. I'm too obsessed with my chai mocha latte. I'm on my way.

I hurried to my bedroom, pulling off the ratty

T-shirt I was wearing on my way to my closet.

I frowned as I looked over my choices of apparel. I wasn't about to lose my comfortable jeans, but I wanted something a little nicer than the T-shirt I'd just tugged off.

Maybe a shopping trip for more clothing was in order.

Selecting a lightweight dark-green sweater I'd never worn, I quickly tugged it over my head.

I had almost no clothing in between my well-worn work-at-home outfits and my power suits.

Dating attire was absolutely not something I'd ever needed in the last few years.

When I found myself fluffing my hair in the mirror, I stopped myself immediately.

This is not a date.

It was just a caffeine run.

I grabbed my purse and went through the garage to get to my cute little red Mazda Miata.

Like Seth, I hadn't opted to buy an outrageously expensive vehicle, but I loved the inexpensive little convertible I had purchased. It was loaded, and it was a pleasure to drive.

I kept the top on, because if I didn't, I'd look like the Wicked Witch of the West by the time I got into town. My fiery red hair was naturally curly and had a mind of its own. Wind was not my friend when it came to my unruly mop.

By the time I arrived at the Coffee Shack, I realized that I was nervous, but had no idea *why*.

Most likely, it was that kiss last night that had me edgy. Or maybe the near-miss embrace I'd *avoided* when Seth had dropped me off.

I got out of my vehicle and grabbed my purse, thinking that all of this would be so damn easier if Seth Sinclair didn't make me want to rip off his clothes and climb him like he was a tree.

I shook my head as I walked to the entrance.

Why did it have to be *him* who suddenly set my body on fire, and had my mind going to erotic places that I'd never even known existed?

Once I stepped inside, I immediately saw him waving his arm in the air.

He was at the same table he'd been at the other two times we'd met up here.

"Hi," I said breathlessly as I sat down across from him.

"The usual." He pushed my chai toward me with a grin that made me squirm with agitation. Seth's smile was heart stopping, and highly intriguing since his smoky eyes didn't give up any of his secrets. There seemed to be so much emotion in their depths, but I had no idea what he was thinking. Quite honestly, he was an enigma.

I picked up my chai. "This is huge," I told him, looking at the supersize cup of chai before I took a sip. "I usually get the regular size."

"You can toss it if you don't want the whole thing," he suggested.

"No!" I exclaimed. "It's not that I don't want it,

128

but it's full of sugar and cream. I try to keep my consumption of it under control. My hips *don't* like it."

He smirked. "Funny that you should say that. I like your hips just fine. I wouldn't like them any less if they got wider, either."

I rolled my eyes, even though I was secretly starting to delight in the complimentary things he said about me.

I watched him as I sipped my chai. There wasn't a thing about Seth that made him unappealing, from the way he filled out his gorgeous gray custom suit to the way his hair was slightly mussed up. But probably the most attractive thing about him was that he didn't seem to *know* just how gorgeous he was, or that his thousand-watt smile was enough to melt almost any woman into a puddle at his feet.

It still seemed strange to me that Seth had never had a long-term girlfriend, even when he hadn't had money. If I was in the market for a man, which I wasn't, I'd be all over him whether he had two pennies to rub together or not.

"How is your day going?" I asked politely. It was more than a courteous question. I really wanted to know.

"I'm distracted," he answered unhappily.

"Is everything okay?" I was worried. Seth wasn't the inattentive type.

"Nope. I'm not. I can't stop thinking about the

hot redhead who rocked my world with a single kiss last night."

My heart skittered. "Maybe you shouldn't see her again so soon, then."

He shook his head dramatically. "Not a chance. We're dating. I want to see *her* as often as possible."

I shifted in my chair uncomfortably. "I'm having a hard time focusing, too," I confessed. "I told you that kiss was a mistake."

"It didn't feel like a mistake, Riley," he rumbled. "My biggest issue is how soon I can taste you again, and all of the places I'd like to do it *next time*."

I tried to ignore his comment, but it was impossible. Just the thought of our bodies melding together, preferably naked and skin-to-skin, sent a shock of heat between my thighs.

I couldn't *not* imagine where I'd like to have those amazing lips of his kiss me. The man was simply too damn tempting.

"Why can't we just be friends?" I said desperately. "It's not like we need to fake the whole 'showing affection' thing anymore."

"Don't get me wrong, I want to be your friend." His eyes drilled into my face. "But if we're going to start off right with this new relationship, I'm not going to bullshit you and say I don't want a hell of a lot more than just a kiss. I want us to be honest with each other, Riley. You won't trust me if I hold anything back. And for me, I wasn't faking it last night."

Maybe I won't trust him if he's not honest. But it certainly *wasn't* comfortable to hear about how he lusted after me, either. I wasn't used to it.

"I'm attracted to you, too," I confessed, determined to be equally up-front with him as well. "But I already told you that I'm not looking for a man or a relationship."

"Then feel free to use me for the time we have. Truth is, neither one of us knows where this is going, but we obviously realize that we'd like to fuck each other until that goddamn desire is gone."

My head shot up to gape at him. "I've never had casual sex."

In fact, I'd only had two lovers in my life: one relationship had ended quickly in college. And then there was Nolan, who made it obvious he wasn't all that physically attracted to me. Obviously, he liked his women younger. *A lot younger.*

I really didn't like to remember screwing my ex-fiancé. Not only did it disgust me, considering he was doing Penny at the same time, but it just hadn't been good overall.

"Never had casual sex?" he questioned. "I've had plenty of it. While I won't say it's completely satisfying, it never hurts to scratch that itch."

"Not interested," I lied. "I have a vibrator."

I shuddered as he looked at me as though he was imagining what I'd look like getting myself off.

"I'd love to see that," he said hoarsely. "But I still think you'd be better off experimenting with *me*."

As I stared back at him, I knew I'd find a hell of a lot more satisfaction with *him*. Naked, rolling around in the sheets, our bodies melting together while we both satisfied *the itch*.

Honestly, for me, the sexual urges gnawing at me were more like an allover body rash that I wanted to scratch hard.

"Please don't push me," I said in a pleading tone that I hated.

I wasn't used to being hesitant about anything in my life. *At all. Ever.* But Seth sucked some kind of vulnerability from me that I couldn't seem to control.

As though he felt it, he reached out and grabbed my hand. "Hey, I didn't mean to push. Take your time. It might kill me, but I'm more than willing to wait, Riley. Truthfully, I'd like to believe that this could be more than just a sexual fling."

A pulse vibrated through my whole body as he stroked the top of my hand with his thumb.

Any contact.

Any touch.

Any sexual innuendos from this man, no matter how subtle, made every rational thought I'd always had fly out of my head.

Truthfully, I wanted him to touch me, but then I ended up regretting it because it breached one of the walls I'd built up inside me.

Safe. Being safe is always better than taking a risk.

I'd craved security for so long. Now that I'd found it in my solitude, it was almost impossible to let that go. Even a little.

I pulled my hand away defensively. "We need to stick with our agreement, Seth."

His lips tugged into a wicked smile. "I'm down with that . . . for now."

I sat back in my chair and sipped at my chai.

Seth changed the subject, talking about his day and asking about mine. *Minus* the sexual innuendos and subtle touches.

I was relieved and disappointed at the same time.

CHAPTER 13
Riley

"I don't know how to do this," I said with a laugh as I watched Seth rig up two fishing poles.

After two weeks of seeing him almost every day, I was losing my hesitance to tell him how I really felt.

I'd laughed a lot over the last couple of weeks, more than I could remember doing in my entire life.

My desire to strip him naked had only grown, but he'd been true to his word, and he never pushed or used the chemistry between us to manipulate me.

Getting together on a daily basis was becoming almost natural to me. To be honest, it was also something I craved now. It would probably feel abnormal not to see his smiling face or experience his wicked sense of humor every day.

It didn't much matter what we did or where we went.

He'd offered to take me anywhere. After all, he *did* own a private jet. It wasn't that I didn't *want* to go everywhere with him, but I'd chosen to just be . . . normal.

We'd checked out several restaurants in the area, including Maya's Bistro, where I'd met

Aiden's wife, Skye, who was quickly becoming one of the friends I'd never had.

There were movies, where Seth had happily discovered that I liked science fiction stuff rather than chick flicks.

I swore that I'd gained another couple of pounds from meeting up with him at the Coffee Shack daily, but I was learning not to sweat it, since I ran every day on the beach. Since Seth always assured me that women with curves were sexy, and encouraged me to eat whatever I wanted, I'd lost the somewhat paranoid notion that I had to be thin.

Seth looked up at me. "You *wanted* to do this," he reminded me.

"I've never fished," I explained. "But I'm going to fumble around like a newbie. And now I'm a little bit worried if this dock will hold both of us."

I *had* suggested that we take a fishing trip on the old dock that sat on his vacant beach property. I'd been taken aback when I saw a flash of disagreement on his face at first. But he'd brushed his hesitance off and complied with the idea almost immediately.

"It will hold up," he said as he stood. "This dock has been here as long as I can remember. It was built for the long haul."

"I guess you would have taken it down if you'd ended up building your resort here."

He nodded as he handed me one of the fishing poles. "I would have," he answered. "In fact, I looked forward to it."

I got distracted when he taught me how to cast my line and didn't think about his statement again until we were both sitting casually side by side on the dock with our lines in the water.

"Why were you looking forward to taking it down?" I asked curiously.

There was a moment of silence before he spoke. "I spent a lot of time here as a kid. Fishing. Just like this. My mom used to bring us here."

"So you have good memories here." I was confused. Did he love the place or hate it?

"Some," he confirmed. "But I always knew she didn't come here to fish with Noah, Aiden, and me."

I turned my head to look at him. Even though I could only see his profile, I could tell that his square jaw was tight with tension. "Then what did she want here?"

"She came here to watch for my biological father," he said huskily. "It's the perfect vantage point to see planes coming and going from the small airport. I think she watched for him every day, but when she really thought he was coming, she'd come here to wait. Only to be disappointed when he didn't arrive."

My heart ached from hearing the raw vulnerability in his voice. "Did you watch, too?" I asked.

"Hell, no. Everybody knew he wasn't going to come except my mother." His voice was tight.

"I'm so sorry," I answered. "It must have been hard to be without a dad."

"Now that we know the truth about him, I think we were better off. My half-siblings went through hell when they were kids because he was an abusive alcoholic. I'm not sure what my mother ever saw in him. But she still hoped he'd come back, because she thought she was married to him."

"He was never around?"

"To tell the truth, I don't even really remember him. He dropped in once in a while, just long enough to get my mother pregnant. But he rarely even acknowledged his bastard kids." His voice was low and thoughtful.

"He didn't even talk to you?" I asked, flabbergasted that Seth had really never talked to his dad about anything.

"Nope. He was more interested in pulling my mother away from us so they could go somewhere alone. She was a beautiful woman."

"Bastard," I grumbled.

His lips turned up in a small smile. "Actually, *we* were the bastards. An entire family of illegitimate kids who had no idea why he rarely chose to visit us. You must know that my father was a bigamist. One family on the East Coast, and the other on the West?"

137

I wasn't going to lie to him. The whole sordid story had been all over the news. "I knew that, but I had no idea that he'd abandoned you."

"He did. Completely. He was a goddamn billionaire, but he never gave my mother a penny to take care of the kids he'd fathered. We always lived dirt-poor."

I hadn't known that, and my heart squeezed at the injustice. What sacrifice would Seth's father have performed by giving his mother plenty of funds to raise his own children? To me, it just seemed . . . cruel. He'd had the money, and he never would have missed it. *At all.*

"But the whole thing made you sad?" I could tell by Seth's reaction that the bigamist thing still bothered him.

"Not so much *me* as it did *my mother.* It makes me a hell of a lot angrier that he always hurt *her.* It killed all of us to see her wait, watch, and never give up hope that he'd eventually come home. She worked her ass off to support all of us, yet my so-called billionaire father never contributed a dime."

"Did she know he was wealthy?" I found it difficult to imagine that she hadn't had some resentment toward the man who had fathered her children.

"None of us really know. Mom didn't talk about him much. I guess she wanted us to be kids and not worry about adult stuff. She was pretty tight-lipped, but she had to have known. On the rare occasions he did show up, he came on a private jet. And she flew on it when he took her away for a while. I suppose he could have come up with some story, but near the end, we know she found out about him having another family and another wife."

I watched him stare out at the ocean, and I instinctively knew that he was caught up in remembering all his mother had gone through.

Now I regretted the fact that I'd pushed to come here. I hadn't known it would dredge up so many bad experiences for him.

"We can go," I offered softly. "I didn't know you didn't like being here."

He grabbed my arm as I went to get up. "Don't, Riley," he grunted. "It's okay. I guess that sometimes there's just some old baggage that can't be thrown away. But I like being here with you. This old dock needs some happier memories to take away the old ones."

"Screw that," I answered angrily as I plopped my ass back down on the wood. "You bring the gasoline, and I'll bring the matches. We can torch the whole thing later."

He chuckled. "You sound like a lioness trying to protect her young."

I smiled weakly because I was still pissed off. "Not that," I denied. "But I'd like to think we're . . . friends. And friends protect each other, right?"

139

"Usually," he agreed. "You say that like you've never had a single friend."

Since he was spilling his guts, I felt okay with doing it myself. "I haven't, actually. Remember where I grew up. My parents wouldn't accept me being with anyone unless they were from our supposed *class*. And there weren't many kids in that circle who I actually liked or trusted."

"Not surprising," he drawled. "What about college?"

I shrugged. "I was too busy studying. I dated a guy for a while, but it didn't work out. We wanted different things, and we were young. He found somebody else who was in his own major who he had a lot more in common with, eventually."

"And then Easton when you got back home?" he guessed.

"Yes," I said sadly.

"You must have felt isolated."

"I did. But I got used to it. Maybe I was so accustomed to being alone that I was actually more comfortable being that way. Plus, I never really knew *any other* way. Even when I was engaged to Nolan, I felt alone. I was still playing the game."

He shook his head. "It wasn't a game for you then, Riley. It was your reality. I think all you ever wanted was to fit in. But you never did, because you're not like them."

"It's really hard to stop wanting my mother's

approval, even though I know that's never going to happen." A pang of pain rippled through my heart.

"You don't need it," he growled. "I know it's hard not to want to try. Fuck knows that my brothers and I wanted our father's approval, too, even though he was an asshole. I think it's an instinct that you have to work hard to shake off. It's normal to want our parents to be proud of us. But at some point, I think you have to break free and tell them to fuck off. She's never been a mother to you, Riley, and I hate to say it, but she probably never will be."

I sighed. "You're right. And I've been working on that since I kicked Nolan to the curb."

"It will happen when you're ready," Seth said in a low, empathetic baritone.

"I get closer to it every day," I answered lightly. "I love it here in Citrus Beach. Nobody judges me, because most people have no idea who I am. To them, I'm just an attorney in town. To be honest, I like that."

"Whether they know or not doesn't matter," he mused. "You can blow off the people who don't care about you for the person you are, and keep the ones close who do."

I shot him a slightly admonishing look. "Like you blow off the women who are chasing you for your money?"

I never saw him making them scurry away.

Ever. In fact, he seemed to have a problem doing it himself.

"Doesn't matter," he answered offhandedly. "I don't like that kind of attention, but I don't take it to heart, either. I know what they're after, and it sure as hell isn't *me*."

I started to fume over the fact that some women treated him like he was nothing more than a bank account. The more time I spent with Seth, the more I knew that he had so much more to offer than just money. "Some of the women in this town are crazy," I mumbled. "You're a true catch, money or not."

"To be truthful, I have to admit I didn't try all that hard when I was broke. A few rejections taught me a lesson, and I really didn't have much to offer a woman," he said in a genuine tone. "There wasn't really anyone I was that interested in, either. I've never been in Aiden's situation, where I met a woman I wanted more than anything else in the world. One of the amazing things about Skye was that she fell for my brother when he was dirt-poor. She saw . . . him. That's pretty rare."

I had to stare straight ahead so Seth didn't see my watery eyes. The fact that no female had ever seen . . . him seemed so incredibly sad to me. Yet I didn't want him to find that woman now, either.

Because I want him for myself.

I balked at the thought, but I knew damn well it was true.

For some reason, I didn't want any woman to be with this gorgeous, sensitive man next to me . . . except me.

I didn't have much time to mull over my revelation.

There was a gigantic pull on my fishing pole that surprised the hell out of me.

"Oh, my God! I have a fish, Seth! I have one!" I got so excited that I stumbled to my feet, not remembering a single thing he'd said about setting the hook or bringing a fish in.

When the monster tugged hard again, I lost my balance in my enthusiasm that I'd actually caught something, and before I knew it, I was plunging forward.

"Riley!" Seth bellowed as he got up and reached for me.

But I was already tumbling ahead, straight into the water, fishing pole and all.

I sputtered to the surface. "Shit! It's cold," I said with a hiss, swiping water from my face.

I looked up at Seth as I treaded in the chilly water. His expression of horror had turned to one of mirth. Probably after he realized I wasn't hurt, and I could obviously swim.

I scowled at him as his laughter boomed through the air. "It's not funny," I said unhappily. "I think I lost my fish."

The pole was still in my hand, but the vicious tugging on the line had ceased.

The bastard just laughed harder, like he couldn't stop.

His hand came out to hoist me up. "Let's go get you warm. That water is probably in the low sixties, and it's not exactly hot out here today."

After the initial shock, I started to adjust to the brisk water. We were in Southern California, and the Pacific was rarely all that warm, even in the late-summer months, but some brave people did swim in it all year long on decent days.

Seth was still smirking, and I had the sudden urge to wipe the smug expression off his face.

I grabbed his outstretched hand, but instead of letting him pull me up, I put a foot solidly on a heavy pile and then yanked with all my strength.

If he was going to laugh at my predicament, he could just end up in the same situation.

I felt elated when I heard a huge splash next to me.

When he came to the surface soaking wet, an evil grin formed on my face.

Just like me, he'd come sputtering to the top.

"How funny do you think this is now?" I asked, trying to keep the humor out of my tone.

He started to laugh again. "You caught me off guard, woman."

"I know," I said cheekily. "That was the plan."

We started to cavort in the water like children.

I dunked his head, and he splashed a wall of water my way.

I felt like a kid.

I felt mischievous.

Most of all, I felt . . . happy.

When he finally swam forward and wrapped an arm around my waist, he said huskily in my ear, "You know, you get sassier every day."

Even though the water was cold, my body heated the moment he touched me.

Weird thing was, he didn't sound unhappy about my behavior at all.

CHAPTER 14
Seth

The whole fucking *friend* thing was about to kill me.

Dating Riley Montgomery was pretty much the most torturous thing I'd ever done.

"Damned if I'm with her, and even more damned when I'm not," I grumbled as I turned my back to the showerhead and rinsed the soap from my body.

My cock was hard, and my balls were blue whether I was with her or not. I'd conjured some pretty amazing fantasies over the last few weeks. Unfortunately, those sexy fictional occurrences just weren't cutting it anymore.

Never really had.

The only thing they accomplished was taking a little bit of the edge off.

I tried not to think about the fact that right now, Riley was down the hall, in another bathroom in my house, stark naked. Once we'd returned to my place after our impromptu swim, I'd sent her to a guest bathroom because she wanted a warm shower.

It had taken everything I had not to yank her into the master-bathroom shower with me.

I promised not to push.

Sadly, I hated myself for giving her my word on that. Every. Single. Day.

There wasn't *ever* a moment when I didn't want to strip her naked and fuck her against a wall. Hard.

Or in my bed.

Or on the kitchen table.

Or in the damn shower, exactly where I was right now.

Problem was, she was in another damn bathroom.

If I wanted to be truthful, I could have easily pulled her onto the dock and banged her on the spot.

After I'd pulled her body against me in the water, I'd been *completely* fucked.

It was the first time those beautiful curves had been plastered against my body, and I'd felt her capitulate almost immediately.

She was starting to trust me.

So even though it had been physically painful to back off, I had.

The trade-offs were worth the pain. In the last few weeks, I'd seen Riley start to let go, have fun, and let down her guard.

Unfortunately, it made her an *even greater* temptation.

Seemed like I favored gorgeous women with curly red hair and curves that would tempt an angel to fall. Not to mention her sharp mind, her quirky sense of humor, and, now that I knew her, her empathy.

"Son of a bitch!" I ground out.

I wasn't used to wanting a woman so damn badly that I could barely rein myself in.

I wrapped my hand around my painfully hard cock, knowing that I needed to blow off some steam.

I closed my eyes as I conjured up an image of Riley, naked, needy, and moaning while I had my head between her quivering thighs.

She was about to come, and I was fucking elated when she started to scream my name.

"Oh, God, Seth. Please. Make me come."

I stroked my cock harder. There was nothing as hot as imagining Riley coming apart because I'd made it happen.

"Yes, please!"

She threw her head back, her fiery hair cascading on a white pillow, her face euphoric as she exploded.

So beautiful.

So damn . . . mine.

She came down from her climax slowly, and when she was finally recovered, she yanked on my hair. "I need you to fuck me, Seth. Now!"

Her voice was low, covetous, and demanding. She didn't have to ask me twice.

I fucking loved seeing her out of control.

Greedy.

Hungry.

Focused on getting what she wanted.

Because I was about to get something I really wanted, too.

I could feel my balls tightening as I slumped against the wall of the shower.

"Tell me what you want, gorgeous," I prompted as I crawled up her silken, curvy body that I couldn't seem to get enough of.

I placed my cock against her tight opening.

She wrapped her arms around my neck. "You," she said in a raspy voice filled with desire. "I just want you, Seth."

I couldn't wait any longer. I gave Riley exactly what she wanted, and was immediately enveloped in the wet, scorching-hot slide that I never wanted to end.

Riley.

So damn hot. So damn beautiful.

I looked at her, and I groaned as I saw the uninhibited, primal joy on her face.

As I sped up my pace, I knew I was claiming her with every single thrust.

Riley was mine. And I was determined that she always would be.

"Shit!" I groaned as I opened my eyes to see my own volatile release fly up and then circle down the drain.

I turned around and slammed my fist against the wall in frustration.

I *never* got to the *end* of the fantasy.

In my mind, it felt too damn good to be inside Riley *not* to come.

Unfortunately, it was pretty much the same with most of my imaginative, carnal illusions about Riley.

As I rinsed myself off, I had to wonder if getting myself off was even worth it anymore, whether having an orgasm was worth the frustration.

I got out and grabbed the first pair of jeans I could find and a navy sweatshirt.

Riley is probably downstairs by now.

I made it out of the bedroom and downstairs in a matter of moments.

I could hear Riley in the kitchen, so I headed in that direction.

Once I hit the entrance, I stopped abruptly, staring at the shapely ass that was currently making a cup of tea.

Her skinny jeans were tight, so how could I resist staring at the way that gorgeous ass was on full display?

Riley's hair was down, and apparently still drying, judging by the slightly darker red color. It was just starting to curl, and I had to clench my fists to stay in place and not move forward to bury my hands in the beautiful damp tresses.

The short, pretty baby-pink sweater she had put on barely reached the waistband of her jeans, and because it slid down one shoulder, I was guessing she *wasn't* wearing a bra.

Jesus Christ!

I knew I was salivating, but what single, red-blooded male *wouldn't be?*

"Sorry I took so long," I said thickly as I entered the kitchen and tore my eyes away from her body. "I see you found something to wear."

She turned, and I couldn't help it, my eyes went directly to her breasts.

Riley *wasn't* wearing a bra. I confirmed it when I saw the subtle outline of her nipples against the pink fabric. It *wasn't* a heavy sweater.

"Eyes on my face, please," she requested firmly.

I'd gotten caught eyeing her breasts, but I didn't feel one damn bit repentant.

"Hard not to look." I moved my gaze up to her face.

I was rewarded by the adorable pink tint that colored her cheeks.

Riley wasn't the flirtatious type, so if I threw her any kind of compliment, she blushed.

Her reaction was incongruous since she was outspoken and blunt in most every other way.

"The jeans, whoever they belong to, are too tight. They're definitely made for someone smaller. The sweater, too," she said flatly as she turned back toward the coffeepot. "Do you want some coffee?"

"Yeah, I'll take one."

Her tone was stiff, so I shot her a curious look. I immediately knew something was off with her.

I could sense it.

"Hey, you okay?" I asked.

"Fine," she said shortly as she slammed a mug into the coffeemaker a little bit harder than she needed to.

Her eyes were defiant as she turned to look at me while the coffee dripped into the mug.

She *wasn't* fine. Something was bugging her.

"It's really none of my business if some woman leaves her clothes at your house," she snapped.

Holy shit!

I assessed her carefully for a minute before I acknowledged what was really going on.

She's jealous.

She thinks those clothing items belong to some current or previous female I hooked up with.

I knew I hadn't imagined the brief flash of hurt in her eyes.

I stepped forward and tipped her chin up so she'd look at me. "You're jealous," I accused lightly.

She tossed her head and huffed as she grabbed my coffee. "I am not jealous. We aren't really involved. It's all a bunch of fiction. Sugar and cream?"

"No thanks. I take it black out of a coffeepot."

I grinned as she handed me the cup of steaming liquid.

I had no fucking idea why it pleased me that Riley was in a snit over some woman's clothing that was in the closet of my guest bedroom.

Hell, I wasn't about to complain if she wanted to throw a little fit over the fact that I might want to screw another woman.

Even if I didn't.

It was a sign that this relationship was becoming more than a sham to her.

However, I had seen that flash of hurt, which bothered me. "Those things belong to my sister Brooke. She keeps stuff here because she and Liam usually stay with me when they come to visit from the East Coast."

She leaned a hip against the counter as she looked at me. "That stuff belongs to your sister?"

I nodded. "If it makes you feel any better, you can look in the other closet across the room. Liam has stuff here, too." I was assuming she'd gotten the right closet the first time.

"I believe you," she said, sounding relieved. "And I was not jealous. I was just . . . curious."

"Don't bullshit me, Riley. It bothered you."

She picked up her tea from the counter and took a sip before she answered. "How can I be upset over it?" she said, her voice tremulous. "You're not really mine. I mean, I really shouldn't be worried because you have another female's clothing in your house, right?"

She looked frightened by the entire realization that she had actually been pissed off.

"Hell, yes, you can be angry. We're dating. Exclusively, right now."

"I don't want to turn into some green-eyed monster," she confessed.

I smirked. "Your eyes *are* green, but you could never be a monster."

"This isn't funny, Seth," she said as she put her mug back on the counter. "I can't remember a time when I was ever jealous. *At all! Ever!*"

I was guessing that right now wasn't the time to tell her how cute she was when she added *at all* or *ever* to her sentences when she was trying to convince herself that something was absolutely true. Or if she *wanted* the statement to be true, but she knew otherwise.

"Emotions happen when you're dating somebody, Riley," I reasoned. "Hell, I'm jealous of every guy you've ever been with, especially Easton."

She blinked hard. "You are? Why?"

"Because at one time, you offered yourself to him, committed to him. You gave a part of yourself that you've never given to me." It was time to get honest, and I wasn't about to stop telling her the truth.

I moved forward and put my hands on the

counter, trapping her body between my arms. She wasn't moving until we got things straight. If we didn't, I was going to lose it.

She stared up at me like she was clueless, and my goddamn heart nearly stopped when she hesitantly wrapped her arms around my neck. "I never really gave him anything, Seth," she whispered softly. "Not really. The only thing he got was my body occasionally, but deep down inside, I knew he wasn't all that attracted to me. He had my loyalty, too, even though he didn't do the same for me. Otherwise, he never really knew me. I never talked to him like I talk to you. He never once made me laugh. And he sure as hell didn't accept me the way that I was. Everything was conditional."

For some reason, her words placated me. Yeah, I wasn't thrilled that the bastard had gotten access to her body. He hadn't deserved it.

I wanted to ask her what in the hell she was doing with him when he didn't make her happy. But I already knew the answer. She'd still been trying to get her mother's approval.

"Nothing will ever be conditional between us. You get that, right?" I needed her to know that I'd never want to change anything about her. Not even a single red hair on her head.

Riley was my idea of perfect.

She nodded slowly. "I think I know that. But please understand that it's not always easy to accept."

"I know," I told her as I wrapped my arms around her.

Fuck the friendship rules.

Somebody needed to *protect* this woman, and I was going to be the guy who did it.

Nobody else ever had.

She'd spent her whole damn life trying to be someone that she wasn't to please a parent who didn't give a damn about *her*.

"Thank you for understanding," she murmured.

She snuggled into my body so trustingly that I knew I was in hell, but I had very little desire to escape my fate.

CHAPTER 15
Riley

"Dinner was amazing, Skye. Thanks for having us over," I told her as we sat on the outside patio of her gorgeous beachfront home.

"I appreciate you having me, too, Skye," Penny parroted shyly. "I'm not exactly family."

It was just the three of us on the patio. Aiden and Seth were playing some music inside the house—Aiden on the piano and Seth on the guitar. Skye, Penny, and I had grabbed a spot outside, close enough to hear them but far enough away from the rest of the family and guests to chat.

"I'm just sorry I couldn't give you much notice," Skye answered apologetically. "And I'm glad you're here, Penny."

Penny's face was glowing because Skye had been so kind to her. Her blue-eyed, dark-haired beauty really shined now that her expression was truly happy.

When Seth had suggested that we go to Skye and Aiden's weekend barbecue a few days ago, I'd already planned to have Penny down to stay with me for the weekend. Graciously, Skye had invited Penny to come along, too.

"Your parties are fun," my young friend told Skye. "Everybody here laughs a lot."

Skye rolled her eyes. "We have to just laugh. Jade and I are overwhelmed by testosterone and male jokes. And now, poor Riley has to put up with it, too."

I smirked at Skye from my seated position across from her. "Believe me, I don't mind." Parties with the Sinclairs *were* fun, so different from what I was used to. "But I did get grilled by Noah today."

Skye gasped. "He didn't!"

I nodded. "He did."

"That's definitely not like Noah. He's usually only interested in getting back to his office."

"I got the feeling he wanted to know my intentions toward Seth."

Skye and Penny busted out in laughter.

"That's like a reverse role," Penny observed. "Like he's trying to protect a daughter."

"He wasn't quite that protective," I mused. "But he did act like he was afraid I'd break Seth's heart or something."

"He probably is," Skye said softly. "Seth isn't exactly a playboy, and it's pretty obvious that he's crazy about you."

"He's not," I said in a rush. "We're more like friends, really."

"Then why is he constantly checking out your ass and your legs in those shorts?" Penny teased.

"I have to admit, I've seen it, too," Skye confessed.

I shrugged. "Maybe he is attracted to me, but that's all."

"Riley, he's more than just *attracted*," Skye said softly. "I think we all see it. Seth has never been a womanizer, and Aiden says he's never seen him serious about a woman. Seth cares about you."

I sighed. "I think I screwed up, Skye. I made 'No sex' and 'No butt touching' rules before we started hanging out together. We barely touch each other. And now that we've been together almost daily for over three weeks, I kind of regret it. Part of me wants to see where this whole thing could go with him, but I'm . . . scared."

Skye nodded her head hard. "I get that. I do. Things get really intimate once something has happened." She hesitated before she asked Penny, "Are you okay with listening to all this?"

I'd told Skye a little about Penny's background with Nolan, so she knew the younger woman had been abused and manipulated by Nolan.

Penny sniffed like she was affronted. "Of course. It's not like I'm a virgin, and I'm nearly eighteen. Riley and I have talked about a lot of unpleasant stuff in our past. I'm better because of that. She helped me get away from my parents. I live with distant cousins now until I leave for Harvard next year."

I turned my head to look at the beautiful young woman sitting next to me. Penny had come a long way from where she'd been two years ago, thanks to a new, more loving atmosphere with her cousins and a couple years of therapy.

"You're an amazing young woman, Penny. And very brave," Skye said encouragingly.

Penny looked at me. "I had a lot of help. I owe Riley some huge favors for what she's done for me that I know I can never really repay."

"Favors aren't done to get repayment," I scolded her. "I'm just happy I'm here with you now. I'm so proud of you."

My heart soared every time I watched Penny reach another milestone. Little did she know that she gave more to me than I could ever give her. It made me happy just knowing she'd never have to go through the same adult hell that I had. And she'd never have to be married to a scum of the earth like Nolan.

Penny was quiet before she said, "You didn't tell me that Seth could play guitar. He and Aiden are pretty awesome together."

"I didn't know he played," I admitted. "He never mentioned it until today."

"Seth and Aiden never broadcast that they're both musically talented. They were self-taught, for the most part," Skye said. "I think they both doubt their talent because they have no real training."

"Which, in reality, makes them that much more gifted," I answered.

Most of the family, and the few friends who were invited to the barbecue, were inside listening. Apparently, it was rare for Seth and Aiden to play.

"I agree," Skye said with a sigh. "But I think Aiden, Seth, and Noah still have a lot of insecurities about their past."

I turned my head sharply to look at her. "Why?"

"I know Aiden still struggles with the fact that they all grew up so poor. That he could never give Jade, Brooke, and Owen all the things kids should have. It's ridiculous, really, considering how much they gave up themselves to keep the family together. Nobody went hungry, and they grew up tight-knit. Maybe they weren't spoiled rotten, but they had the basic necessities."

Penny spoke up. "I really think it's better that they didn't grow up spoiled. I've seen the bad results that can happen when a kid has everything. Money becomes way too important to them, and they expect to be pampered the rest of their lives. Women really need to learn independence by counting on themselves more and marrying rich a lot less."

"Exactly," I grumbled.

"You're wise for your age," Skye said softly to Penny.

She shrugged. "Not really. I was kind of

pushed out into the world suddenly, and I didn't know what to do. Riley taught me to be more independent. If she hadn't, I'd be married to some old guy who treats me like a possession."

"You give me way too much credit, Penny," I told her. "If you hadn't done the work yourself, you'd still be exactly where you were two years ago."

"And hating it," she said emphatically. "I'm glad you're with Seth now. He's pretty amazing. I like him a lot. None of the Sinclairs are pretentious, even though they're megawealthy."

I picked up my glass of wine on the coffee table in front of us and took a healthy slug.

Skye smiled. "None of them will ever be snobs. I guarantee it. I'm a Sinclair now, too. In this family, you don't have to be blood to be part of the family."

I had to agree with Skye. Even Noah was extremely down to earth, even if he had run me through the mill trying to see if I was going to be good for his brother. Not that he needed to do that. I made it clear to him that Seth and I were just friends.

Unfortunately, I wanted more *now,* but it seemed impossible for me to have that. For the most part, Seth had his shit together. I was working on that, but I had a long way to go. He *deserved* someone a lot better than me. A woman who already had her head on straight and wasn't bogged down by her past.

I relaxed as I sipped my wine, listening to the music flow through the open patio door.

Seth and Aiden were good. *Really good.* It was hard to believe that they hadn't grown up with the benefit of lessons. It sounded like they'd both studied their craft for years.

"I'm not *really* with Seth," I finally said. "I told you that, Penny. It's a game. An experiment."

She rolled her eyes. "Please, Riley. I have perfect eyesight. Like Skye said, he's crazy about you. Don't you feel the same way?"

I suddenly had two sets of inquiring eyes waiting for my answer.

I swallowed hard. "Maybe. But that doesn't mean that I'm the right woman for him. I can't be."

"Is this about your dad?" Penny asked softly. "Is that why you don't think you are good enough?"

I shot her a panicked look and shook my head. Even though Skye and I were becoming friends, I hadn't told anybody except Penny about much of my early childhood. And I'd only spilled my guts to her because I thought it might help her. "No. It's not."

Even as I denied it, I knew I was lying.

"What happened?" Skye asked curiously. "Is it something I don't already know? You can talk to me, Riley. For God's sake, I was once married into the Mafia. I carried a hell of a lot of fear and pain during those years. But I've learned that it's much better to talk about it instead of trying to bury it."

"It's a long story," I said shortly.

"Not that long," Penny drawled.

"Just remember I'm here if you want to talk," Skye said gently. "I don't want to push you to talk about anything you don't want to share. When you're ready, I'll be here."

"Oh, my God!" Penny exclaimed. "Were you really married to a Mafia guy, Skye?"

I was almost envious when Skye nodded and started to tell Penny about her history.

I wished that I could be that open, that secure.

Skye could talk about her past without really letting it affect her present or her future.

Unfortunately, I couldn't. Not yet.

When Penny was done asking questions, and expressed her admiration for Skye's bravery, they started to chat about Penny's future.

"What's your major going to be?" Skye asked her.

"Computer science," Penny said, her voice animated.

"She's talented," I shared with Skye. "Penny taught herself to program, so she's way ahead of the game."

"Are your parents on board?" Skye queried.

Penny shook her head slowly. "No. They're not. When I refused to have anything else to do with Nolan and left home, they paid me off with millions of dollars if I'd agree to not show my face in their world again. Which wasn't exactly a sacrifice for me. I'm grateful to have the money to get my education, though. So that's something."

I had to blink back tears as I listened to Penny. I knew damn well she was still hurt that she'd been so easily dispensable.

Skye's eyes looked troubled, but she didn't push for more information. Through my budding friendship with Skye, I already knew she was incredibly intuitive and empathetic. I was thinking that she knew when there was nothing else to say.

Personally, I thought Penny would be better off in the end *without* her parents. *Conditional.* Everything was conditional in our world. She'd been through enough.

I opened my mouth to change the subject, and then slammed it shut when I heard a male voice I'd never wanted to listen to again sound behind me.

"Hello, Margaret. Fancy seeing *you* here. I was attending a little get-together down the beach. I was just taking a walk when I saw you three sitting here. And here you are. And Penelope, too. It's nice to see you two again, I must say."

The horrified look on Penny's face was enough to make me stand up and put myself between her and *the voice.*

Meeting the stare of the brown-eyed man made me want to retch. But my protective instincts were too strong to turn away.

"Nolan," I answered, my voice dripping with ice. "It's not nice seeing you at all. Leave. Now."

CHAPTER 16
Riley

It was obvious that Nolan probably *had been* at a beach party. He was dressed in slacks and a polo shirt, attire he usually didn't wear. But who was going to wear a tux to a beach affair?

"I've missed you and Penelope," Nolan said in the irritating nasal tone that I despised.

"How did you *really* find us?" I demanded to know.

I didn't buy the I-just-happened-to-be-in-the-area bullshit.

He shrugged nonchalantly. "My host may have mentioned that the Sinclairs looked like they were having a party. I've never had the pleasure of meeting any of them."

I was fuming. He'd obviously been feeling slighted that he hadn't made the acquaintance of the family who had more money than he did. So he'd decided to see if he could get into their good graces. Maybe the family didn't attend any of the rich crowd's parties, but nobody wanted to piss off a Sinclair, either.

Not now that they were filthy rich.

"You weren't invited. Leave," I said angrily.

The *last thing* Penny needed was to have this

asshole show up. The frightened look on her face was enough to make me want to lay Nolan on the cement.

"Exactly how did you and Penelope get invited?" he asked casually.

I knew *that voice.* He was envious, which was pretty normal for Nolan. No matter how much he had, he always wanted more.

Skye stood. "They're friends," she said coldly. "And you're not."

"Oh, I'm definitely *more than friends* to both of these two women," he said in a chilly tone. "I've missed them both. I'd like to see them . . . more often."

Jesus! Did the bastard really think we were both going to do a threesome or be a couple of women in some kind of harem?

He's out of his tiny mind.

"Neither one of us want to see *you!*" I snapped.

He started to move forward, but I stood my ground as he said, "Come on, Margaret. You can't possibly be happy here. Your mother told me you have a shack on the beach, and that you rarely attend any events anymore. Do you really want to live as an old maid and close to pauper status any longer?"

"Yes. As a matter of fact, I do." I didn't owe him any further explanation.

My little "shack" had cost more than 99 percent of the population could afford, and the cottage

168

was beautiful. But he was so obsessed with having "things" that it looked like poverty to him.

"You still want me, Margaret. And so does Penelope. You're both too afraid of rejection to approach me. So I'm approaching you." He made it sound like he was doing us a huge favor.

"You're scum," I said bluntly. "And I'm sure Penny and I are *too old* for you now, since you seemed to like your females young. *Very young.*"

His face was shocked, and then it turned to rage.

Maybe there were *whispers* about child abuse, but nobody ever really confronted Nolan about any of that.

"You're a child molester, Nolan," I continued, my anger burning way too hot now to stop. "A lowlife piece of crap who should be in prison right now. And maybe I don't circulate in your group anymore, but believe me, I'm keeping track of you. If you ever end up with another underage girl, I'll know it. I still know enough of the good people in your circle to get the news, and I'll make damn sure you end up in jail."

"Like your father ended up there?" he answered sarcastically. "Do you really think those rumors went unnoticed, Margaret? And he got away with it *for years*. Nobody could touch him. People have to press charges, and nobody will. Now, let's talk about getting together. You, me, and Penelope."

169

"You'll touch her again over my dead body," I growled.

Nolan lurched forward and slammed me against the brick wall of the patio.

For a moment, I saw stars, and then everything went dark, but it was momentary, and when I came to my senses, all I could feel was his slimy lips on mine.

"You've got to be fucking kidding me." I heard the angry comment come from Seth, but I didn't completely register it.

I was too busy trying to get my eyesight back to normal.

"Get the fuck off her," Skye screamed as she yanked Nolan back. "Aiden! Please come help us!"

When my vision was semiclear, my rage that he'd had the gall to so much as touch me flooded my being.

I was out of control, but I didn't give a damn.

My hand flew hard, and I heard the satisfying crack of my palm slapping against his face. While Nolan was momentarily stunned, I lifted my knee and slammed him in the balls with enough force to lodge them in his throat. And then I did it again. And again. Until he fell to the cement with a pathetic howl of pain.

"Get up, you bastard," I demanded, even though I felt myself swaying.

I wasn't done causing him enough pain that

he'd never get within a hundred miles of Penny ever again.

"Riley, don't," I heard Aiden rasp into my ear as he pulled me back by my shoulders.

"She's hurt, Aiden," Skye said, sounding a bit frantic. "He slammed her head against the brick wall. She needs medical attention."

"I'm fine," I muttered. "I need to take Penny home."

I turned around to go sit by Penny. "Are you okay?"

She took my hand in hers. "It wasn't me who just got smashed against a wall. Riley, you have to get to the hospital."

"I'm fine," I reassured her, even though my vision was still a little blurred.

My adrenaline continued to course through my body, and I was trembling with some residual unspent rage.

I took a deep breath and tried to calm down as Noah and Aiden came to haul away Nolan.

His wailing was still bouncing off the patio walls, and it was grinding on me, so I was grateful that they were taking him away.

"He came from some kind of event here on the beach," I told the brothers shakily, loud enough to carry over Nolan's groans.

"I know where it is," Aiden informed Noah. "We were invited, but they aren't the kind of folks we have much in common with. We refused it."

"I say we take him back there personally, and let *his host* deal with him," Noah said.

"Whoever is having the party told him where you lived," I said to Aiden. "He wasn't initially here for Penny and me. He wanted to get to know you and your family. I guess we were just a bonus."

"Bonus, my ass," Aiden rasped. "I'll let his host know if this piece of shit even puts a toe on the sand again, *he'll* be the next one screaming."

"Where's Seth?" I asked shakily.

"Gone," Aiden said shortly. "He said he had to go since he wasn't going to compete with your ex. He said you were kissing him. I think he knew it was Easton. God knows that this idiot isn't shy around a camera."

Nolan was a media whore, so I was certain that Seth did know what he looked like.

"She wasn't kissing *him*," Skye said in my defense. "She was half-unconscious. The only reason her hands were on his shoulders was to try to steady herself after Nolan crashed her head against the wall. God, Aiden. I could hear her skull hit the damn wall. Did Seth really think she'd kiss anybody else?"

"I wouldn't," I said tearfully, my mind still not completely functioning.

"No way she would," Penny commented. "He's a complete prick."

"You certainly knew how to kick the crap out

172

of him," Noah mentioned with appreciation in his tone.

"I was . . . angry," I tried to explain.

"With good reason," Aiden grunted as he and Noah hauled Nolan to his feet. "Just remind me never to piss you off." He turned his head and shot me a mischievous wink.

"Call an ambulance for Riley, please," Noah said to Skye. "We'll take out the trash." He nodded toward a still-screaming Nolan.

"I don't need an ambulance," I argued.

"I'll drive her," Skye said firmly. "It's only a few minutes to the hospital from here."

"I'm going, too," Penny insisted. "And we aren't taking no for an answer, Riley. I'll be fine. I'll be with you. I'm not afraid of him anymore. I was just . . . shocked. But I am worried about *you*. Please get checked out. For me. I can't go back to San Diego until I know that you're okay."

My greatest fear was that Nolan would find a way to get to Penny. Considering his condition right now, my thoughts were probably irrational, but he obviously knew where I lived.

I was grateful when Nolan's screaming stopped as Noah and Aiden dragged him into the house to get to the garage.

"Can you walk?" Skye asked as she put her hand underneath my upper arm.

"I'm sure I can," I said in a much calmer voice.

Now that Nolan was gone, I felt like I could do almost anything.

Penny got up, let go of my hand, and spotted me from the other side.

"I should have helped you," she said morosely. "I just . . . froze, Riley."

"There wasn't enough time for anybody to help, hon," Skye crooned. "It happened too fast. Don't think about that now. It's not important. Let's just get Riley to the hospital."

The two females were so upset that I wasn't going to argue anymore.

Penny would be with me, so Nolan wasn't going to approach her. More than likely, he'd never come near either one of us again.

There was a certain satisfaction in that theory.

I walked slowly into the house, one woman clutching each of my arms.

I stopped when we got to the garage door. "What about Seth? Did he really think that I'd actually kiss Nolan? It hurts that he even considered that possibility."

Skye nudged me forward, and she didn't answer until we were all settled into the car. "I honestly don't imagine he was *thinking* at all. But that's not to say I condone his ridiculous behavior."

She opened the garage door before she continued, "When you blanked out, from his angle, it probably did look like you were kissing him. You couldn't fight right away, and you put your hands on Nolan's shoulders."

"He couldn't have stopped to find out?" I questioned unhappily.

"He should have," Skye murmured. "You need to talk to him about making a snap judgment. Aiden and I went down that road once, and it only causes unnecessary heartache."

"I'm not sure I even want to talk to him again. I thought he trusted me."

Even though I'd been slow to give Seth my trust, I thought we'd gone beyond not having faith in each other.

"Men are stupid when they're jealous. Sometimes they turn into green-eyed monsters in seconds. I guess women can do that, too."

Green-eyed monster?

Hadn't I morphed into one of those over the female clothing I'd found at Seth's place?

In my case, I hadn't walked away.

Seth had.

I could have very easily left his house without making a cup of tea or hanging around to see if there was some kind of explanation.

He could have given me the same courtesy.

"The thing is, Seth was jealous because he doesn't see you two as friends anymore, Riley," Skye pointed out as she maneuvered her way toward the hospital.

"I'm not his possession," I answered.

"I agree. And I don't think he believes you are for one second. His actions were completely motivated by hurt. I saw his face. He looked entirely destroyed before he got pissed off."

My heart squeezed. "Any disappointment he experienced was unintentional. I'd never do it deliberately."

"I know that. Once Seth has a chance to reason it out, he'll know that, too. Sinclair men tend to react before they think sometimes. And then they're so repentant that it's almost annoying." She paused before she added, "Don't worry about Seth right now. Let's take care of you."

"I'm okay," I grumbled. "I'm only doing this for you and Penny."

"I'll take that if it gets you to the hospital," Penny chirped from the back seat.

"Me too," Skye agreed with a smile as she pulled up to the emergency room.

I smiled weakly at both of them.

They had no idea how good it felt to have *real* friends.

CHAPTER 17
Seth

What in the fuck is she thinking! She can't go back to that asshole!

I was thoroughly exhausted, but not enough to curb my anger and frustration.

Thump! Thump! Thump!

I'd been out for a very long run, and I was currently in my home gym beating the hell out of a punching bag that was mounted from the ceiling.

Maybe I was wiped out physically, but the rest of me was still so furious that I couldn't seem to get enough activity to keep the image of Riley willingly kissing Easton out of my head.

Thump! Thump! Thump! Thump!

"Son of a bitch!" I cursed, slamming my hand into the bag one more time before I bent over to catch my breath.

I shucked off my gloves and straightened, trying to decide on what kind of torture I could put myself through next.

I eyed my Peloton bike and decided that would be next on my list. I could work up a hell of a sweat once I got going.

Right now, I'd go through every piece of

equipment in my gym if it meant I'd be so exhausted and sore that it would take my mind off Riley.

No doubt, I'd never scrub the visions of Easton devouring the woman I wanted from my brain, but I sure as hell wished I could make it hurt . . . less.

I'd seen it.

The memory was fresh in my head.

Riley had been fully cooperating in that embrace.

If she hadn't, I would have killed the bastard.

Truth was, I cared too damn much about her not to want her to have whatever made her happy.

He'll make her fucking miserable.

That was the part that killed me.

Maybe she'd never stop seeking her mother's approval.

Maybe she couldn't.

Shit! I knew damn well I'd find myself at her doorstep eventually, trying to convince her that she didn't want to be with a piece of slime to feel like she belonged.

Truth was, she belonged with me.

Riley had been mine from the first moment I'd seen her. Maybe I hadn't realized that back then, but I knew it now. No doubt in my mind.

I could make her happy. She'd been smiling, laughing, lighthearted at the barbecue until that cockroach had crawled out of the wall.

Had she invited him?

There was no other rational explanation as to why Easton was even there.

"What in the fuck are you doing here?" my brother Noah's voice asked from behind me.

I swung around. "I fucking live here," I shot back, not in the mood for any of Noah's patriarchal advice. I already knew I shouldn't be thinking of talking to Riley after she'd been kissing another guy. "What are you doing here? How did you get in?"

He held up a full key chain. "You gave me a key. And you didn't answer the door. Your Range Rover was in the garage, so I figured you were here somewhere."

"I'm working out. I don't have time to talk at the moment," I grumbled.

He gazed my way, apparently assessing me. "Looks to me like you've already done your workout. Your entire body is dripping sweat."

"I don't give a fuck," I rasped. "It makes me feel better."

Noah ignored me and went to the small refrigerator in the corner. He pulled out some bottled water, opened it, and handed it to me. "Drink or you'll be dehydrated."

I swiped it from his hand. I hadn't slowed down long enough to realize that I really was dying for some water.

I sucked down the whole container, crunched

179

it, and tossed it into the garbage. "You obviously want something, Noah. You've never exactly just dropped in for a brotherly chat."

We generally had to seek *him* out.

"I'll ask you again . . . why are you here?" he repeated.

"And I told you that I live here."

He shot me an irritated glare. "You should be at the hospital."

My head shot up, my attention shifting in an instant. If somebody in our family was hurt or sick, of course I wanted to be there. "What happened? Is it Aiden?"

Noah shook his head. "As much as you seem to care about Riley, I had assumed you'd want to be with her while she was being treated."

Riley?

What the fuck?

"Are you trying to tell me she's in the hospital?"

He simply nodded.

"Isn't Easton with her?" I asked drily.

Noah frowned. "Why in the hell would he be there? After what happened, I doubt he'll ever be within swinging distance of her again."

"They were locking lips well enough at the barbecue," I informed him huskily. "They were damn friendly."

Noah looked disappointed. "You know, for a guy smart enough to build up a commercial-property business as fast as you have, you have your moments when you can be completely brainless. Like right now. She wasn't willingly kissing the asshole."

My heart sped up. "Looked like she was."

"You missed the part where Easton slammed her head against the wall. For God's sake, Seth, the woman was pretty much unconscious when he was kissing her. Okay, maybe she had her hands on him, but only because he'd scrambled her brains. You also missed the part where she kicked his ass after she'd gotten away from him. She was protecting Penny for some reason, but I'm sure she didn't mind putting her knee in his groin a couple of times, hard enough to make sure he sings soprano for the rest of his life. Personally, I was impressed. She fights dirty. I like her."

My mind flashed back to the scene that had only lasted a couple of seconds before I couldn't take watching it anymore.

Her hands were on his shoulders.

Easton had been all over her.

But . . . her back had been against a brick wall.

And . . . she hadn't been fighting him, but she hadn't really been participating enthusiastically, either.

I shook myself to get rid of the scene in my head. *Jesus!* What if Noah was right?

I gave him a suspicious glance. "Are you sure?"

"Of course I'm sure. Aiden and I saw the last bit

181

when she kicked his ass. She walloped him hard enough to snap his neck nearly off his shoulders, and then she put his balls in his throat. She was a crazy woman, and she would have kept going if Aiden hadn't stepped in. I'm not exactly sure what happened between them, but she apparently has a lot of suppressed anger regarding him. Aiden said she has a right to hate him, because he's heard some gossip that he cheated on her, and I believe him. But I'm not sure there isn't even more to that story, since she was protecting Penny."

"You have no idea," I muttered as my mind kept racing. "So all of it was nonconsensual?"

"Rage inducing," he corrected. "Not only was it nonconsensual, but she released the wrath of hell on him even though she'd already taken a pretty big hit to her skull. Like I said, I like her, and I don't like very many people other than my family. The woman has some major fortitude and she's gutsy. I certainly wouldn't want to piss her off."

I shook my head. "I've never seen Riley like that."

"Thank God," Noah drawled. "It was a little bit frightening."

"Is she okay?" My heart was pounding out of my chest. I had to know that Riley wasn't badly injured. "Tell me the truth."

"I talked to Skye, and they're keeping Riley

overnight for observation. She has a concussion, but luckily, it didn't break her skull. Skye told me she heard it crack against the wall." As he finished speaking, Noah went to the fridge again and handed me another water. "Drink. You need to hydrate. You look like shit."

I took a huge slug. "I need to get to Riley. What in the hell did I do, Noah? I just . . . left her. Easton was hurting her, and I just walked away."

Nausea rose up in my throat, and I took another gulp of water to hold it back. I was starting to believe that Noah's account was real. It had to be. And I felt like a bigger asshole than Easton at the moment.

How could I just . . . leave, when Riley had been hurt and in trouble?

"You didn't know. And believe me, that woman can protect herself," Noah said grimly. "Do not start beating yourself up over your reaction. Learn from it. If you'd stopped for just a moment, you would have realized that your thoughts made no sense. Riley hates Easton. Why in the hell would she be cuddling up to him again?"

To please her mother?

Hell, now that I was rational, even *that* excuse didn't make sense.

I knew Riley.

I knew she was breaking away.

I knew she hated that life where *everything* was conditional.

"I fucked up," I said hoarsely.

That woman can protect herself. That's what Noah had just said. And yeah, I had no doubt that Riley could take care of herself, because she always had.

The thing was, I should have been there to help her. It was time that Riley knew that somebody would be there *for her.*

And I . . . hadn't.

"Then fix it," Noah suggested. "And don't go off half-cocked next time. She doesn't have any family in Citrus Beach. She'll probably need some help until her brain is right again. Skye is more than willing to be there for her, and Aiden is, too. They're both trying to talk Penny into going home, since she has school in the morning."

"I'll be taking care of her." I couldn't stand the thought of Riley ever thinking she was alone.

Noah smirked. "I thought you would be. If you could just pull your head out of your ass."

Maybe I did hate myself for walking away from Riley when she needed me, but I wasn't going to compound that mistake and ever do it again.

"Are you sure she's okay?" I asked Noah again.

"When have I ever bullshitted you?" he asked.

"Never," I admitted.

"Then take my word on this. She's got one hell of a headache, and she's a little fuzzy. But the doctor said she'd be fine. Keeping her overnight is precautionary, just to make sure she's watched. They don't expect any complications."

I looked my older brother in the eyes. "She might end up hating me for being a jerk, but I'm not leaving her again."

Noah shrugged. "I can't say that I understand how you feel. I don't get making a big deal out of any relationship with a female. But I think she's worth caring about."

"Way worth it," I informed him emphatically. "I gotta get going. I want to get to the hospital as soon as possible."

"Finish that water and please take a shower. If Riley isn't nauseated already, she will be. You stink."

All I really wanted to do was get to Riley, but Noah was right. For her sake, I needed to wash the stench off me.

"I'm on it," I said as I jogged toward the stairs.

"Seth!" Noah hollered.

I stopped on the third step impatiently. "Yeah?"

"If she's really pissed, get the girl a kitten," Noah instructed. "It might soften her up."

I looked at my brother like he was crazy. "What?"

"Riley has always wanted a cat. But her parents would never let her get one. It came up in a conversation I had with her today. She's been meaning to get one, but she hasn't gotten around to it yet. So if she's really mad, get her a

185

kitten. It might work," he said, trying to sound unconcerned, when I knew he really wasn't.

I shot him a grin. "Thanks for the tip."

He shrugged. "What are brothers for?"

Without another word, I sprinted up the steps.

As I ran, I thought I heard Noah grumble, "I'll just let myself out."

CHAPTER 18
Riley

I couldn't say that I really *wanted* to see Seth when he walked through my door at the hospital.

Now that my brain was getting unscrambled, I was pretty damn mad that he made a snap judgment.

Although the worried look on his face made me cave just a little.

I'd grudgingly agreed to stay overnight in the hospital, not because I wanted to, but because it was the only thing that had made Penny leave to get back to San Diego for school the next day.

Aiden and Skye were still sitting at my bedside, and they both greeted Seth as he came through the door.

I wasn't quite as cordial. "What do you want?" I mumbled as he stopped beside the bed.

He reached out and stroked my hair gently. "I know you're pissed, Riley. And you have a right to be. I made a quick judgment—"

"Way too quick," I answered.

Aiden and Skye stood up.

"I think we should go," Aiden said.

"I was going to stay with Riley tonight," Skye protested.

"I'm staying. I don't plan on ever leaving this room tonight," Seth said in a firm tone.

"Riley needs to be okay with that," Skye insisted.

Oh, God. I really wanted to say I *wasn't* okay with it, that I wanted Seth to go away. But then Skye would have to stay here all night because she thought somebody needed to be here with me. No amount of persuading was going to change her mind, even though the nurses had told her they'd watch me closely.

I smiled at her. "It's fine. Go home. Thanks for being here for me."

"Call me if you need anything," she answered. "We're so close that I can be back in a matter of minutes."

Aiden took Skye's hand and guided her out of the room.

Seth pulled up a chair so he could sit right next to the bed. "Listen to me, Riley. I know I fucked up—"

"You hurt me," I told him bluntly. I was tired of always needing to say the right thing. I was learning that it was much easier to just state the whole truth.

His eyes were full of regret. "I know. I'm sorry. I should have been there for you, but I wasn't. I thought you were kissing Easton back. The thought of losing you wasn't pleasant. I just . . . lost it."

I crossed my arms over my chest. "The fact that

188

you didn't trust me enough to stay and see what was really happening pissed me off. I suppose you already have the *correct* story now?"

Somebody must have told him, because he was here. And very repentant, just like Skye had predicted.

He nodded. "Noah stopped by my place. I swear I'll kill Easton for this."

"No, you will not. You won't go near him. He's not worth going to jail over, and I got my own shots in." Okay, I was getting a *little* alarmed by the fury in his expression.

Seth looked like he'd been dragged to hell and back. His hair was mussed up, like he'd just rolled out of bed. He was dressed in a pair of old jeans and a ratty-looking sweatshirt. The most concerning things were the lines on his face and his troubled eyes.

Not to mention the fact that he looked completely exhausted and spent.

"If I agree *not* to kill him, will you let me stay here with you?"

I glared at him. "Blackmail, too?"

"It's not blackmail. It's a compromise."

I rolled my eyes. "I suppose you can stay, but I really don't need anyone. I'm in the damn hospital. I have plenty of people watching out for me. That's why I'm here."

"Consider me your personal nurse," he suggested.

"You are *not* taking me to the bathroom," I told him, mortified at the thought.

He nodded. "I'll get the real nurse for that one."

"Fine. Now tell me why you were such a jerk. The truth. You know how I feel about Nolan and what he did to Penny. What would ever make you believe that I'd go right back to him? God, I can't even stand to look at his face, much less let him touch me in *any* way," I informed him.

"There wasn't a rational thought in my head when I saw you two together," he rasped. "All I could think about was you going back to him."

"None of this is even supposed to be real," I said softly.

"It's not pretend anymore, Riley. I think you already know that, but you don't want to say it."

I knew I couldn't lie. The weeks we'd spent together were the happiest time in my life because of Seth. "I don't want to talk about our relationship," I insisted. "Not right now."

"We don't have to," he said as he reached for my hand and entwined my fingers with his. "All you need to do is get well."

"I'm fine. Why is nobody listening when I tell them that?" I sounded miffed.

"Probably because they care about you," he replied. "From what I understand, you took a pretty good hit to your head when the asshole flung you against the wall."

"I did," I explained. "I was incapacitated for

several seconds, which is when you saw what looked like a mutually desired kiss. But it wasn't. I nearly gagged when I figured out what was happening. His tongue was down my throat."

"Noah said you kicked his ass," Seth said.

"As hard as I could," I confessed. "I think I displaced his balls. That's such strange behavior for me, but the worst part was that I couldn't seem to stop. I wanted him to get up so I could hurt him again. But he hit the cement and whined until Aiden and Noah finally took him away. I guess, in a way, I was completely irrational, too. All I could think about was Penny, and everything he'd put her through."

"It wasn't exactly easy for you, either," he pointed out.

I shrugged. "Maybe not. But Penny was just a child. I was an adult."

"I should have been there for you instead of acting like an idiot," he said. "You were hurt, dammit!"

Seth looked distraught, so I took pity on him. "I lived. I didn't expect anyone to rescue me. Nobody ever has. You didn't do this. Nolan did."

"Still wish I'd been there," he rumbled.

I peered at his face again. "I think you should get some sleep. Go home, Seth. I'm in good hands."

"I'm not leaving you again, Riley. I'm going to be here in case you need me this time. Every damn time," he growled.

"Then you can stretch out on the recliner or hop into the other bed. The nurse already told me she isn't putting anyone else in this room."

"I'll take the recliner. I'll be closer in case you need anything."

I looked at his huge, completely ripped body, and wondered if he shouldn't have chosen the bed. "It won't be comfortable."

"I deserve to be uncomfortable at the moment," he said gruffly.

Yeah, I'd been angry, but for some reason, I did not want to see Seth suffer.

I sighed. "No you don't."

"You said I hurt you."

"I was just being honest. I don't want to be afraid anymore. I want to say what I really mean and feel." I'd spent years trying to placate everyone in my life.

"I *want* you to be honest," he insisted. "I think we need to really talk when you're feeling better. I care about you, Riley. A lot. I swear I'll do whatever I can to make this up to you."

I didn't want him to feel like he needed to make amends. I only wished he would have believed me in the first place. "I don't know what I want right now, Seth."

I was confused, and I needed time to think. Preferably when my head was clear.

A yawn escaped from my mouth.

"You're tired," he accused.

I nodded sleepily. "It's probably because of the pain medication. I got some right before you got here."

He squeezed my hand. "Sleep, Riley. I'll be here."

I yawned again as I watched Seth put the recliner into the flattest position.

I lowered the head of the bed, not sure how much longer I could keep my eyes open. They were suddenly *very* heavy.

Seth reached for the light switches and turned the overhead light off, but left the small one on.

"Can I ask you a question?" Seth said in a low baritone voice.

"What?" I asked.

"Are you ever going to forgive me? I mean, we don't have to talk about our relationship right now. But I want to gain your trust back. I need to. I just want to know if you'll give me a chance to do it."

I'd probably end up letting him off the hook. Eventually. But I wasn't about to make it too easy.

"I'll think about it," I replied as my eyes fluttered closed.

He chuckled. "I'll take that."

CHAPTER 19
Riley

Over the next several days, I found it *really* difficult to stay mad at Seth.

First, he'd stubbornly hauled me back to his house instead of my home, claiming the doctor insisted someone keep an eye on me for another day or two.

Second, he'd worked at home so he could do just that.

Third, he spoiled me rotten. My damn heart melted every time he'd bring me a chai mocha latte when he went out. Or lunch. Or dinner.

I hadn't lifted a finger for days except to do some work on my computer.

In short, he'd been nothing short of amazing.

Of course, I'd probably egged him on, since I hadn't admitted that I'd gotten over his leap to judgment.

"Am I forgiven yet?" he asked from his desk at his home office.

I was kicking back in a recliner across the room, trying to catch up on some work. "I'll think about it," I replied for about the millionth time since I'd gotten out of the hospital.

Skye hadn't exaggerated about the Sinclair

men being incredibly contrite when they made a mistake.

He'd been getting the same answer for days, but it didn't seem to faze him. Really, it was more like a joke for us now, since I'd already decided to cut him some slack.

"I'll keep trying," he said lightly.

"For how long?" I asked, my heart tripping.

He shrugged. "For as long as it takes."

His eyes were still on his laptop, and I took the opportunity to study the man I certainly didn't understand, but absolutely adored.

I wasn't trying to kid myself that he was just an experiment anymore. Although, at the moment, I had no idea exactly what we were to each other.

I cared about him a lot, and I was starting to wonder if I could ever manage to just walk away in a month, once our contracted time was over.

I noticed that he looked a lot more relaxed than he had when he'd come to the hospital. Working at home, he didn't bother with a suit, so he was dressed in jeans and a navy-blue polo shirt that made his eyes stand out every time he looked at me.

He was gorgeous, but still rough around the edges at times, something I actually loved about Seth.

Okay, maybe I *could* do without *some* of the stubbornness, like his mulish refusal to let me go home alone. We'd argued about that, but I'd eventually given in. Not because he'd bullied me, but due to the fact that I could see the deep concern in his compelling silver eyes.

Usually, we worked in silence, comfortable with each other's company. But my mind was wandering today.

I closed my eyes and took in a deep breath, savoring the hint of his scent that always seemed to linger in the air here in his office, which was kind of closed off at the end of the house.

When I opened them, he was staring right at me as he asked, "What are you doing?"

Caught!

"Nothing," I answered shortly and directed my gaze back at my laptop.

Did he have any idea how difficult it was to work when I was surrounded by the sexy pheromones he exuded, even when he wasn't really trying to catch my attention?

Now that I was recovered, it was getting harder and harder to ignore the unrelenting pull, the powerful chemistry between the two of us.

"I'm thinking it might be good if I could get back home to my own office." I lifted my eyes to look at him again.

"Why?" He lifted a brow.

"I could work better there."

"You're not comfortable?" He looked concerned.

"I am. But I can't keep working here forever, Seth."

"You're staying," he said gutturally.

He sounded very much like a caveman who would absolutely drag me back to his cave by my hair if I tried to step outside the house.

That should probably be terrifying, but it wasn't. I was getting used to Seth's unreasonable demands because he was worried about me.

I wasn't about to tell him directly, but the way he'd treated me over the last several days had made it considerably easier to get past the fact that he'd wavered in his trust for a short time.

I took a deep breath. "I forgive you," I told him. "You really don't need to watch over me anymore. I've been fine since the day you brought me home. I'm not used to anybody taking care of me, Seth."

"Get used to it," he grumbled. "Since you wouldn't let me kill Easton, the only solution is to keep you in sight—even if you do forgive me, which I'm grateful for, by the way."

I sighed in exasperation. "You can't watch me forever."

He stood up and walked over to my chair. He moved my laptop to the floor. I squeaked as he lifted me up, sat down, and pulled me into his lap. "I can't let you be alone, either. What if he comes back?"

He stroked my hair, and I melted into his strong, muscular body. Seth felt so good that I couldn't resist. And really, I'd wanted to be close to him like this for days. Without thinking about it, I wrapped my arms around his neck and stroked his nape, luxuriating in the feel of his coarse hair on my fingertips.

"He's not coming back," I said, trying to placate him. "He ran into Penny and me by chance. Him being here in Citrus Beach wasn't a plot to find us. But I have to admit that I enjoyed the chance to kick the crap out of him, even if I did bump my head."

"You didn't *bump your head,*" he said tightly. "The bastard bashed it against a brick wall."

My heart squeezed. Seth was pissed off . . . still. "I'm not used to anybody taking care of me. Nobody ever really has. I've been alone for a long time. I was self-sufficient even as a child."

I shivered as Seth tightened his arms around me, and one of his big hands stroked up and down my back.

"Let me care about you, Riley. I already do, but I want you to accept it as your right, as something you deserve. I can't go back to not touching you and pretending we're friends. I'll lose my fucking mind." His voice was husky and persuasive.

And damned if I could bring myself to say *no.* "What's going to happen if we do change everything?" I was so damn tempted, but scared at the same time.

"Whatever we want to happen, baby," he answered. "We don't have to plan things. We just have to find out where it will go. In my case, I know what I want. I've wanted you ever since you sat down at my table in the Coffee Shack for the first time."

I felt myself giving in. Maybe I was still afraid, but I couldn't deny that Seth and I had been building to this exact moment for weeks.

I'd felt it.

He'd felt it.

And going back to the way we'd been would be excruciatingly painful.

"I felt the same way," I confessed as I threaded my hands through his hair. "But I didn't want to be consorting with the enemy," I teased.

He took my head between his hands, encouraging me to look at him.

I did.

And I was completely lost.

The grimness in his expression and the heat in his eyes were so damn real that I felt a flood of warmth between my thighs. My nipples tightened painfully as our eyes locked and held for so long that I lost track of time.

Finally, he said huskily, "You will never be my enemy, sweetheart. Never going to happen."

I shuddered. I could feel his hard erection underneath my ass, and see a gut-wrenching hunger in his stormy gaze.

Me. This beautiful man wanted *me.*

"What do you want?" I asked in a mesmerized whisper.

"I want you to fucking kiss me before I lose it," he growled.

And because I couldn't wait any longer, I did.

He put a hand behind the back of my head, and I lowered my mouth to his.

I moaned against his lips. The relief of finally being able to express my emotions physically was a reprieve, an alleviation of a pain that had been gnawing at me since the moment we'd met.

His tongue invaded my mouth, his hand holding my head steady like he was afraid I'd move away.

I'm not going anywhere. I can't. I've wanted this man for too damn long.

Our embrace became hungry, needy, full of a desire that couldn't be appeased until we were both naked and skin-to-skin.

"Seth," I murmured when his mouth moved down my neck, tasting every inch of the sensitive skin.

He was exploring me like he had to learn exactly what was going to turn me on.

"Seth," I said in a stronger tone.

He lifted his head. "What's the matter, Riley? What do you want?"

You. All I want is you! I want you to fuck me until my body is satisfied. Until I'm not overwhelmed by the uncompromising demands of my body.

I moved back a little, even though my body balked at the action. "There's something I need to tell you. Something important."

Seth and I were combustible, so I had to get out a truth that I needed to tell before I wasn't able to tell him anymore.

My mouth opened, and reflexively closed again.

I blinked tears of frustration from my eyes. "Dammit!" I cursed, angry because something always thwarted me when I wanted to tell the truth about my childhood. Not that anybody knew about it except Penny and my counselor, but it had been difficult even when I'd told them.

So I started a different way. "I don't have much sexual experience," I blurted out. "I mean, I'm definitely not a virgin, but it's never been . . . good."

"I'll make it good for you, Riley," he promised in a sexy baritone.

I took a deep breath. "There was a guy in college, but he finally walked away because he was interested in somebody else. Deep inside, I know it was because I didn't respond well to . . . sex. I didn't really like it, and I don't do . . . oral sex. *At all. Ever.*"

He was silent, so I continued, "And then there was Nolan." Tears started to flow from my eyes as I spoke. "It was awful every single time, but I don't think he really cared. I just lay there praying for it to be over. So feeling this way with you is . . . unexpected. I don't know what will happen."

To my mortification, I started to sob, something I'd never done in my entire life.

Seth pulled my head down to his shoulder. "Let it go, Riley. Let it go."

He just stroked my back and held my body against his as I started to wail uncontrollably.

I felt like I was expelling years of torment and pain with every breath I took, every convulsive cry that left my mouth.

I wasn't sure how long I bawled against his shoulder like a child, but he was with me every step of the way.

I could *feel* his compassion. And I could hear his pain mingling with mine as he crooned, "Everything will be okay, baby. I swear. I know something is wrong. Just tell me. Whatever it is, we'll deal with it."

"That's the problem," I said tearfully against his shoulder. "I've never been able to deal with it until recently. Even after the intensive counseling I've gone through for the last two years."

My cries had quieted, but my tears were still flowing, soaking his shirt as they kept coming unceasingly.

I felt Seth's body tense beneath mine. "Tell me. Get it out."

I want to tell him.

I need to tell him.

Our relationship really couldn't go any further

until he knew, yet it was going to be difficult to discuss.

I drew on all that I'd learned over the two years of treatment I'd had for my issues. But it was the hardest thing I'd ever done when I blurted out, "I think I've never liked sex because my father molested me for three years when I was a child. From the time I was six, until I was almost ten years old. I think you need to know that I'm emotionally damaged from it, Seth. I'm not sure I can be the woman you need. *At all. Ever.*"

CHAPTER 20
Seth

I would have been less surprised if Riley had told me she was secretly an alien from another planet in a different galaxy.

I could have probably handled that.

Unfortunately, I had no damn idea how to rationalize what she'd just told me.

All I knew was that somehow, I needed to make things right for her again. Her emotional pain was killing me.

She started to sob all over again, and every ragged breath she took was like a knife plunging into my soul.

I felt destroyed.

I felt savagely protective, to the point where my arms tightened around her body in an effort to protect her from things that had already happened to her as a child.

But I couldn't do that. I couldn't shield her from the events of her childhood.

All I could do was make her understand that as of today, she was mine to protect for the rest of her life, or until the end of mine.

I could feel how difficult it had been for her to share something like that with me, and I'd hurt as

I'd watched her struggle bravely to spit out the truth.

I stood up with her in my arms, took the stairs, laid her gently on the bed, and wrapped us up together until our limbs were so entwined that she wouldn't know where she ended and I began. She rubbed her head against my shoulder. "Seth?" she murmured uncertainly.

"I didn't bring you here to have sex, Riley," I promised. "I just want you to rest. And I want to hold you when you do. If you want to talk, then we'll talk. But the last thing I want to do is push you."

"You probably don't want to have sex with me anymore, right?"

"Wrong," I said harshly. "I want you so much it fucking hurts. But that isn't my first priority. It never was. Baby, my balls aren't going to fall off if we don't have sex, even though it might feel like it. From now on, it's all about what *you* want. This goes at your pace."

"I think you need to find a woman who's . . . whole," she whispered close to my ear.

"I have the woman I want," I rasped. "And I'll move a damn mountain to help her realize that she's already whole. I'm so fucking sorry about what happened to you as a kid, but it makes no difference to who you are *now*. It wasn't your fault, Riley. It never will be. You were a little girl. And an adult in a position of power in your life used it against you. You must know that by now."

"Rationally, I do," she answered weakly as she cuddled against my body. "But there are still glimpses of the guilt and shame I've carried since childhood, even though I've been in counseling for two years. My father has been dead for a decade, and I still remember everything. I've never been able to have pleasurable sex. I felt . . . dirty."

"You're not dirty," I answered, anger coursing through my entire body. I tamped it down. The last thing Riley needed was to deal with my emotions about what had happened to her. "You're beautiful inside and out, baby."

"I never felt like I was," she murmured softly. "I thought I'd forget it, Seth. It did happen a long time ago. But later, I started having flashbacks, and I was mired in depression and anxiety when I was finishing law school. I was spiraling downward, and I think that's what led to me accepting Nolan's proposal. I thought that maybe if I could just . . . belong, I'd be okay. Except I think it had the opposite result. I felt . . . trapped. And even more anxious. It wasn't until I started seeing a counselor here in Citrus Beach that I realized I was probably having a form of PTSD. I started to understand that those kinds of things can't be buried. Ever. I had to learn to deal with it before it completely controlled my life. I needed to talk about it."

"Do your brothers know? Does your mother?"

"No," she answered softly. "I haven't told them. I'm not sure if my mother knew, but I'm sure she heard the rumors. My father was caught crawling into my bed by one of the staff one night, and the activity got circulated around. A lot of people started to whisper about it, but like cowards, they never confronted him because he was a billionaire. He was almost untouchable. I never knew that people suspected until I was older. I thought it was *my fault*. That I'd done something to deserve it. I never told anyone because I didn't know if they'd even believe me."

"Fuck that shit about people knowing but not saying a word about it," I cursed. "That's why you dragged Penny away, right? Not to say that you wouldn't have done that anyway, but she reminded you of yourself?"

"Yes," she agreed softly. "I didn't want another kid to go through what I did. Just like me, I don't think she really understood that she was being abused until she was outside of that small world. Maybe I felt a little bit better about my circumstances by helping her, too. I'd finally stood up to fight against what happened to me, even though it was too late for me. But Penny knows, and she understands Nolan's actions for exactly what they were. She had me to talk to, and she didn't suppress it. Penny is the only person in my life who knows. I wanted her to

207

know that I'd always be there to support her because it had happened to me, too."

I buried my face in her hair and breathed her in, wishing like hell I could understand why anybody could have hurt Riley as a child. But I couldn't. "You're so damn brave, baby. So incredibly brave. There shouldn't be any shame about what happened to you. You were all alone. You didn't have anybody to rescue you like Penny had you to help her. I get why you didn't tell your mother. I doubt she would have been sympathetic."

"She would have probably called me a liar," she answered. "She never loved my father. She just wanted his money. She didn't grow up rich. So status and money were things she would have hung on to at any cost."

"Your father was in a position of trust. He violated that. I'm actually glad he's dead, or I would have wanted to kill him, too, maybe *before* I offed Nolan."

I heard a small laugh come out of Riley's mouth, and it was the sweetest sound I'd ever heard.

No wonder she didn't laugh much.

I was going to change that.

"Are you always going to want to commit murder if anybody hurts me?"

"Yep," I said honestly. I wasn't going to lie. "I have a protective streak miles wide when it comes to you, sweetheart. Probably always will."

"I always wanted to feel safe, but I never did," she explained. "It feels really good to have somebody watching my back, but you can't protect me forever. I've pretty much learned to stand on my own two feet."

"You can be independent but still have somebody who wants to keep you safe, baby."

"Maybe you're right," she said. "I'm pretty sure I'm addicted to you."

"Ditto," I said hoarsely, the dull pain in my gut becoming more acute because she sounded like she was willing to take me on in the future.

"I'm sorry to dump this on you, but you needed to know the whole truth if we want to take this relationship any further. I have . . . limitations. I'm not exactly a great lover. You had to know that," she said hesitantly.

Obviously, Riley's father had forced her to put her mouth on him, which was why she couldn't stand to give a man oral sex. Like I gave a damn? For Riley, I'd probably become celibate if it meant she felt safe.

"Riley, you're the most incredibly responsive, sexy woman I've ever met. The ball is in your court now. Nothing happens unless you really want it. And I'd never encourage you to do something you weren't comfortable doing," I said sincerely.

I didn't just want Riley's *body*. I wanted *her*. If I couldn't have all of this woman, I'd damn well

209

wait until I could. I knew it would be worth it.

If I had to keep getting myself off, so be it.

"Are you really willing to be that patient?" she asked, sounding surprised.

"What do I have to do to make you understand that all I want is you, sweetheart? I have since the day we met. I'd rather be here like this with you than to be fucking any *other* woman." When I eventually took Riley, and I knew I would, she was going to be just as eager as I was.

Honestly, even if I wanted it—which I sure as hell didn't—I wasn't certain I was even capable of being with any female *except* Riley.

"My counselor said I'm ready, but I'm kind of afraid. What if I end up not being the woman you want, Seth?"

It killed me to hear her talking like that. "Don't, Riley. You're the gutsiest woman I know. All you need to do is realize that's what *I see,* and always will. You *are* the woman I want. No fear, okay? We'll figure this whole thing out together."

"Okay," she conceded. "Just don't say I didn't warn you."

I chuckled. "Duly warned, but not the least bit afraid of diving into this relationship whole-heartedly anyway."

"You're just a little bit crazy, you know," she answered. "I have issues."

"We *all* have issues, sweetheart. Why do you think I wanted to tear down that dock on that

210

beach lot and build a superstructure? Things that happen to us when we're children can fuck up our whole life."

I understood her better than she would ever know. Even though my early childhood had been nothing like hers because I'd always had my mother, I got that a person could carry bad memories around for a lifetime.

However, I was *determined* to help Riley get beyond the childhood trauma she'd endured. Maybe it would always be there in the back of her mind, but I damn well wasn't letting it interfere with her happiness now.

She pulled back a little, and it felt like a swift kick in the gut when I looked at her swollen eyes. "Don't let those things hurt you anymore, Seth. Don't. None of the stuff with your biological father was your fault, either. He should have been there for you, but he was a dick. *You* weren't unlovable. He was the one unable to love because he was a narcissist. He couldn't love *anyone*."

It ripped at my heart that Riley was trying to console *me,* even though she was the one who really needed to be heard and understood.

I gently stroked back a lock of hair that was hanging in her face. "I wouldn't tear down that dock now even if I could. I have a fond memory of you there, now. I know that my father wasn't capable of caring about any of us. I guess it was just some residual childhood anger that was driving me. No way am I going to let him ruin my future. I think making new memories that outweigh the bad ones for me did help. Shit will always pop up from time to time, but it never lasts that long."

"I wish I could say the same thing," Riley said wistfully.

"Be patient," I suggested. "You'll get there. Go easy on yourself."

She nodded slowly. "I'm trying. I've come a long way in two years."

Considering that she had a heartless bitch for a mother, and a cruel bastard as a father, Riley was fucking incredible.

"You have," I agreed. "Even though you don't realize it yet, you *are* whole, Riley."

She raised an eyebrow. "How did I ever end up with a guy like you in my life? You seem to accept me just the way I am."

"You don't get that I feel the same way about you?"

She shook her head.

I continued, "You see me, Riley. You're not looking at my bank account. It's pretty rare. That's why I liked you at first. You didn't hesitate to tell me off or fight for what you wanted. Becoming wealthy has made me pretty damn cautious. I can't say it's exactly changed any of us, but being rich is new, and it has changed the way we look at other people in our lives. I wonder what they want, because they generally do want *something*. When you strolled into my life, you changed all of that for me."

"I was a challenge?" she asked carefully.

"You were *real*," I corrected. "And maybe I like a woman who challenges me."

"Okay. I think I like that better than *being* a challenge to conquer," she teased. "But I do have my own money."

"I have more." I tried not to make that comment sound arrogant. "Does it really matter that you have your own money? It seems like a lot of rich people always want more."

I could see the little crinkle in her forehead that told me she was thinking.

"Usually, yes," she finally said. "At least in my world, they do. Personally, I don't care. I have enough money to last me several lifetimes of lavish spending. What's the point of having more?"

I nodded. "Exactly. I don't work at building Sinclair Properties for the money, you know. I do it because it's a challenge, and I like it. Money just happens to be a by-product of my success."

"I do most of my work pro bono," she said reluctantly. "Maybe that's a little crazy, seeing as I'm a Harvard graduate. But I'm doing something that means the world to me."

"It's *not* crazy. You're making yourself happy and helping a lot of furry or feathered friends

213

along the way." I loved that she was doing what she was passionate about. I couldn't see Riley doing anything else.

She snuggled against my shoulder. "I feel so . . . tired. It's not even dinnertime yet."

I knew *exactly* why she was exhausted. She was emotionally drained. She'd cried out a bunch of sorrow and pain that had been hanging around inside her for way too long.

"There's no crime in taking a nap, Riley."

"I don't do that. *At all. Ever.*"

I smirked against her flaming-red hair. "You should try it."

"Of course I won't," she said, sounding miffed. "It's a workday, Seth."

I grinned when I heard her even breathing a few moments later.

Riley was out cold.

CHAPTER 21
Riley

I was confused when my eyes opened and it was dark.

It took me a couple of minutes to get my head straight.

I told Seth about my history of sexual abuse.

I cried like a hysterical child.

I told him I wouldn't fall asleep.

And then, I conked out.

I squinted at the clock on the bedside table.

Four a.m.

How long had it been since I'd slept for nearly twelve hours? Since I wasn't an early-to-bed kind of woman, and I got up relatively early, it had been a very long time since I'd slept *that much*.

I slowly registered that there was a very bulky, hard, and incredibly warm body behind me. I knew exactly who it belonged to. If I didn't, I'd be terrified by now.

The two of us were actually . . . spooning. His arms were wrapped around me, his hands resting right beneath my breasts.

I wriggled just a little, trying to get closer to him than I was already.

God, he felt so good.

So damn tempting.

In that moment, as I leaned back against him, I knew that for the first time in my life, I felt . . . safe. My heart was also much lighter than it had ever been before. Like an enormous weight had finally been lifted from my soul.

Seth had listened to me without judging me and reassured me that I wasn't any less attractive because of what my father had done. He'd told me that it wasn't my fault, and that it was my father who had betrayed *my* trust.

Those were all things I already knew and had been trying desperately to solidify in my thoughts and emotions. Still, there was always *some* remaining shame.

But it felt smaller, less important.

Telling Seth had helped. It had just been terrifying while I was doing it. I suppose I should have known that he'd understand.

The room was dark except for the light coming through the blinds, but I slowly shimmied my way onto my other side so I could face Seth. Unfortunately, when I'd completely shifted, I realized that I couldn't really see his face all that well.

However, I was more than happy about the fact that I could feel the hot, smooth skin of his shoulder and back.

He's not wearing a shirt.

I closed my eyes as I stroked the soft skin,

savoring every inch underneath my fingertips.

"What are you doing?" Seth grumbled sleepily.

I was startled by his voice, but I couldn't seem to stop touching him.

"Feeling you up," I murmured. "I'm sorry. I woke up and you were just . . . there. I couldn't resist."

Sorry-not-sorry.

It wasn't like I could really regret what I was doing. I'd waited too damn long to be able to touch him like this.

"Baby, if you're going to feel me up, I could think of a lot of better places for you to grope," he said in a low, sleepy voice.

"I could kiss you," I offered, my heart kicking up its pace a notch.

I wanted this man. Badly. I just didn't really know how to take the lead, and he was obviously waiting.

He'd said everything could happen when I was ready.

Well, I *was* ready.

Now more than ever.

I just wasn't quite sure exactly what to do.

"You could definitely kiss me," he said in a sexy baritone. "I'm all yours, sweetheart."

All mine.

The thought was exhilarating and terrifying at the same time.

I wrapped my arms around his neck and kissed

him, trying to communicate exactly how I was feeling without words.

He was passive only for an instant, and then he took control, his tongue exploring my mouth thoroughly, assertively, and with so much passion that my core flooded with liquid heat.

"Seth," I said breathlessly as he broke off the embrace to explore my sensitive earlobe.

"Jesus, Riley. I want you so damn much that I'm not sure how long I can do this," he rasped beside my ear.

I could feel his warm breath wafting over my ear, the tension in his body, and the way his voice sounded like he was about to lose it.

There was something about knowing that he wanted me as badly as I wanted him that broke me.

"I can't do it anymore, either," I confessed. "I can't. I want you to fuck me, Seth. Please," I begged. "I ache. I have for a long time. But you'll have to help me, at least this time."

He rolled away from me for a moment, and I practically grieved the loss. Seth turned on a soft light at his side of the bed, and then rolled back to me again.

He gently pushed me onto my back. "Look at me, Riley," he insisted. "I need to know that you're doing this because you really want it. I don't want to rush you. I didn't really mean to say that. I can wait."

I stared at him defiantly. "I don't do things I don't want to do. *At all. Ever.* Okay, maybe I *used to,* but not anymore. I can't be with you and not want more. To get closer to you. It hurts for me, too. But I don't really know what to do, other than counting the moments until the sex is over. I don't know what to do with the way you make me feel, Seth."

"Baby, you'll never fucking be counting the minutes until we're done," he told me in a gravelly voice.

His mouth came down on mine almost immediately, and I let out a moan of relief against his lips. I needed to be connected to him so badly that I couldn't breathe.

I actively participated instead of just letting it happen, wanted him to know how much I needed him.

I shivered as he nipped at my bottom lip and then soothed it with his tongue.

"Be sure this is what you want, Riley. Because once this happens, there's no going back. Not for me," he growled.

There's no going back for me, either.

Maybe I'd always known that it was going to be all or nothing with this man, which had terrified the hell out of me.

Until now.

Until tonight.

Until I trusted him.

I knew at that moment that I was in love with Seth. Completely. Totally. Irrevocably.

I couldn't voice it right at the moment.

I wasn't ready to be quite that vulnerable, because it was new to me.

"I don't want to go back," I whispered. "I just need both of us naked."

"I'm not about to argue with that," he said with a grin that made my heart skitter.

Our gazes met and held, speaking without saying a word, before he rolled off the bed.

I licked my dry lips when I saw his entire body. All he was wearing was a pair of sweatpants, and one jerk of the string holding them in place on his hips allowed him to strip them off.

Sweet Jesus!

He hadn't even looked this tempting in my *fantasies*. He was completely ripped, but not puffed up in a bodybuilder sort of way. Seth had strong muscles in his biceps, thighs, and six-pack abs that any woman would drool over.

My eyes finally dropped to a very large erection that almost made me wary.

When my gaze drifted up again, he was smirking.

The man had no shame about baring every inch of skin he had. And I loved that.

I smiled back at him as I sat up. I grabbed the hem of my shirt and whipped it over my head. I tossed it away, not really caring about where it landed.

Seth was on me before I could blink.

"I'll take it from here, gorgeous," he rumbled, his fingers seeking and finding the clasp of my bra. He unhooked it and threw it in the same direction as I had my top.

He cupped my bare breasts, and then rubbed the hard, sensitive peaks of my nipples between his thumbs and forefingers.

My head flopped back onto the pillow with a strangled moan of pleasure.

He took his time, his mouth exploring every inch of my breasts. Seth bit softly on one nipple and soothed over it with his tongue. Then he moved to the other, and did the same thing.

He moved back and forth, tormenting me until I felt like I was losing my mind.

"Seth. Please," I whimpered.

I felt him unsnap the button on my jeans and lower the zipper. I raised my hips to help him strip them off. He took my panties at the same time.

When he was done, Seth didn't leave his kneeling position.

He just . . . stared. "You're so damn beautiful, Riley," he ground out, his voice sounding like sandpaper had been applied to his vocal cords.

It probably should have made me uncomfortable that he was assessing every inch of my naked body, but it didn't.

"Fuck me, Seth," I demanded, feeling on edge and impatient.

"I'll get to that, believe me," he warned. "Does your aversion to oral sex go both ways?"

He was going to . . .

He wanted to . . .

Oh, God.

"I don't think so," I confessed. "But nobody has ever done that before."

"Then I'll be more than happy to be your first," he said in a rough, feral tone.

I trembled as he spread my legs and his hands drifted up my thighs. Just that light touch of his fingers so close to where I wanted him to be made me buck my hips.

When he lowered himself down and buried his head between my thighs, I squealed from the shock of the sensation, and the carnal need it wrenched from me.

He speared his tongue between my folds and ran it the entire length of my pussy.

"Oh, God," I cried softly, unused to the feel of a man's mouth going down on me.

But it felt so good I wanted to cry.

He explored my pussy leisurely, and so thoroughly that my breaths began coming from my mouth in tiny puffs.

"More," I demanded, spearing my hands into his hair and fisting it so I could somehow ground myself.

Finally, he nipped gently at my clit, and then gave me the burst of pleasure I'd been craving by stroking his tongue firmly, over and over, against the tiny little bundle of nerves begging for his attention.

The big ball that had formed in my belly started to unfurl, and I arched my back. I pushed my hips up, begging for every touch of his tongue that I could get.

"Seth. Yes. Please," I screamed with abandon as the weight left my stomach and shot straight through my body before exploding in my core relentlessly.

I let go and allowed myself to enjoy the satisfaction of my intense climax.

Before I spiraled down, Seth came on top of me, and thrust inside me until he was buried to his balls.

It was exactly what I wanted, what I needed. "Yes!" I hissed as I wrapped my arms around his neck.

"This is better than any fantasy I've ever had about you, Riley. Way better," Seth growled.

I didn't have time to contemplate the excitement that ratcheted up inside me from knowing he'd actually had lustful fantasies about me. But he wasn't letting me think rationally.

He pulled himself almost out, and then back in again.

I felt stretched, the muscles in my channel relaxing to accommodate a man of his size.

I let out a gasp of pleasure as Seth began a

smooth rhythm, every stroke inside of me harder than the last.

And God, how I'd craved his fierceness, his primitive instincts that seemed to be overtaking both of us.

He made me feel alive, and I welcomed that.

Lifting my hips experimentally, I caught his rhythm and pushed back, intensifying the strength of each and every thrust.

I wrapped my legs around his hips by instinct, desperate for both of us to find release.

Our skin was damp with exertion, and our bare bodies slid together erotically, his chest abrading my nipples as he moved.

I was on overload. Nothing could ever have prepared me for feeling like I did.

Ferociously hungry.

Wild.

Willing to do anything to satiate both of our greedy longings for each other.

And then, it happened. I was submerged in the sweetest, sharpest pleasure I'd ever experienced.

"Seth. Oh, God," I gasped.

I could feel my climax rushing toward me when he took my mouth and used his tongue to mimic the actions of his enormous cock.

I dug my short nails into the bare skin of his back, clawing as I felt the first spasm in my core. Then, I got lost in my overwhelming climax.

I couldn't think.

I couldn't do anything.

All that I was capable of doing was *feeling,* riding every surge of bliss that rocketed over my body.

My orgasm was so volatile that my inner muscles cinched hard around his cock.

He groaned loudly. Seth sank his cock into me one more time and let go of his own hot release deep inside me.

We were both panting and speechless, but he managed to roll over, taking my weight, leaving me sprawled out on top of his body.

"You weren't watching the clock," he said, his chest still heaving.

When my breathing slowed, and my heart rate started to return to normal, I finally spoke. "No. I don't give a damn what time it is. I'm pretty sure that my sexual issues are nearly cured," I joked.

Honestly, I'd been in counseling for so long that I'd worked through most of them. I'd just been wary of testing out the real thing. It had never felt right until I'd met Seth.

He laughed in a low, wicked voice. "Damn glad they are, baby. I'm sure a *lot more* experimentation will make it even better."

His wicked baritone was teasing, but I could hear a serious note in the sexy, low voice, too.

Seth took my head between his hands and kissed me, a slow, satisfying embrace that curled my toes.

More experimentation? Hell, yes. I was *completely* on board with that.

CHAPTER 22
Riley

"We didn't even talk about birth control or protection last night," Seth said casually later that morning.

I'd decided to take pity on him and cook breakfast, since we'd both been famished after sex in the bed and then sex in the shower. Oh yeah, and then sex right before we'd gotten dressed. Which had sent us back to the shower again.

I'd drawn the line at doing the sex-after-the-shower thing . . . *again.*

Not to say that I hadn't been *tempted,* but a woman could only take so much before she couldn't walk straight.

I'd shooed him out of the bedroom before we got ourselves in trouble again, and started to make some food.

It was nearly lunchtime, and neither one of us had even had our morning shot of caffeine yet.

Seth was in the process of remedying our lack of a pick-me-up. He was brewing up my tea and his coffee while I fixed the bacon and eggs.

"Don't panic," I told him. "I'm on the pill. I didn't stop taking it after I called it quits with

226

Nolan. I'm not exactly eager to have a child. I never have been."

I held my breath for a moment, not sure how he'd take my honest statement.

He shrugged as he slid my tea over to me. "I'm good with that," he rumbled. "I spent most of my life raising siblings, and then getting them through college."

I understood what he meant. Seth had never had time for *himself*. He'd still been a child himself when he'd started to take responsibility for his younger siblings. It was perfectly understandable that he didn't want to raise kids of his own, too.

My fear about having kids sprang from my childhood. I didn't know if I even *had* the capability to be a good mother. I hadn't exactly had good parenting examples, so just the thought of having a child and screwing him or her up was enough to make me take my birth-control pills like it was a mandatory religious experience every single day.

I turned to him as I said, "I don't know why we didn't discuss this before we had sex . . . several times."

I didn't make critical mistakes like that. *At all. Ever.*

He shot me a wicked grin that made my heart trip.

"I know why," he drawled in a deep, mischievous tone.

I smiled back at him. I couldn't help it.

Seth was irresistible under *any* circumstances, but he was doubly sexy when he was standing shirtless in his kitchen, dressed only in a pair of jogging pants.

Why did he have to be so damn . . . attractive? Even after exploring every inch of his massive chest and those six-pack abs, I still wanted to trace each hard muscle all over again with my tongue.

"I suppose this is where you tell me why?" I asked, my voice breathless from ogling his gorgeous, half-naked body.

He paused before speaking. "I've never done that before. Not talked about birth control or protection before I took a woman to bed," he explained as he moved stealthily forward.

I backed up until my ass hit the counter and he was invading my space.

He added, "But you? You aren't like any woman I've ever known, Riley. I think I forgot my own damn name last night. Nothing mattered except getting inside you before I lost my damn mind."

He was so close that I could feel his warm breath on my lips. "Is that so?" I asked as I wrapped my arms around his neck.

"Your fault," he grumbled. "You made me temporarily insane."

I laughed and pulled his head down to kiss him.

There was something incredibly seductive about knowing I could make this beautiful, perfect man forget everything except . . . me.

He kissed me tenderly, thoroughly, and I closed my eyes and savored the taste of Seth.

I'd never get used to the way he got me all off balance. But I trusted him enough to know he'd catch me if I tumbled.

I'd never really had that kind of faith in any man before, but then, I'd never known a man like the one kissing me like his life depended on it.

I was disappointed when he finally lifted his head.

"Are you okay?" he asked as he looked down at me. "I mean, after what happened with your father—"

I put a finger to his lips. "I'm fine. The only reason I mentioned it was because I thought you had the right to know. I've never really liked being that intimate with a man before, and I had no idea *what* would happen. I've always tolerated sex, but I've certainly never enjoyed it."

The fact that I'd suddenly become orgasmic had actually been a surprise. Yeah, I was mega-attracted to Seth, but I was afraid he'd be disappointed—or I would be—once we'd finally done the deed.

"And did you like it?" he asked with a slight frown.

I snorted. "If you didn't figure out the answer

to that question over the last several hours, then I'm worried about you."

He looked relieved. "I guess I just wanted to hear it from you."

"You rocked my world," I confessed. "It makes me happy to finally feel normal."

He tucked a strand of hair behind my ear. "You're anything but *normal*, Riley. You're one of a kind."

My heart tripped as I looked into his silvery eyes, so full of sincerity that it made me want to cry. I could see the way he saw me in his gaze.

Seth made me feel wanted, adored. Even though the way he looked at me made me uncomfortable at times, it also made me feel like I could fly.

Eventually, I might get used to being treated like I was valuable to someone I was dating, but I was certain I'd never take it for granted.

Finally, I answered, "You're pretty special yourself, big guy."

He grinned. "I'm ready to take you back to bed."

"Oh, no you don't," I said with a delighted laugh. "I'm sore. I haven't had sex in a few years, and now that we've done a marathon with several sessions, I can hardly walk."

"Does it hurt?" he said unhappily. "I'm sorry, gorgeous. I should have thought about that."

I shot him a mischievous smile. "I'm not complaining, but I may need a break. At least for a few hours."

"We'll take all the time you need."

"It won't be long," I assured him as I raised my hand to run my palm against his five-o'clock shadow. For some reason, I thought the rapid whisker growth was a very good look on him.

"I want more than just sex, Riley," he said huskily. "You should know that."

"What else do you want?" I said, my voice barely more than a whisper.

"Everything," he said in a warning tone. "I like waking up with you in my bed. I like seeing you at the end of the day just so we can talk about what happened while we weren't together. I like meeting you at the Coffee Shack when we need a break. I like seeing you laugh. Really, I like everything about you, even your temper."

"I don't have a temper," I told him with mock indignation.

"Bullshit," he said teasingly. "You busted Easton's balls. I wish I'd been there to see it."

I rolled my eyes. "You didn't miss much. He cried like a baby. And I had a reason to kick his ass. I wasn't about to let him near Penny. Maybe I did have a little suppressed rage about what he did to me, too."

"If that was just some residual anger, I'd hate to see you furious."

"If you stick around for a while, you'll see it someday."

"I'm not planning on going anywhere."

I searched his eyes, trying to see if he was telling the truth. Now that I knew that I was completely head over heels for him, this whole relationship thing was pretty damn scary.

Seth was capable of destroying me, but I was going to have to learn to put my fears aside. "So this relationship is going to be monogamous?"

"Are you kidding?" he asked gruffly. "Of course it is. I can't even think about being with another woman anymore. Hell, yes, it's monogamous *and* committed."

Committed?

Did I want commitment?

With Seth, I was fairly certain that I did.

I nodded. "Okay. I guess I just wanted to know exactly what we're doing."

"Isn't that what you want, too?" he asked, sounding slightly apprehensive.

"Yes," I answered swiftly. "I slept with you, Seth. If I didn't want it, I wouldn't have done that. But I'm a little bit scared. I've had a total of one man in my life. I can't really count the college thing. And look how *that* turned out."

I'd ended up being nothing except an ornament to Nolan.

But this time everything was different.

Seth was *different.*

"I'm not Easton," he rumbled.

"I know that."

"I'm not even going to pretend that I might not

be a somewhat jealous boyfriend. I'll also be an overly protective one, too, because I can't stand to see you hurt again. But I'll be loyal. Always."

I thought for a minute before I answered. "Then I guess we're monogamous."

"Glad you got that worked out," he answered, like *he* never intended to take any other answer.

I shrugged. "I don't want to be with anybody else, either."

"Thank fuck!" he said hoarsely. "I doubt I'd handle it well if you did."

My attention was momentarily distracted as I sniffed the air. "Oh, my God! The bacon!"

The noxious odor I'd smelled was smoke.

I pushed against Seth's intimidatingly large form so I could rush back to the stove, and quickly turned off the gas while I waved my hand in the air above the bacon to dispel the thick smoke.

"I ruined it," I said wistfully as I used a fork to stir the blackened mess.

Seth put his hands on my shoulders. "It doesn't matter, gorgeous. Don't sweat it."

"Of course it matters," I mumbled. "We're both starving. It's your fault for distracting me."

He chuckled. "Did I ever mention that I really like my bacon extra-crispy?"

I was still pissed at myself for doing something so stupid, but I couldn't help myself.

I snorted.

And then I laughed.

CHAPTER 23
Riley

Dear Ms. Montgomery:

I'd like to make you a proposition.

Even though you're the sexiest attorney I've ever laid eyes on, I find myself wanting something other than your legal expertise.

In fact, it may very well involve groping your ass, and having hot sex, something you were previously against in our old arrangement.

Let me know if you'd like to continue breaking that previous contract—as soon as possible.

Sincerely,
Seth Sinclair

"I'm very much interested in *destroying* that old contract forever," I said with a laugh as I read Seth's email.

Over a week had passed since we'd first been intimate, and it seemed like we couldn't get through a workday without some kind of communication from each other.

Pathetic, right?

I leaned back in my office chair with a smile on my face.

When I'd kissed him good-bye this morning and made my way back to my own home office to work, I'd known damn well that *one of us* would break down and text, call, or even email—the form of communication he'd decided to use *today*.

I let out a huge sigh, knowing I was useless for the rest of the day. My mind was now focused on every single dirty thing I'd like to do in order to keep breaking my previous contract with Seth. Luckily, it was late afternoon, and I'd done everything I really needed to do for my clients.

Every single day, I seemed to find myself crazier about Seth than I had been the day before. Strangely, I wasn't as scared as I used to be about my situation. I was convinced that he was into this relationship just as deeply as I was.

I practically lived at his house now, coming back to my cottage only during the day to work. If I didn't turn up at his home when he got back from the office, he'd come over to my place to find me.

Is that normal? Is it really healthy to be so connected that we want to be together almost every moment that we aren't working?

Since I had very little experience with *normal*, I wasn't certain what a couple should really be doing together.

Does it really matter what other people do?

Probably not. Seth and I were both pretty content to keep on doing what we were doing now.

I leaned forward and read the few lines of his email again.

It occurred to me that Seth was usually the one to reach out during the day. Not that I didn't want to, but I usually waited until he did.

Knowing *exactly* what I wanted to do, I got up, grabbed my keys, and headed for the garage door.

After making a quick pit stop, I ended up at his office building about twenty minutes later.

"Good afternoon, Edie," I greeted Seth's secretary as I came through the door.

Edie smiled up at me from her desk. "Ms. Montgomery. It's so nice to see you in person."

I'd only stopped by Seth's office once, when we'd planned on going out to dinner after he left work. Any other communication I'd had with Edie had been on the phone.

I smiled at the older woman. "It's good to see you, too. I brought you a coffee. I don't know if you indulge."

She beamed. "I do. I love anything from the Coffee Shack. That's so thoughtful of you."

I set the mocha latte on her desk. "Is he in?"

Edie nodded. "He's in a meeting with your brother Hudson."

"Just Hudson?" I asked.

Edie nodded as she picked up her coffee. "Yes."

I grinned at her. "Then I'll interrupt."

"I doubt either one of them will mind. I know Mr. Sinclair definitely won't," she teased. "You go right in, Ms. Montgomery."

"Riley. Please." *Ms. Montgomery* sounded way too much like my mother.

"Riley," she agreed. "Let me get the door. Your hands are full."

I had a coffee in each hand, so I was grateful when she opened the door to Seth's office.

"Delivery," I said cheerfully as I closed the door with my butt. "Since you usually bring me my fix, I thought I'd return the favor."

My heart skittered as Seth's eyes immediately went from Hudson to me, and he grinned.

He was breathtaking in a blue custom suit that made his smoky eyes more pronounced than usual.

And his covetous gaze was centered . . . on me.

That was one of the many things I loved about him. When I was in the room, it was like nobody else existed for him. He gave me his total attention.

"Hey, gorgeous," he said huskily as he stood up.

"Hi," I said breathlessly. "I didn't want to interrupt. I just wanted to return the many Coffee Shack favors you've done for me." I moved to set his coffee on his desk.

He caught me around the waist and kissed me like Hudson wasn't sitting right across from him. The embrace was short, but I could feel his passion even in the short show of affection.

"There's so much sweetness in this room that I'm getting nauseous," Hudson drawled.

I could feel my cheeks turning pink as I turned to my older brother. "I think I'm starting to enjoy a little bit of sugarcoating in my life."

"Can't say that I blame you," Hudson said thoughtfully as he stood up and gave me a hug. "You certainly never got any of that in our family." He hesitated before he asked, "No coffee for me?"

"I didn't know you were here. What are you doing in Citrus Beach?"

"Convincing your boyfriend that he needs the Montgomery brothers as investors."

I looked from Hudson to Seth. "And did it all work out?"

Hudson nodded. "I think we've discussed everything. And since I have another meeting in San Diego, I'll leave you two alone."

"Great idea," Seth replied.

Hudson's eyes narrowed as he shot a warning glance at Seth. "Just remember what I said about what happens if you hurt my little sister."

"What happens if she breaks my heart?" Seth inquired with mock innocence.

Hudson shrugged as he walked to the door. "I

don't give a shit. If she does, you'd probably deserve it. I'll call you tomorrow after I talk to Jax and Cooper."

Seth snickered as Hudson exited.

"I can't say that your brother isn't painfully blunt," Seth said, casually leaning against the desk as his office door closed.

I took a sip of my chai before I answered, "All my brothers are like that. But at least you know exactly where you stand with them."

He picked up his coffee and chugged it. "I'd rather know where I stand with you."

"I think you already know," I teased. "I'm here with coffee before the workday is even over. I got your email."

He raised a brow. "You came here to break the contract . . . again."

"I came to bring you coffee."

He put his cup on the desk. "Much appreciated, since I couldn't get out today. The coffee was a bonus. What I *really* like is seeing you."

I finished my chai and tossed the disposable cup in the trash.

As usual, he left me tongue-tied. Joking around was easy, but I had a hard time knowing what to say when his tone was so serious.

Seth was just . . . like that.

He could blurt out a compliment or lay his emotions out there so much easier than I could.

"I missed you," I mumbled awkwardly.

He wrapped a steely arm around my waist and tipped my chin up. "Hey, don't get all shy on me now. You're welcome to come here whenever you miss me. I missed you, too, gorgeous."

I smiled. Seth had a way of making me feel . . . valuable. And wanted. I could never be reticent in his company for very long.

Coming here had been totally spontaneous, and I didn't do unplanned events. *At all. Ever.*

So it was nice to feel welcome when I'd actually given in to being unconstrained.

I wrapped my arms around his neck, and my body suffused with heat.

I tried not to remember all of the intimate things we'd done the night before, but I was failing miserably.

He lowered his head and kissed me, and it was a much longer version of his previous embrace.

I reveled in the pleasure of Seth taking control with a ferocious hunger that he never failed to express whenever he touched me.

I got lost in the kiss as he stroked my back sensually, and then moved his hands down to cup my ass.

"Seth!" I gasped as he released my mouth.

"Jesus, Riley," he said like he was in pain. "All I have to do is see you, and I get hard. When I actually touch you, I'm fucked."

I was relieved when he expressed the fact that seeing me turned him on. Maybe because it was nice to know that I wasn't caught in this madness alone.

I squeaked as he nipped at the skin on my neck, and then soothed it with his tongue.

"I needed to see you," I confessed. "I needed to touch you."

He groaned. "I think I feel that way every damn minute of the day, Riley."

"Is this crazy?" I panted as his warm, soft lips caressed the space where my neck met my shoulders.

His fingers threaded into my hair. "If it is, I sure as hell don't want to be sane again," he said hoarsely.

I speared my hands into his hair, closing my eyes because the feeling of those coarse strands between my fingers felt so damn good.

This man completely consumed me, and I was more than willing to let him.

I'd never felt this way.

Hadn't even known that I could.

Seth squeezed the cheeks of my ass through the denim of my jeans and jerked me forward to feel the effect I had on his body.

The moment I felt his erection against my lower belly, I moaned.

"Seth, we have to stop," I said weakly, making no attempt to pull away because I just . . . couldn't.

I needed to feel his enormous body against me.

I was enmeshed in a beautiful web of need that I couldn't escape.

"I don't want to stop, gorgeous," he said gruffly. "At all. Ever."

His mouth came down on mine with a force that stole the breath from my body. I tugged his head closer and tried to get as much satisfaction from his kiss as possible.

Seth's tongue delved deep, owning my mouth like it belonged to him.

Molten heat flooded my core, and all I wanted to do was climb inside this man and never come out.

He nipped at my bottom lip, and then ran over the place he'd nibbled on with his tongue again, which made me absolutely insane.

"Seth, please," I begged, not even knowing what I wanted. I was in his office, not home in his bed.

I ached with need. But I was in the wrong place if I needed satisfaction.

I felt my back hit the wall, even though I hadn't even been aware of him pushing me toward it.

When he moved back, I almost whimpered over losing contact with him.

He reached for the zipper of my jeans and pulled it down after he'd swiftly opened the button at the top.

"We can't, Seth. Not here," I said, sounding slightly panicked.

"Right here. Right now," he growled. "Neither one of us wants to wait. I own the damn building, so I can do whatever I damn well please."

"Edie?" I said, my breathing ragged now.

"Don't move," he answered, and then went to the office door. He flipped the lock in place and came back before I could take another breath. "She can't get in. So the only way this stops right now is if *you* want it to stop."

He met and held my gaze, his fierce expression reflecting the way I was feeling at the moment.

His chiseled jaw was tight, his eyes assessing as they swept over my face. "You make the call, Riley. I can't. If I had my way, I'd already be fucking you up against this wall until you begged for mercy."

Oh, God, yes!

I could see the image of him pounding into me, my legs wrapped around his waist, both of us lost and straining for relief.

Without taking time to think, I yanked the shirt I was wearing over my head and dropped it on the floor. Then I shucked my bra and tossed it down, too.

"I. Can't. Wait." I yanked my jeans down, taking my panties with them, and kicked them to the side. "Fuck me, Seth. Make my body stop aching for you."

His chest was heaving as he slapped a hand next to each side of my head, trapping me in.

"You almost gave me a damn heart attack, Riley. When in the hell did you get so bold?"

I was always incredibly responsive to him, but I had no idea when I'd decided to be adventurous.

He'd always taken the lead, but I was tired of waiting. And I didn't give a damn where and how I got close to this man.

Me.

Riley Montgomery.

The woman who planned everything.

I grabbed his tie and yanked him closer. "Right now," I finally answered. "You got a problem with it?"

He grinned down at me. "That's my girl. Hell, no. You can get naked in my office any damn time you want to do it. I'm not complaining."

CHAPTER 24
Riley

Seth's expression changed as I reached down and liberated his cock.

I stroked it gently, and then wrapped my fingers around the shaft. "You're so hard," I murmured.

He grabbed my wrist. "You're going to realize just how hard it is firsthand in a matter of minutes," he growled. "If you keep touching me like that, I'll lose it."

I wrapped my arms around his neck. "Maybe I *want* to see you lose it."

Nothing made me hotter than watching a powerful man like Seth relinquish all semblance of control.

"Baby, you see that every damn night."

Honestly, I *did* see it. I relished the moment when Seth was no longer rational.

He cradled the back of my head and kissed me, his other hand moving down my body languorously.

I shuddered when his fingers teased between the folds of my pussy, his touch like a lightning bolt sizzling every single nerve I possessed.

His touch was slow and teasing, his finger sliding over my clit with long, light strokes.

I put my hands in his hair and fisted the strands, my body taut.

"Now, dammit!" I insisted between gritted teeth.

"You really are becoming incredibly bossy," he grumbled. "You're so damn wet, Riley. Perfect. It's like you were made for me."

I whimpered as he caressed my clit a little bit harder, but not enough to satisfy me.

Desire was gnawing at me and ready to swallow me whole.

I jumped up and wrapped my legs around his waist. "No more tormenting me," I insisted. "Fuck me, Seth, before I lose it."

"I want you to be ready, gorgeous," he whispered huskily against my ear. "I want you to enjoy this as much as I will. And I want to know that you want me as much as I want you. And that's one hell of a lot."

He thinks I don't want him just as much as he wants me?

Impossible.

I inhaled deeply, the musky scent of him enfolding me.

"I ache, Seth," I told him. "Make it go away. I already want you so much that I can't take it."

His hand went underneath my ass to support me, and a second later, he was buried to his balls inside me.

"Yes!" I hissed, my muscles slowly relenting to accept his massive cock.

"This is going to be a wild ride," he grunted.

My body was so primed that I knew exactly what he meant.

There was no slow buildup, no leisurely thrusts as we climbed higher together.

We were frantic, frenzied as he pummeled into me, and I rocked forward against him, both of us straining to find the release we both desperately needed.

There was something incredibly erotic about being completely nude, while Seth was still dressed in an expensive suit. My sensitive nipples abraded against his jacket as I undulated against him, every action hurtling me toward an orgasm that had been delayed too long.

"Seth," I moaned.

I wanted to scream, but I bit my lip to stay as quiet as possible since we weren't alone in the building.

I wanted to cry out about how much I loved him, but I swallowed the words.

My head lolled back, and hit the wall, but I didn't care.

All I wanted was to keep up the frenetic pace he'd set.

"We belong together, Riley," he snarled. "You. Belong. With. Me."

I wrapped my arms around him tighter as he slammed into me with a force that rocked my body deliciously.

"I know," I panted. "You belong with me, too."

There was nothing more to say.

Not now.

Maybe not ever.

Seth Sinclair owned me body and soul, and I had no doubt that we were meant to be together.

It was more than just carnal lust that was driving both of us.

I love you. I love you so damn much!

I wanted to say the words, but I already felt too vulnerable.

"Yes!" I said aloud, my body tightening as Seth continued his frantic pace.

I savored the feel of every hard plunge of his cock inside me as I felt my climax rushing toward me.

I buried my face into his shoulder, trying to muffle the sound of my moans of euphoria as I came so hard that my body trembled.

"Christ, Riley. You feel so damn good that I don't want this to end," Seth groaned.

My muscles clamped hard around his cock, causing him to find his own powerful release.

"Holy fuck!" he rasped roughly, his chest heaving as he just held me tight against him, his fingers digging into my ass.

I wasn't sure how long we stayed suspended in that position, his body pinning mine to the wall as I panted to recover my breath. My heart was thundering so loud I could almost swear I could actually *hear* it.

Minutes later, Seth finally spoke. "I'm squashing you. Can you stand up?"

My whole body felt like jelly, but I nodded anyway. "Yes."

I really wasn't sure I could stand, but I did feel like I could fly.

He lowered me slowly back to my feet, and then picked me up and carried me to a leather chair in the corner of his office. Seth sat and pulled me into his lap. He cradled me there, his touch gentle as he pushed a few locks of hair away from my face.

"You're so damn beautiful, Riley," he said hoarsely.

I'd never felt all that attractive before, but Seth made me feel like a seductress. "You're pretty attractive yourself," I replied. "Too attractive. You're dangerous."

I stroked some slightly damp locks of his hair from his forehead.

"We're a mess," I told him. "I have a feeling we look like we've been screwing around in your office."

My heart skittered when he shot me an evil grin. "Probably because we were," he answered as he stroked a hand up and down my naked back.

"You shouldn't have sent me that email," I said with mock displeasure. "It made me want to find out exactly how we could keep breaking that old contract."

"Baby, that contract is dust," Seth drawled. "I tore it up a long time ago. I'm way beyond experimenting. This is real, Riley. For me, I think it always has been. I'd be completely destroyed if you walked away now."

My heart felt like it was in a vise as I met his earnest gaze. God, I wished I could express my feelings as well as he could. I wished that I could make myself that vulnerable. "I'm not going anywhere."

"You better not. If you do, I'll find you," he rumbled as he pulled my head down to kiss me.

I sighed into his mouth, luxuriating in the feel of his soft lips teasing mine.

It was an embrace full of emotion and promise, and unhurried, sexy discovery.

It was a kiss I could lose myself in, and I did for several moments.

Finally, I pulled back to look at him. "I'm still kind of damaged, you know," I revealed candidly. "Sometimes I'm not sure if I'll ever be normal. But I'm starting to feel so much better. And it's all because I'm finally discovering who I really am. Because of *you,* Seth. Because of *us.*"

He looked at me like there wasn't one single thing wrong with me as he replied, "Then I'll help you put yourself together again, Riley, if that's what you want. But to me, you'll always be the only woman I want."

I tried to blink back the tears that sprang to my

eyes, but I couldn't. One fat drop landed on my cheek. And then another.

"I don't really even know what normal is, Seth. I realized that today. Everything that has happened in my life has been so dysfunctional that I really don't know what it's like to be completely whole," I said stoically.

"You don't have to be somebody else's definition of normal, Riley. You just have to be you. I get that sometimes you don't know how special you are, but you're the smartest, strongest, gutsiest woman I know. I wish to hell I could take away everything that's happened to you that makes you feel broken. Because there really isn't a damn thing wrong with you." Seth swiped away the tears on my face with a gentle finger.

"Okay. So maybe I'm *not* completely broken, but sometimes I just have problems expressing myself. Not when it comes to work or legal stuff, but personal stuff," I shared.

He shook his head. "Hell, you weren't exactly encouraged to be demonstrative as a kid or as an adult. I've met your mother, Riley. And your father was an asshole pedophile. You learned to keep everything inside you. But that will eventually change now that you've changed your environment. Give it time, gorgeous."

I shot him a small smile. "Maybe sometimes I just think you deserve a woman who completely has her shit together."

He shrugged. "I wouldn't want her."

I lifted a brow. "Why?"

"Because she wouldn't be you," he answered earnestly. "It would really suck to have a woman who thought she was perfect. Who would I talk to about my own imperfections?"

"Are you saying you have some of those?"

"You know I do," he said. "I told you why I wanted to take down that dock and build a superstructure on that property. Most of us have had some dysfunction in our lives. It helps to have somebody who understands and doesn't judge because of it."

My heart squeezed inside my chest, and I wrapped my arms around Seth and hugged him so hard that I was surprised he didn't protest.

It was hard to believe someone as gorgeous, intelligent, and empathetic as Seth still harbored *any* insecurities, but he did have a few from growing up poor, and his childhood. "You can always talk to me," I told him fiercely.

"Ditto," he said as he held me tighter. "I'm here for you, baby. Just talk to me."

"I will," I promised. "It's just difficult sometimes. I guess I'm always waiting for the backlash if I say something that isn't acceptable."

"I think you might need to tell your mother to go to hell," he said thoughtfully.

"I've wanted to," I told him. "I really do. But I guess there's always some hope that she'll just accept me as I am someday. Rationally, I know that's not going to happen. But that little girl in me still wants her to love me, I suppose."

"I think she does to the extent that she's capable of loving you, Riley."

"But it's always conditional, and I've never been able to be enough for her to love," I mused. "I know I need to accept that she's just not able to care without some kind of perfection no person is capable of achieving. But I hope I'll get there."

"You will," he said encouragingly.

I smiled at him. "You're a pretty extraordinary guy, you know."

I wished I had the words to tell him just how unique he really was in comparison to every other man I'd ever met.

"I'm not special, Riley. You've just known some real assholes. I look good in comparison," he said teasingly.

I laughed as I squirmed in his lap. "I need to get dressed. I can't believe we're sitting here having this conversation when I'm naked in your office."

"I don't know, I'm enjoying these nude conversations," he drawled.

I rolled my eyes and got to my feet. "I'm the only one who's naked here," I reminded him.

He smirked. "Exactly. That works for me."

"You're such a pervert," I accused jokingly as I went to snatch my clothes from the floor.

"You're the one who stripped without hesitation," he answered. "Not that I had a single problem with you doing it. In fact, you could do it more often."

I snorted. "Maybe I'm learning to throw off my inhibitions."

"Please feel free to toss every one of them aside. That whole *take-charge* attitude is pretty hot."

I laughed as I pulled on my panties and my jeans. "Maybe I'll throw caution to the wind later," I teased.

Seth stood and righted himself and zipped up his pants. "God, I hope so," he said enthusiastically.

My heart swelled, and I knew that from the minute I'd entered his office until this very moment, I'd fallen just a little bit more in love with Seth Sinclair.

CHAPTER 25
Seth

"I want to ask Riley to marry me," I told Noah as we sat down to coffee at his house a week later.

Aiden hadn't been able to come drop in on my eldest brother today, but I'd really felt the need to talk.

As usual, I'd turned to Noah when I was considering something monumental in my life. We were too close in age for me to see him as a parental figure, but he'd always been the head of our household. Workaholic tendencies aside, my eldest sibling had always been there for all of us when we really needed him.

He shot me a dubious look. "Seth, think about it before you do something that you might regret later. You've known Riley for a month or two. I don't think that's long enough to decide whether you want to spend the rest of your life with her."

I shook my head. "I know I want that. Hell, I think I've known almost from the first time we met. There isn't a woman in the world like her, Noah. We just . . . fit. I can't really explain it, but I can't imagine my life without her anymore."

"Why the rush? Riley is still going to be around in another year or two."

I shrugged. "I can't explain that, either. All I know is that I need her to be mine."

Generally, I wasn't all that impulsive, especially when it came to huge decisions like marriage. However, my need to make Riley mine was pretty fucking relentless.

Noah leaned back in his chair and just stared at me. "I like Riley. She's gutsy. Definitely protective of the people she loves, judging by what happened at the barbecue, and she's highly intelligent. I just don't think you need to rush into anything."

"I'm not saying I'm rushing things, exactly. I just know what I want, and it fucking eats at me not to go after it."

Noah shook his head. "You've always been like this, I suppose. I still remember when you were so damn determined to get secondhand bikes for Brooke and Jade when they were younger. But we just couldn't afford it. So in addition to your construction work, you decided you'd work in the bicycle store putting together bikes at Christmas in exchange for those two used ones that Jade and Brooke really wanted. You're stubborn as hell when you set your mind on something."

"The girls were over the moon that Christmas," I explained. "It was worth it just to see them smile. They didn't get much as kids."

"None of us did," Noah reminded me. "But you busted your ass to make up for that. So the last thing I want to see right now is for you to destroy your life. You have it good now, Seth. Everything you've ever wanted."

"Except her," I told him. "Maybe you don't quite get it, but Riley is the woman I always wanted but could never manage to find. She doesn't give a damn about my money. She wants to be with *me*. I know she wouldn't have treated me any differently when I was poor, Noah."

My brother released a deep breath. "I agree. She's fiercely loyal when she commits herself to somebody. That's not the point. I'd just like to see you wait a little longer before you jump in over your head."

I smirked at him. "When have I ever done that?"

"Unfortunately, never . . . until you met Riley."

I folded my arms over my chest. "Someday, you'll meet a woman who knocks you on your ass. And you'll know exactly how I feel. I think Sinclairs fall hard and fast. Look at the rest of the family."

He grimaced. "Not going to happen. I don't, never have, and never will lose my shit over a woman. I don't have the time or inclination to have my head up my ass."

I didn't speak as I watched his grim expression. Noah had always been the one to sacrifice everything for his family. He worked too hard, and all of his focus and dogged determination had been on seeing every one of us get what we needed. Sure, Aiden and I had helped, but Noah had taken the responsibility for all of us on his own shoulders. "You know you don't have to work this hard anymore, right? In case you missed it, we're billionaires, Noah. All of us are grown up."

He looked at me, puzzled. "What else would I do?"

"Relax?" I suggested.

"I'm not sure I know how, and I'm positive I wouldn't like it."

It suddenly dawned on me that even though our circumstances had changed, Noah was still doing what he did best. He worked until he was ready to drop.

Maybe being head of our family wasn't exactly a good thing. My big brother was conditioned to work and look after all of us. He'd been doing it since he was eighteen. He had no idea what else to do with his adult life.

"You're just not used to taking a damn breath," I told him. "You've always been there for us. Let us be there for you now."

I couldn't change the fact that he was the oldest, but I could try to make him realize that everything had shifted. We could finally be like normal siblings. He didn't have to be a father figure anymore.

"I'm good," he grumbled. "I like what I'm

doing. There's a lot of satisfaction in developing new programs."

"Not when you're completely obsessed with doing it," I pointed out. "We fucking miss you, Noah."

"I'm right here. Does one of you need something? Is it Brooke or Jade? What do we need to do?"

I got Noah's complete attention just because he mistakenly believed that one of us needed him. I hadn't meant to do that at all. "We're all fine. We just want you to join the family now. Not that you haven't always been ultraresponsible. But we just miss you being there when we're all having a *good time.*"

That would be a change, since all he knew were the *bad times.*

"Unlike the rest of you, I'm not about to meet some kind of life partner or soulmate," he said gruffly. "It's not part of my personality. You aren't the only one who had women treat you like you were invisible when we were dirt-poor. What female wants a guy who has the responsibilities I had? Not that I'm complaining, because I'm not. I'd give up women all over again to have all of you happy. I don't want a female now that I'm rich beyond my wildest imagination. I'd rather keep working on my projects."

"How long has it been since you've gotten laid?" I asked.

"No comment," he said harshly. "Let it go, Seth. And let's get back to you and Riley. I'm perfectly content."

No, he's not.

Noah was disillusioned, just like I'd been before I'd met Riley. Our positions might be a little bit different. Noah had been the only one old enough to make the sacrifices in the beginning to keep our family together. But I understood him more than he knew.

I wasn't about to give up on him. None of us were. We just needed the right opportunity to show Noah that we could be a family now, without him shouldering all the responsibility.

It wasn't that we didn't *need* him. We did. But we didn't need him to resolve every problem we had.

"There isn't really much more to say," I explained. "Riley is it for me, Noah."

His eyes drilled into me. It was a look that I knew and had never felt comfortable under. He'd always been able to get us to toe the line with *that* expression.

"I won't tell you *not* to marry her," he said thoughtfully. "I trust you to make your own decisions. I just need to play devil's advocate here. God knows I want you to be happy. And I think Riley is an exceptional woman. I just don't want to see you do something you'll regret later. You'll need a prenup if she agrees."

"I won't," I contradicted. "If she agrees to marry

me, I'm never going to let her go. Besides, the money has never been that important to me. It's changed my professional life and personal life, but it really hasn't changed who I am, Noah. If Riley were to leave me, I wouldn't give a damn about the money. What good would it do if I was miserable?"

"You're crazy," Noah rumbled unhappily.

"Did Jade get a prenup? Did Brooke?"

"They were marrying someone who was already rich."

"Riley isn't looking for money. She's a Montgomery. Like in *Montgomery Mining*. Jaxton, Hudson, and Cooper Montgomery are her brothers. They bought her out of her portion of the company because she didn't want it. She's happy being an attorney fighting for the rights of endangered species."

I quickly explained everything I could about Riley without breaking her confidence. I could never share some of her history, but I tried to make Noah understand that so much of her childhood and adult life had been anything but happy.

He paused for a moment before he spoke. "So it was no coincidence that she happened to be engaged to a prick like Easton?"

"No. Until a few years ago, she was part of the elite crowd. She's wealthy in her own right, but she hated that whole scene. It was like trying to fit a round peg into a square hole for her. Nothing she ever did could make her mother happy. Riley turned herself inside out to try to please her, but she never could."

"What parent wouldn't be proud of a woman who graduated with high honors from Harvard?" Noah mumbled unhappily.

"I don't get it, either," I agreed. "But I respect the hell out of the fact that she broke away from something she'd been raised to be her entire life. She dumped Easton and started all over again here in Citrus Beach."

"How are her brothers?" Noah queried.

"Protective," I said with a grin. "But they'll make good investors in Sinclair Properties. And they care about Riley. They're pretty much rebels themselves."

"What are they going to do if you ask Riley to marry you so soon after you've met her?"

I shrugged. "I don't give a shit."

The only thing I really cared about was seeing Riley happy for the rest of her life. Fortunately, I was sure I was the guy who could make that happen, since I'd make it my mission for the rest of my life. There had been way too much sorrow and pain for her so far. I never wanted to see her cry again. It ripped my damn heart out.

"You sure about this?" Noah said, still sounding skeptical.

I nodded. "Yep. I didn't come here to ask for your permission. I guess I just wanted you to be the first one to know."

"Okay," he said, resigned. "What can I do to help you?"

"Nothing, really. I have no idea if she'll even say yes. But I have to ask the question anyway. If it's too soon for her, I'll wait."

I wasn't the least bit surprised that Noah was going to back me up or help me out if I needed it. He always had.

"Let me know what happens," he demanded. "If she breaks your damn heart, I won't say that I told you so."

I downed the last of my coffee and stood. Having Riley as my wife was going to happen eventually. Any other result was unacceptable.

Noah got up and clapped me on the back. "Good luck."

I grinned at him. Noah might seem uninterested most of the time, but it was a sham. He heard and remembered everything. "Thanks."

"Seth," Noah said as I started for the door.

I turned around. "Yeah?"

"After everything this family has been through, nobody deserves to find happiness more than you do."

I nodded sharply and made my way to the door.

Maybe I disagreed, but I didn't say anything more.

The one who really deserved to find what he needed was Noah, and I'd make damn sure that he got it someday.

CHAPTER 26
Riley

I sat on my couch watching Seth play with my new kitten that he'd brought me a few days ago. I'd named the feline Bandit, and both he and Seth were currently on the living room floor.

I still wasn't quite sure why Seth had brought me the adorable male fluffball. It had come out of the blue. He'd mentioned something about knowing I'd always wanted one, but he hadn't elaborated.

I absolutely adored the black furball with some spots of white on his face that really *did* make him look like a bandit.

Hence, I'd given the kitten that moniker soon after he'd made his arrival at my house.

The kitten was a rescue from the shelter, which made me love Seth just a little bit more—if that was even possible.

"You're so mean," I accused with a laugh as Seth teased Bandit with a stick and dangly strings that he never let the little cat quite reach.

Seth grinned up at me from his position on the floor. "He loves it."

I had to admit that Seth was probably right. The kitten looked overjoyed as he kept bouncing around in pursuit of those untouchable strings.

I reached down and plucked Bandit off the floor when he got close to me. "He's a kitten. I think he's tired."

Seth flopped next to me on the couch. "He didn't look all that exhausted to me," he said skeptically. "I think you just want to hold him."

"Maybe I do," I confessed as I felt the tiny body start to purr.

My heart warmed as Bandit snuggled up against my breasts.

"Lucky cat," Seth said in mock complaint.

I shot him an amused glance. "Like you don't get enough of that yourself?"

He shook his head. "It's never enough."

I'd been with the man I loved long enough to know he was sexually insatiable.

However, I'd be the last one to complain.

"I don't understand why you've never gotten a cat if you wanted one," Seth contemplated.

"I always wanted a kitten as a kid. Desperately. But of course my mother had never allowed it. She hated animals in general, and cats most of all because they might scratch her furniture. Obviously, I couldn't have one while I was in college. I lived in the dorms."

"What about the last two years? You've been living alone."

I shrugged. "I wanted to, but I was hesitant."

"Why?"

"Maybe because I wasn't sure if I was ready.

I was kind of a mess in the beginning when I moved here. Recently, I've been meaning to get one. I've been thinking that I was ready. I'm leaving old memories behind."

"Something upset you at one time. Something about cats."

His words were a statement and not a question. He seemed to always know when there was more to the story.

I nodded as I cuddled Bandit just a little closer. "When I was sixteen, my father was working on a mining project in Florida. It was rare when he took my mother and me with him. But that time, he did. He was doing phosphorus mining, something my brothers stopped when they decided they wanted to focus on gems and diamonds. Understand, my father had no scruples when it came to getting things done on time and making a maximum amount of profit. When the mining project was all set up and ready to start, one of his managers told him that a Florida panther had been spotted on the mining land."

"They're endangered," Seth commented.

"Very much so," I answered. "And they're still critically down in numbers, even today. Because my father was worried about the panther sighting disrupting his start schedule, he hunted it down and shot it. He buried it and swore the manager to secrecy. For some reason, he took me along on that hunt. I didn't know what he had planned until it actually happened. I watched him kill a precious, majestic animal that was nearly extinct. He did it without a single ounce of remorse. I was heartbroken and traumatized. That incident led to my current passion for protecting endangered species."

"Jesus, baby. I'm so sorry. As much as you love animals, it must have nearly destroyed you at that age," Seth commiserated.

"I sat by that big cat, just petting it, until my father made me let go so he could bury it. I think I cried myself to sleep every night for two weeks. Not only was the panther beautiful, but I knew there would be one less to help their numbers recover. That's when I became obsessive about saving every single animal I could from extinction." I still had occasional nightmares about the horrible incident with my father, but knowing I'd helped dozens of other endangered species live on helped considerably.

Seth was quiet, so I continued, "It's in the past now. I work to protect wildlife, and I feel good about doing it. Not that the work I do is actually atonement for that lost cat, but it just feels . . . right."

"It wasn't *you* who needed to atone," Seth rumbled. "But I do know that you're a damn tough, stubborn opponent."

I smiled. "I can be. I took it a little easy on you since I was fairly certain Jade was going to talk you into giving up that property, eventually. She would have, right?"

"Baby, you didn't take it easy on me over the summer. I've seen you play hardball. And yeah, I would have given Jade the property. If not, she would have gotten upset and cried. I've always hated that. All of us do."

"So not seeing your sister cry is worth a multimillion-dollar deal?"

He nodded. "In a heartbeat. I'd like to think I've learned how to be ruthless in business. But this wasn't about business. It's about family. Family always comes first."

I knew that now better than I'd known it a couple of months ago. Seth would cut off both his hands before he'd see his siblings hurt for *any* reason. "So why did you even put up a fight after she found out?"

He sent me a mischievous smile. "If you haven't figured that one out yet, I guess maybe I need to spell it out. It was always about you, Riley. If I gave Jade the property easily, I would have had no reason to communicate with you. Maybe in the beginning, I didn't want to admit what my motivation really was, but I learned what it was soon enough."

My heart skipped a beat. "So you wanted to keep fighting with me?"

He shrugged. "I think I liked fighting with you more than I would have liked not hearing from you anymore at all. I was pretty certain I wouldn't just be able to give away the property and ask you on a date."

"Probably not," I said regretfully. "I wasn't exactly receptive to getting involved with any guy. And I knew *you* were trouble."

"How did you know that?" he asked curiously.

"Because I was attracted to you and had been from the first time I met you. However, you *were* a foe at the time," I teased. "Like I said . . . *trouble*. Normally, I'd never even speak to a defendant again after I'd kicked their ass in court."

"I figured," he drawled unhappily.

I laughed. It was almost incomprehensible to me that someone like Seth would go through that much trouble to get to know me better. Maybe I should be upset that he'd tricked me, but I couldn't help but actually be grateful that he had. If not, we wouldn't be together right now.

"Should we eat here or my place, or just go out?" he asked.

"Here," I answered. "My brothers are coming for dinner. Will you stay?"

"I didn't know they were coming," he replied.

"It's Saturday, and this isn't about business," I joked. "They're just coming to see me. We have a lot of time to make up for, since we haven't seen that much of each other."

"I thought that was just during your childhood."

I shook my head slowly. "They've pretty much always been away except for the last year. Even now, they go away frequently. But at least I see more of them. My brothers are all gifted. Their boarding school was designed for gifted children, and all three of them were graduated from college by the age of twenty. After that, they went into the military, Special Forces. I know none of them wanted to get out of the service. But they pretty much had to do it. After my father died, my brothers left Montgomery Mining in the hands of an unethical, crooked CEO who slowly degraded the company. They nearly lost Montgomery Mining because of it. Now, they're all back, and the company is thriving again."

"I didn't know it was ever in trouble."

"They had a lot of problems to wade through, issues that had escalated over nine years or so. I doubt they'll ever turn the company over to anyone again."

"I'll definitely stay for dinner. I'd like to see them in a relaxed mode. They're all smartasses, but I like them. They're definitely intelligent, and great with business. And Riley, it's not just *them* who are ultrasmart. *All of you* are gifted. You're the smartest woman I know. I wish I had gone to college, but it wasn't in the cards."

I put my hand over his, and he threaded our fingers together. "It doesn't matter, Seth. You're just as smart as I am, but you've learned in a different way. I had opportunity. You didn't. That doesn't mean you aren't brilliant."

Never did I want to see Seth feeling like he was "less than" because he hadn't been given the chance to go to college.

"I'm learning a lot from Eli and Hudson," he admitted.

"You soak information up like a sponge," I told him. "It isn't about the time you've spent in school. It's drive and experience that are really important."

"I get that," he answered. "I wouldn't trade the decisions I've had to make in my life. I might have a few regrets here and there, but I wouldn't do things any differently."

Of course he wouldn't. Seth was a guy who would protect family at any cost.

I was just leaning in to kiss him when my phone rang.

I glanced at my cell on the coffee table. "My mother," I said, my heart sinking.

"Answer it," Seth said. "Don't let her affect your life in any way, Riley. She's sucked enough of your happiness. Don't give her any more of it."

His words hit me hard, but not in a bad way. I'd just never thought about my mother's actions like that.

He was right.

I had a choice.

I didn't need to be a frightened child anymore.

Maybe she'd taken my past away, but there was no way I was giving her my present or my future. Not now that I was happier than I'd ever been.

"Hello, Mother," I said firmly as I answered her call.

"Margaret! Where have you been? I've been calling you for days."

"Busy," I replied.

"Too busy for your own mother?" she asked in a bitter tone. "I needed to talk to you about Nolan. I think he may be willing to take you back."

I shuddered at the thought.

I took a deep breath. "Why would you think, even for one single moment, that I'd want to spend my life with a child molester, Mother? I would think you'd want me far away from all that. *And* him."

We'd never really talked about what Nolan had done to Penny, but it was *beyond time*.

My mother made a tutting sound. "Penelope was a little young, but Nolan is still a good catch. He's rich, and his family is extremely prominent. They have been for generations."

I felt nausea rising in my throat. "Penny was fifteen. Not a *little young*. She was still *a child*."

"Grow up, Margaret. Sometimes a woman needs to overlook these things to gain power. That's the way it is in our world."

I swallowed hard. Even though I didn't want to face this particular fear, I knew I had to ask the question. "Like you had to overlook what Father was doing to me when I was a child?"

There was a long silence, and in that moment of complete quiet, I knew that *she'd known*. She'd *always* known. She just hadn't stopped it, because she loved her reputation and money more than she'd ever loved me.

Seth squeezed my hand, and I appreciated the support, but this was something I had to do myself.

She finally sniffed. "It wasn't for very long. And there was no way I could control *anything* your father did. More than likely, he would have just cast both of us aside if I'd said anything. You survived, Margaret. He didn't *beat* you. There was no lasting damage."

He didn't beat me? Did she really think being molested was so much better than being hit? I would have much preferred that he had beaten me up. Instead, my father had left invisible open wounds that had never healed.

Fury built inside me. "It wasn't for very long? It lasted FOR YEARS! And even after it was over, I had to live with the shame of what had happened."

"You're being dramatic, Margaret."

I lost it. "You are not *a mother*. You're a *monster*. All these years, I've given you the benefit of the

273

doubt. I'd hoped you never knew the truth, but *you did*. How could you just let that happen?"

"That's not important," she answered in a brittle tone. "Nolan—"

"I don't give a flying fuck about Nolan," I told her angrily, my voice getting even louder. "He's a sick, twisted individual who I can't even be in the same city with, much less in the same room."

I was seething with the most ferocious rage I'd ever experienced, and I couldn't seem to put a lid on it. I wouldn't. Not anymore.

"Margaret, it would make me happy if—"

"*Nothing* will *ever* make you happy. Ever. I twisted myself inside out for years to make you happy with me, even just a little bit. No child should ever have to do that. Love for a child should be unconditional."

"Margaret," she started in an admonishing tone.

I stopped her. "My name is *Riley*. Riley Montgomery. I have no desire to be Margaret. She was the child who was sexually assaulted by her father. She was the child who could never get her mother's approval. She was the child who never fit into *your* world. There is no Margaret anymore. That child no longer exists."

"You could fit in if you really wanted to—"

"I don't *want* to fit in anymore. I know exactly where I belong. I also know exactly who I am, and I like that woman. I like her a lot. But I don't like . . . you."

For once, my mother didn't say anything.

I continued, "Don't call me again. Don't even try to communicate. I'll never be the daughter you want, and I don't care. Why should I ever give a moment of thought to a mother who was *never* a parent? Who *never* protected me? This is the end of the road for us."

Finally! I felt every word I'd just said. I meant them.

"Good-bye, *Mother,*" I said drily before I hung up.

Seth pulled me to him right after I dropped the phone on the coffee table. "Are you okay?" he asked, concerned.

"Actually, I think I'm better than just okay," I told him. "She knew, Seth. She . . . *knew*. And never once did she try to stop it."

"I'm so sorry, Riley," he crooned as he pulled me into his lap. "I know that was a tough call."

I put my arms around his neck. "It actually wasn't. I feel . . . free."

I wasn't sad about saying good-bye to my mother. Maybe because she'd never given a damn about me.

The hurt might come later, but I could deal with it. What I couldn't handle was spending one more moment of my life letting her control me in any way. I couldn't continue to twist myself inside out for the rest of my life looking for parental approval that would never come. After intensive counseling, and seeing the Sinclair siblings together, I finally understood what a family *should* be.

"Do you mean that?" Seth asked as his eyes drilled into my face.

I nodded. "I do. I really do. I love the woman I am now. And I do know exactly where I belong."

"And where might that be?" he asked gently.

I dropped a gentle kiss on his lips before I murmured, "With you. Always with you."

"Damn straight," he rumbled in agreement, right before he kissed me.

CHAPTER 27
Riley

"My period is late," I said bluntly to my nurse-practitioner, Layla, as I sat half-naked on her exam table.

I'd only taken four of my placebo pills so far, but I was never late. *At all. Ever.*

Panicked, I'd called Layla, and I'd been lucky enough to get an appointment time the same day due to a cancellation.

"You're only four days overdue," Layla said gently as she sat down on a stool several feet away.

"I'm never late," I said grimly. "The pill has always made me as regular as clockwork."

"You have reason to be concerned," the pretty blonde answered, giving me her complete attention. "But don't get yourself upset yet. There are any number of things that could be the problem."

I liked Layla. I always had. It wasn't that I *didn't* like Dr. Fortney, her colleague, but I'd never been comfortable with having a strange man doing pelvic exams.

Layla was more like a casual friend than a medical professional to me.

"Like what?" I asked.

"You're on a hormonal pill, Riley. Just because you haven't missed a period yet doesn't mean you can't. In fact, it happens fairly often."

I had my first glimpse of hope. What if Layla was right? What if I was just skipping a period?

"Hey," she said comfortingly. "Would it be that bad if you were pregnant?"

I nodded. "Catastrophic," I mumbled. "I come from a pretty dysfunctional background, Layla. I don't want to screw up a kid of my own."

She nodded like she understood my fears. "What about your significant other?"

"He doesn't want children. He spent his entire adulthood raising and educating younger siblings. He's gotten to the point where he's free to do what he wants," I explained. "I can't do this to him. I can't tie him down with another child to raise."

"No offense," Layla said drily. "But it takes two to make a baby. An egg doesn't get fertilized all by itself."

"I know. But I'm on birth control. This wasn't even on *his* radar or *mine*."

"Granted, getting pregnant while you're taking birth control properly is rare, but it happens, Riley."

I rolled my eyes. "So I'd be in that less than one percent of women who gets pregnant on the pill?"

"It's possible."

"Great."

"Is your fear of screwing up your child's life the only reason why you don't want to have kids?" Layla pushed softly.

I thought about her question for a minute, wishing she wasn't so into women's issues. I wasn't sure I wanted to think about my desire to avoid children right now.

"I'm not sure," I confessed. "I've never gotten past that one very compelling reason."

"You don't have to answer this question if you don't want to, but you said you come from a dysfunctional background. Were you sexually assaulted?"

I nodded. I was done feeling ashamed of what happened to me when I was younger. "My father."

"You know that wasn't your fault, right? And it doesn't mean you won't be a good mother to any child you have."

"Rationally, I know it. But psychologically, I'm still getting over my issues. He was *my father*."

"He broke your trust, Riley. You were a kid, right?"

I nodded. "In grade school. My brothers were all sent off to boarding school, but my father kept me at home."

"Did you ever consider that it was probably

his plan to keep you at home? He tore you away from anybody who might have protected you."

I'd never really thought about it, but . . . "You might be right."

Maybe I'd always convinced myself that I hadn't been sent away because I was a female, but Layla's rationale made perfect sense.

I guess I'd never wanted to even contemplate the possibility that my abuse had been carefully planned.

"Did your mother know?" Layla questioned.

I nodded my head slowly. "I found out recently that she knew about everything. She just never stopped it."

"Are you going to counseling, Riley?"

"I am. It's helped a lot. I've come a long way in the last few years. But I have occasional moments when I'm still that scared, confused little girl."

Terrified.

Uncertain.

Still looking for approval from my mother.

Thank God I'm not even remotely looking for my parent's love anymore.

Layla smiled at me. "I think it's normal to feel that way sometimes."

"I wish it would go away. I don't think it's ever good for a relationship."

"Does your boyfriend understand?"

I nodded. "He's amazing. Supportive. That's why I hope I'm not pregnant. He doesn't deserve to be a father when he doesn't want to be."

Even though I knew Seth didn't have a single regret about busting his ass to raise his younger siblings, I didn't want to saddle him with a responsibility that he didn't care to take on.

"What about you?" she prodded.

"Like I said, I don't want children."

At one time, I'd known I'd probably *have to be* a mother when I'd been engaged to Nolan. There had been no doubt in my mind that he'd want a male child to inherit his business.

I can't say that I'd ever been okay with that, but I'd managed to block the thought completely from my mind.

Now, I could make my own decisions.

And I'd chosen not to have kids.

Or at least, I had *thought* I never would have a child of my own.

Until . . . today.

"If you're pregnant, there are alternatives, Riley," Layla said.

I put my hand to my flat abdomen reflexively.

If there *was* a baby, I couldn't stand the thought of terminating a pregnancy, or giving Seth's child away. "No," I murmured. "I'll figure it out if it happens."

If I was pregnant, the child had been created from love, at least on my part.

It would rip my heart out to do anything other than love and nurture any baby who had been created because I loved Seth Sinclair body and soul.

"Whatever happens, I'll be here to help you, Riley. Shall we get on with it?"

I looked at the pretty blonde gratefully. Layla had always gone above and beyond for her patients.

Honestly, I'd never had a reason to spill my guts to her like I was doing now. But I was pretty damn glad she was my health-care professional.

I couldn't imagine having this conversation with the elderly, male Dr. Fortney.

"What do we need to do?" I asked, trying to build up my mental strength for whatever might be coming.

I appreciated the fact that Layla was trying to prepare me just in case I *was* pregnant.

Really, I'd been so stressed that I hadn't thought about what would happen if I was going to have a child.

The reality was . . . I'd never be able to part with a child who belonged to Seth and me. *At all. Ever.*

If necessary, I'd raise the baby on my own. It wasn't like I didn't have the resources to take care of him or her.

"First, I'd really like to do a blood test. It's a little more sensitive in picking up HCG if you're pregnant. It's the best test, since this would be extremely early. And you'd know the truth without a doubt."

"Let's do it," I agreed, steeling myself for whatever the truth might be.

Good or bad, I'd handle it.

I didn't mind having blood taken.

But the wait was excruciating.

By the time I finally left the doctor's office, I was utterly devastated.

CHAPTER 28
Seth

"I haven't heard from Riley for four damn days," I told Aiden and Skye as I sat in the living room of their home. "She sent me a two-line email four days ago and said she needed some time alone. After that, I've called, I've emailed, I've texted. *Nothing*."

"If that's what she wants, she deserves to have that time, Seth," Aiden said. "Maybe she's just busy."

"Busy, my ass. Something's wrong," I grumbled. "We're together every damn day. Neither one of us was ever too busy to find time."

"Maybe that's the problem," Skye contemplated from her seat next to Aiden. "She could be overwhelmed, Seth. She shared her history with me last week when we met for coffee. She might need space."

My head turned to Skye sharply. "She actually told you?"

She nodded. "Yes. I've always told her I'd be there if she wanted to talk. She finally did. Honestly, it sounded like she was doing well with coming to terms with her past. So I'm a little surprised that she's suddenly backed off."

"What happened?" Aiden said, looking baffled.

"Never mind," Skye said to her husband.

"It's personal," I told him. "She had a rough childhood. That's about all you need to know."

I wasn't about to explain everything that had happened to Riley.

"She cares about you, Seth. She'll come around in her own time," Skye said softly.

"I'm willing to wait," I explained. "But I can't shake the feeling that there's something wrong, something more than her just needing time in general."

How could I explain that I *felt* Riley in that way? I couldn't.

So I didn't want to even try.

There was something off about her initial email. I'd known it since I'd read the short missive.

Riley had changed. It wasn't like her to be elusive or vague. Not anymore.

It certainly wasn't her style to back away from things she needed to confront, either.

She knew she didn't need *time*.

Not with me.

Hell, if she was mad at me for some reason, she'd have no problem telling me off to my face.

And if she *wasn't* angry, she'd talk to me about whatever was bugging her.

"I'm not sure how much longer I can wait," I confessed.

Aiden lifted a brow. "You been by her place?"

"Every. Damn. Night. I walk down the beach and check out her cottage every evening just to see if she's in there."

"And?" Aiden prompted.

I shrugged. "I see a shadow or two in the kitchen, so I know she's there."

"Look, bro," Aiden said calmly. "When I needed you to talk me down from a ledge when I was losing it over Skye, you were there. You told me to talk to her, not to judge without knowing everything. I'm giving you the same advice."

"You did that?" Skye looked at me, obviously shocked.

"He did," Aiden answered for me. "He encouraged me to go after what I wanted, and not to jump to conclusions."

"It was good advice you gave him, Seth," Skye said gently. "Can you just be patient? Riley's face lights up every time she talks about you. I know she has feelings for you."

"I wanted to ask her to marry me. I've had the ring in my pocket for a while now," I said gruffly.

"So she's the one?" Aiden asked.

"She is," I answered stiffly. "Maybe you think I'm crazy—"

"I don't," Aiden answered. "I think Sinclairs in this generation only love once, and they love hard. Maybe I would have blown off that theory if we didn't have an army of Sinclair siblings and cousins. But once we fall, it's game over."

"I was thinking the same thing," I confessed. "You were waiting for Skye for years. I didn't realize it, but I think you were."

"Subconsciously, I was," Aiden replied. "There was never another woman like her, so I pretty much gave up looking for one."

I watched as Skye reached for Aiden's hand automatically with a huge smile on her face.

"I knew I was screwed from the time Riley sat down across a table from me in the Coffee Shack. It just took a while to realize how screwed I really was."

There was silence for a moment until Aiden broke it. "So why didn't you ask her to marry you?"

"After I'd decided to do it, she broke ties with her mother. It was a huge step for her, and I didn't want to jump right in and ask her after that happened. I decided to wait. If she hadn't started to ditch me, I probably would have done it by now."

"You're in love with her," Aiden stated.

"Completely," I said miserably.

"Do you think she needs time because of what happened with her mother?" Skye queried.

"No. I think she might be a little sad about the mother who never existed for her, but I doubt she's mourning the mother she had. Honestly, I'm pretty sure it was a long time coming. Her brothers came over later that night, and she told them everything, including the fact that she needed to sever ties with their mother."

"What did they say?" Skye questioned.

"They were justifiably furious. They barely speak to their mother themselves, so I don't think it was a big deal for them never to talk to her again. They probably told her off first. Riley's brothers might be filthy rich, but they've never operated in that circle of rich snobs unless they absolutely have to." It was something I admired about the Montgomery brothers, actually.

"So they'll probably never speak to her again, either," Skye surmised.

"Never," I verified. "I think they'll end up blaming themselves that they weren't there to protect Riley, though it wasn't their fault. But they really deserved to know the truth."

"I'm not even going to pretend that I understand what you two are talking about," Aiden said, sounding disgruntled. "I'm assuming they didn't know about whatever happened to her during her childhood."

"No," I stated simply.

"I'm glad she told them," Skye told me. "It's too hard to keep family secrets like that."

"I think she's over not talking about it. Or feeling like it was somehow her fault."

Skye nodded. "I think so, too."

"Since I have no idea what did happen to her,

let's get back to the problem at hand," Aiden suggested.

"I think he should give her a little more time," Skye suggested. "She's had a lot of family stuff happen. Emotional things."

"I'll give her one more day. And it's probably going to kill me. But if she isn't communicating by tomorrow, I'm going to get her to talk to me somehow. We were perfectly happy, and then she bolts with no warning? It doesn't make sense. There's something she's not telling me." I raked a hand through my hair in frustration.

Skye rolled her eyes. "Why are all of you Sinclair men so stubborn?"

I answered morosely, "Because we only have one damn chance to be happy. We *have* to be persistent."

"I agree," Aiden rumbled. "But take it easy, Seth. The last thing you want to do is scare her away. I know how you are when you're hotheaded and determined."

"I'm not that bad," I denied.

Aiden gave me a knowing look. "The hell you aren't. Do you remember that time—"

"Don't go there," I warned.

My younger brother would probably go through every bit of my history if I'd let him, to prove his point.

"I was just going to offer up examples to jog your memory," Aiden said nonchalantly.

"None needed," I said through gritted teeth. "I better get going. It's late."

I knew they both had to be up in the morning. Their daughter, Maya, went to school pretty early.

"Stay if you need to talk," Aiden said adamantly, his tone sincere.

"Yes, do," Skye encouraged. "I'll go to bed so I can get Maya up early, and you two can talk."

I stood. "I'm good," I assured them both. "I think I'll take a run or a swim."

I needed some kind of physical exercise to wear my ass out, or it would be another night that I'd spend staring at the ceiling, wondering what in the hell was up with Riley.

I'd leave it for tonight, but no promises about what would happen tomorrow.

Sure, I wanted to respect Riley's request, but I couldn't stop the gnawing concern that she needed me. Whether she wanted to reach out or not.

Aiden and Skye got to their feet. "You sure?" Aiden asked quietly.

"Yeah. I'm hardly going to beat her door down this time of night."

Not saying I didn't want to do that, but I wouldn't.

It would probably scare the shit out of her.

"Call if you need me," Aiden demanded.

"Absolutely," I agreed.

Absolutely not!

By tomorrow, I'd be chomping at the bit to see Riley. It got worse every day. The last thing I wanted to hear was that I needed to keep waiting.

I noticed the concerned look on Aiden's face.

Hell, I was grateful that all of my family was there when I needed them. Problem was . . . a voice of reason just wasn't working for me right now.

Probably because I was far from thinking logically.

Skye hugged me tight, and Aiden slapped me on the back when she was done.

My nighttime run was extremely long, but even though I was exhausted, sleep still eluded me that night.

CHAPTER 29
Riley

Bang! Bang! Bang!

I flinched at the pounding coming from my front door.

It was so loud that I could hear it from the kitchen.

"I know you're in there, Riley." Seth's agitated, booming voice rang out just as loud as his insistent hammering did. "Open the damn door. You've been avoiding me for five days now. Something is wrong. I can feel it." Seth's voice was loud and angry.

I chewed on my bottom lip nervously as I weighed my options.

Answer the door?

Or ignore it?

I actually *had* been ducking Seth for the last five days, trying to put distance between the two of us. The only communication I'd made with him was a very short email asking him to back off for a while.

I couldn't think when he was around, so I'd stayed home.

No more cozy dinners together.

No overnight stays.

I didn't answer his emails.

Or his texts.

And I *certainly* didn't answer the phone.

If I'm going to make a clean break, I have to rip off the Band-Aid and get it over with.

Seth deserved to hear what I had to say *in person.*

Truth was, I'd avoided him because I hadn't been able to tell him the truth.

Unfortunately, that meant I'd spent days moping around in a state of depression and missing him so badly that it was killing me.

I'd gotten very little work done in the last several days, which wasn't like me at all. I could work through almost any emotional state. God knew I'd done it many times.

That was before Seth.

Before I'd lost the ability to compartmentalize my emotions.

I turned off the dinner I'd been cooking on the stove and went to the door.

When I opened it, my heart sank to my feet.

Seth looked like he'd been to hell and back.

I could see the agitation and frustration so clearly on his weary face.

He was dressed in a pair of jeans and an old T-shirt, his hair sticking up on the top of his head like he'd raked his hands through it more than once.

Still, he looked so damn good to me that I

wanted to throw myself into his arms so I could feel the heat and hardness of his incredible body.

I fought the compulsion with everything I had.

He strode through the door as he said, "What the fuck is wrong, Riley? You don't answer your phone, emails, or texts. I was worried that something bad had happened to you."

I closed the door. "I'm fine. I've just been . . . busy."

Yep. I'd been totally occupied with getting through my depression about missing Seth like a piece of my heart had been clawed out of my chest.

Every day had gotten more difficult than the last.

He took me by the shoulders, none too gently. "Just tell me what I did. I don't buy the bullshit that you've been *too busy*. We've never been too busy to see each other every damn day."

I shrugged out of his hold. "Okay. Then I'll tell you the truth. I don't think we should see each other anymore, Seth. It's just not working for me."

"Why?" he asked. "What in the hell brought all this on?"

I shrugged as I walked into the living room. "I've just been thinking about it. I care a lot about you, but I don't think we were meant to be together. We want . . . different things."

"Since when?"

I plopped down on a chair because my legs didn't feel like they would hold me anymore.

I felt like my entire life was ending.

And maybe it was, in many ways.

Seth had opened a whole gamut of emotions I'd never experienced before, and there was no way I'd ever be able to compartmentalize or bury them ever again.

I was completely, utterly, no-doubt-in-my-mind in love with Seth Sinclair. I wanted his happiness more than I cared about my own.

"I feel like we should both be headed in a new direction," I said weakly.

He sat down on the couch, his elbows on his legs, and simply stared at me for so long that I started to get uncomfortable.

Shit! I wish that I didn't feel like he could see right through me.

Finally, he said somberly, "I don't want to head in any direction except *toward you,* Riley."

My heart squeezed until I thought it would explode. I got to my feet and started to pace the small living room. "Why are you making this so damn hard?" I asked desperately. "We need to *break up,* but I'm having one hell of a hard time *doing it*. This isn't going to work, Seth. Not over the long run. We'd end up miserable."

I'd never had a man who wanted to be stuck to me like glue.

Somebody who would always be there when I needed him.

A guy who I could tell anything to, and he'd just be there to support me without any kind of judgment.

It was pure torture to just throw that all away.

"What happened? Tell me," he said persuasively. "I'm not leaving until I get the real story, Riley."

I continued to pace. "You make me crazy, do you know that? You came barging into my life, all hot and gorgeous, and then proceeded to turn that life upside down. I've never once heard you say a single thing that I'd consider a criticism. You're pretty much perfect. Well, maybe except for the fact that you're the most stubborn guy I've ever known, but even *that's* usually an asset for you, since it helped you get your siblings raised." I took a deep breath. "Some woman should have snapped you up a long time ago and been damn grateful she had you in her life, rich or poor. I really don't understand why that hasn't happened."

"Maybe because I've been waiting for you?" he suggested.

I stopped and glared at him. "See! You see that? Even when we're both pissed off, you *still* say something nice. Y-you're almost flawless, Seth. And I have a ton of faults. Lots of them. A ton."

I felt my body running out of steam, but I was still walking back and forth like a woman possessed, releasing emotions that I hadn't even realized were gnawing at my soul.

All of the things coming out of my mouth had never been planned, none of them the reason I'd been avoiding Seth. Or so I thought.

At first, I'd thought that distancing myself from Seth was for *his benefit,* and maybe it partially was.

Now, I realized it was my way of running away from something that was going to demolish me in the future if it didn't work out.

All of my other excuses aside, it was *me* who didn't feel like I was *good enough* for him.

I wasn't protecting *him,* I was guarding *myself* after my visit to the clinic.

"I'm still waiting for you to tell me exactly what happened, Riley," he said in a husky but patient voice.

"You even know when something is eating at me," I mumbled unhappily.

"You know when something is bugging me, too," he answered. "We're connected like that, sweetheart."

He was right. *We were.* And it scared the shit out of me.

The way I loved him, the intensity of those emotions that I'd never felt before, was terrifying.

"Well, we need to get *unconnected,*" I told him.

"Not going to happen," he said doggedly. "Now explain."

I stopped, folded my arms across my chest, and stared at him. "Can't it just be a case of me figuring out that we're all wrong for each other?"

He shook his head. "No. You're running. But I'm not letting you go very far."

Seth reached out, snaked his arm around my waist, and tugged.

My ass landed beside him on the couch ungracefully.

"Talk," he demanded.

"Okay. Fine. You want to know what happened? I'll tell you. I-I missed a period. So I went to the doctor. The chances of me being pregnant were pretty damn slim since I'm on the pill, but I had to know the truth. Neither one of us wanted children. I knew it was going to be a disaster for both of us."

Seth tightened his arm around my waist, buried his other hand in my hair, and forced my head up. "Look at me, Riley," he demanded. "Fucking look at me."

Our eyes met, and I got lost in the fierceness of his gaze.

I saw a thousand different emotions in those expressive, ashen eyes of his, and I had no idea which one was the strongest.

"Are. You. Pregnant?" he rasped. "Goddammit! Tell me the truth. Do you really think I'd let you walk away from me if you are? That I'd just ignore the fact that you are having my child?"

Deep inside, I knew he wouldn't. Seth would be the polar opposite of a deadbeat father. Like it or not, he'd be a good father.

"Riley," he growled, his eyes drilling into mine.

My heart was galloping in my chest, and my body shuddered. "I'm not, Seth. I'm not pregnant."

"Then why are you so upset?" he asked gruffly.

"Because when I heard that I *wasn't* pregnant, I was actually *disappointed.* I should have been *relieved,* but I wasn't. Somewhere between my panic and the final results, I warmed up to the idea of having a child. *Our* child. I don't know what in the hell happened, but I nearly mourned a baby who was never there. It's crazy. You don't want kids, and neither did I. But something . . . changed. Now I'm afraid that if we stay together, and I get pregnant in the future, I'll be happy, and you won't. It would tear us apart, Seth." I felt tears rolling down my cheeks, and I didn't even try to stop them.

When I'd realized how badly I wanted his child, it had killed me to know that he *wouldn't* have wanted it. Yes, he would have stepped up as a father. But it certainly wouldn't have been something that he'd initially wanted.

He wrapped both arms around me and pulled to bring my body flush with his. "So you're upset because you might want to have my child someday?"

I nodded. "I'm sorry. I didn't think I'd ever feel that way."

"Jesus, baby. Don't be sorry. I'd love nothing more than to see a beautiful, redheaded child with your eyes looking back at me."

My head jerked up. "You said you didn't *want* to have kids. You've raised your siblings. I thought you didn't want to be a dad. *At all. Ever.*"

I searched his face, but I didn't see a moment of hesitation or doubt in his expression.

He was deadly serious as he said, "I never said that I *didn't want* kids someday. All I said was that I was completely okay with *your* decision not to have any. And I *was* okay with that. Just like I'd be fine if you changed your mind. You're my priority, sweetheart. With or without kids in our future, I want *you*."

I let out a sob and slammed him in the chest with my fist. "God, I hate it when you say something like that."

Okay, I loved it, *and* I hated it.

"Why?" he asked, sounding genuinely confused.

"Because you're so willing to accept me either way," I wailed.

He pushed my head into his chest as I cried. "I know your history, Riley. And whether or not I have kids isn't really all that important to me. Although having my baby in your belly definitely isn't an unpleasant thought. I'd love to have children, but I'm good if you *don't* want that, too. Why would I make a big deal over something that isn't all that important to me as long as I have you?"

What in the hell could I answer to *that* statement? Maybe if I hadn't freaked out, I probably would have accepted him either way, too, if his decision was that important to him. Granted, I'd warmed up to having children, and I realized that I really *did* want to have Seth's child, but I would have respected that he didn't. He was my priority, too.

I sniffled and raised my head. "I have to tell you something."

"Shoot," he encouraged.

"I'm in love with you, Seth. Crazy, head over heels in love. I'm not saying that to pressure you. I just want you to know that I want you to be happy, too." I didn't look away from him, even though I wanted to.

I faced my emotions head-on with as much honesty as possible. I realized that before the pregnancy scare happened, I'd been waiting for him to say it *first*. It was less risky. But since he'd never been the one to falter, I owed him the truth.

No bullshit.
No running.
No hiding.

Relief flooded his face, and he grinned. "Damn glad to hear that, gorgeous. Because I'm beyond hope myself. I think I've been in love with you since the first time you sat across from me at the Coffee Shack and chased that woman away."

I hugged him hard. "I said it first," I teased, my heart soaring now that he'd said it, too.

"Yes, you did," he agreed. "But you'll hear it plenty for the rest of our lives. I love you, Riley Montgomery. There's never been anyone else for me except you. Promise me you'll never run away again. We'll face shit together. Whatever happens."

"I promise," I said readily as I put a hand behind his head and pulled him down so I could kiss him.

The minute his lips touched mine, I knew that hiding was a thing of the past for me.

I had absolutely no intentions of going anywhere. *At all. Ever.*

CHAPTER 30
Riley

I laughed as my ass hit the bed Seth had just tossed me on.

"It's been five very long, very hard days for me, woman," he growled as he pulled the T-shirt he was wearing over his head.

I watched shamelessly as he revealed those six-pack abs and massive chest that made me salivate.

God, he's beautiful.

A sigh escaped from my lips as I scrambled to sit on the side of the bed. I grabbed his belt and yanked him forward so I could grope his cock through the denim of his jeans. "How hard was it?" I asked in a sultry voice, running my hand over his crotch greedily.

"I think you can feel that for yourself," he rasped.

"I'm going to," I informed him as I unbuckled his belt and then freed his cock.

I went to my knees in front of him as I pulled his jeans and boxer briefs down his muscular legs.

He kicked them off while my hands went everywhere.

I was hungry to touch every inch of his ripped body. I settled for running my palms up his thighs, and then traced the delineated muscles of his abdomen. "You're so damn gorgeous, Seth," I told him breathlessly as my fingers followed the happy trail of hair that ran tantalizingly down to his groin.

I'd never tried to taste him before. I'd never done the intimate act on any man. But I desperately wanted to do it now.

My desire took control, and I wrapped my fingers around his cock.

"Riley, no," Seth croaked as he reached for my wrist. "Not that."

"Don't," I said as I batted his hand away. "Unless you really don't want it."

"There isn't a red-blooded guy in the world who wouldn't want it," he rasped. "But I know damn well this is something you don't want to do. And I don't need it."

I stopped for a moment, realizing that when I'd told him I didn't do oral sex, he'd assumed I'd never want to do it.

He doesn't realize that everything is different with him.

"I do want to. Help me," I pleaded. "I've never done this before, but I need to."

I looked up, and Seth's intense gaze focused on my face with so much love in his eyes that my heart skipped a beat.

"You're doing just fine," he said between gritted teeth.

I broke eye contact and focused on what I was doing, leaning forward to taste the tiny drop of moisture at the very tip of his cock.

He tasted slightly salty, masculine, and so good that I opened my mouth to take as much of his cock as I could between my lips.

"Riley," he groaned, the sound low and animalistic.

I wanted to hear those sounds of pleasure coming from his gorgeous lips more than I wanted to breathe.

Putting my hand on the root, I licked up and down the silken surface of his cock, loving the feel and the taste of Seth.

Taking him into my mouth, I faltered a little because of my inexperience.

It was awkward at first, but became more natural as Seth buried a hand in my hair and guided me up and down his cock.

"Fuck, baby! You're killing me," he rasped, his voice scratchy with arousal.

His lustfulness just stoked mine, and I could feel warm heat flood between my thighs.

He demanded more.

And I gave him whatever he wanted, following his lead as he urged me to speed up the pace.

My pleasure felt merged with his as I moved faster and faster, relishing every sound that came spontaneously from his lips.

My free hand went to his perfect, muscular

ass, and I dug my nails into his skin as I tried to get a solid grip on him that would keep us from parting.

He let out a hiss, and I knew it wasn't because of the pain of my fingernails.

Seth loved it.

I lost myself in the frenzied rhythm of pleasuring Seth, no longer feeling awkward or inhibited at all.

"I can't take it, Riley. Move your mouth unless you want a mouthful. I'm going to come," he warned me harshly.

Move? Oh, hell no. I'd been waiting to taste him, and I wasn't backing off now.

My eyes flew up to watch him, and I was rewarded with the hottest thing I'd ever seen.

Seth threw his head back, the muscles in his throat straining, as he orgasmed.

"Riley. I fucking love you so much!" His voice was feral, uncontrolled, and so incredibly carnal that my core clenched as his scorching release flowed into my mouth and down my throat.

I relished that orgasm, and then licked his cock clean after it was over.

Seth yanked me to my feet and wrapped his arms around me, and we collapsed onto my bed together.

His chest was still heaving as he said, "You realize you just put me out of commission for a little while."

I pressed myself against his side. "Wasn't it worth it?"

"For me, hell yeah. For you, probably not so much. But I can think of other ways to make you come, sweetheart. A whole lot of them."

"It was good for me, too," I told him. "Sometimes, I just want to make you happy."

"Baby, I'm ecstatic right at the moment," he answered huskily.

I smirked as I disentangled myself from him to go to the bathroom.

When I came back, I smiled as my eyes saw his bulky form on the bed.

Seth was out cold, his breath even and relaxed.

His exhaustion tugged at my heart, because I instinctively knew that he'd probably had several sleepless nights.

I knew I'd hurt him by trying to run away, and it floored me that he was so quick to forgive me.

That he loved me so easily.

A tear trickled from my eye, but I swiped it away.

I wasn't going to question why Seth loved me, or how lucky I'd been to find him. All I really wanted to do was love him back with just as much strength.

I stripped off my clothes, turned off the light, and crawled into bed beside him, pressing my bare skin against his side.

"I love you," I whispered softly.

His arm came around my waist, and he pulled me harder against his powerful body with a grunt of contentment.

I closed my eyes with a smile on my face.

When I woke up, it was daylight, but all I could focus on was the warm breath on the back of my neck.

I squirmed a little when I realized it was Seth and we were spooned just as close as we could get.

At some point during the night, he'd pulled me into his body, and his arms were tightened around my waist. We were skin-to-skin everywhere, which made me move sensually, rubbing my back against him like a cat.

"I didn't mean to wake you up." His voice was sleepy and sexy next to my ear.

God, I wanted to wake up with this gorgeous man next to me every day.

I'd never feel alone again.

Seth invaded my personal space, but for the first time in my life, I didn't care. I *wanted* to share it with him.

"You didn't." We'd both conked out early, so I'd probably slept way more than eight hours.

I rolled over so I could see his face, and then reached a hand out to stroke his whiskered jaw. He had a wicked five-o'clock shadow.

It looked good on him.

It was even better when my eyes moved to

his, and I saw the adoration and love in his gaze.

Having a man look at me that way seemed like some kind of miracle.

And I almost threw it away.

"I'm sorry for what I did," I blurted out.

A smile curved up on his sexy lips. "I hope you're not talking about the way you blew my mind before I so rudely fell asleep. I do plan on making that up to you."

I made a face at him. "Not *that*. About running away. The way I love you is scary sometimes. And honestly, the way you love me is terrifying. This is all new to me, Seth. I guess I just . . . panicked. I'm not used to anyone . . . loving me. Not the way you do."

"Get used to it, gorgeous. I'm not going anywhere. And it was easy to forgive you since you cut me slack when I fucked up. We're both going to make mistakes. You're exactly where you belong right now, and I'll do whatever it takes to keep you here. I get that your life hasn't exactly been rainbows and sunshine, and I'm not going to guarantee we're never going to butt heads. We're both stubborn, but no matter what happens, my love is *not* conditional. *At all. Ever.*"

I smiled at him, amused because he was copying my common expression. "I'm not going anywhere, either. You're stuck with me. After realizing that I was protecting myself more than I was protecting you by creating some distance, I recognized that it was beyond time for me to stop running away from the best thing that had ever happened to me. *At all. Ever.*"

He smirked. "When I didn't see you for a few days, I figured you just needed space. When I didn't see you for four days, I started to worry, Riley. You should have just told me what happened. I'm always going to be there for you."

I saw the light of sincerity in his eyes. "I know. I'm sorry. What can I do to make you understand that I'm over questioning us? What can I do to make it up to you?"

He grinned. "Apology already accepted. But I woke up with a very large boner because I had a beautiful woman in my arms."

Somehow, Seth always seemed to know when things were getting just a little too heavy. I was amazed by how easily he just accepted the fact that I'd made a mistake. "So you'd like me to fix this very large erection you have?"

He rolled on his back and grinned at me. "Not just that. I want you to ride me, take what you want, whatever you need to get off. I left you high and dry last night."

I climbed on top of his ripped body, savoring the feel of his overheated, silken skin sliding along mine. "I didn't mind, Seth. I'm starting to understand that a relationship isn't all about fifty-fifty. Sometimes you'll give more, and sometimes I'll give more. I think there are . . . cycles. I know

I haven't quite gotten over what happened to me. But that's my old life. There will come a time when you need me to give everything to you, and I'll do it happily."

"Doing what you did last night was hard for you," he grumbled as he pulled my head down close to his. "You gave plenty, and it was pretty damn brave."

"It wasn't that difficult. I wanted to do it because it was *you*. Between us, I want to share every kind of intimacy that we can."

He put his hand behind my head and pulled it toward him until my mouth collided with his. I sighed against his silken lips, and then opened so he could do a more thorough job. I tangled my hand in his hair, relishing the sensual embrace.

The kiss was raw, carnal, but unhurried, which drove me completely insane.

It went on forever. Seth nibbled at my lip, and then my jaw. When I felt his warm breath wafting over my ear before he nipped at my earlobe, my body flooded with molten, incendiary heat.

I undulated my hips, my wet pussy sliding against his ripped, rock-hard abs.

The erotic torment went on until I finally moaned in his ear. "Seth. I need you."

He put his hands on my hips and guided me over him. "I need you, too, gorgeous."

I let out a gasp as I slid down on his cock. "Yes," I whispered in relief.

This man filled me so completely, loved me so amazingly.

"Take what you want, Riley," he grunted.

All I really wanted was to stay just like this, so connected to him that it filled up my body, my heart, my soul.

Eventually, I had to move, and Seth's strong grip on my hips guided me into a steady, mesmerizing rhythm.

Not slow.

Not fast.

Just . . . perfect.

I used my hands to push against his chest until I was sitting up, which pushed him deeper inside of me.

"You look so damn beautiful," Seth groaned. "Take everything you need, baby."

When I looked at his face, he was watching me, his eyes focused more on my face than the rest of me.

Watching me obviously aroused him even more than he already was, so as he guided my hips, I cupped my breasts and caressed my nipples.

Pleasure coursed through my body as I did exactly what he wanted.

I reached my climax as Seth sped up the pace until he was lifting his hips to meet every slapping thrust.

Pinching my hard nipples, I threw my head back, completely uninhibited as I closed my eyes.

"Fuck!" Seth cursed, and then put his fingers

underneath me so my clit rubbed against them with every downward stroke. "I'm about to rush to the finish line," he grunted.

It didn't really matter. I wanted him to come because I couldn't control the climax that was slamming over me with a vengeance.

"Seth," I screamed, letting go of everything, allowing myself to just enjoy the powerful release. "I-love-you-so-much!"

"I love you, too, Riley," he said in a desperate, frenzied tone that I adored.

Our skin continued to pound together until Seth hurtled into an orgasm with an animalistic sound that could have been heard out on the beach.

Spent, I collapsed on top of him, my breath sawing in and out of my lungs, my heart ready to pound right out of my chest.

We were both covered in a sheen of sweat, but I was pretty sure neither one of us cared.

He gave me a long, sweet kiss once we'd recovered, and stroked a gentle hand up and down the damp skin of my back.

"I need you, Riley. Don't ever fucking leave me again," he rasped fiercely as he buried his face in my hair.

"I won't," I murmured. "I promise."

Because I needed him just as much as he needed me.

I was stuck to Seth like a powerful magnet.

No way was I ever letting go. *At all. Ever.*

CHAPTER 31
Seth

"I *am not* going to Mexico," Noah said in a voice he'd always reserved for putting us in our place as kids.

Adamant.

Unbending.

It meant—absolutely not happening.

I'm not doing it.

Etc. Etc. Etc.

Only this time, I knew my big brother *wasn't* going to get his way.

We were well into the holidays, and Brooke and Liam were home. Even though it wasn't Christmas yet, we'd wanted to give Noah one of his Christmas gifts from all of us.

A two-week resort vacation in Cancún, Mexico.

We'd all gathered together at Aiden's place. We figured there was strength in numbers, but I knew *exactly* what was going to break Noah. The same thing that got me every damn time.

I looked around Aiden's living room, waiting for the guilt trip to start.

The room was packed with family, but I didn't mind being on the floor with Riley between my legs and leaning back against me.

Brooke turned a sad face to Noah. "You don't like our gift? We tried so hard to get you something you could use."

Aiden and I snickered quietly as Jade's eyes welled up with tears. "I'm sorry, Noah. We just wanted you to get away and relax."

I could see Noah squirm in his recliner as he said, "Don't be sorry. It isn't that I don't like it, exactly."

My eldest brother was such a liar. He hated it, all right. Noah would detest *anything* that got him out of his office for two weeks.

Problem was, he *couldn't* break Jade's and Brooke's hearts.

He was just as big a sucker about making them unhappy as Aiden and I were, but he'd probably never admit it. Not that he had to. It was pretty damn clear at the moment.

"But you said you wouldn't go," Brooke said in a tremulous voice.

"I feel so bad," Jade chimed in.

I glanced at Eli, and he was smirking. My brother-in-law knew damn well that his wife was crying crocodile tears. He was obviously amused by the performance.

Liam didn't look concerned about Brooke, either, so he was apparently in on the farce.

"I'm way too busy to get away," Noah said gruffly. "I can't take two weeks off."

"Yes, you can," Aiden argued. "You're a damn

315

billionaire, Noah. It doesn't matter if one of your projects gets behind. You don't contract with anyone. It's not like some company is waiting for your next big thing. Okay, maybe *they are* waiting for your next project because you've pushed out some brilliant stuff, but you aren't on a deadline."

"I have self-imposed deadlines that I set myself," he disagreed.

"Then maybe you should stop doing that," I told him. "You need a vacation. It will clear your mind."

"I don't want to clear my mind," he grumbled. "I'll lose ideas."

"But couldn't you just go *this time?*" Skye pleaded, getting into the drama.

Maybe Noah was particularly sensitive to his little sisters, but he cared about Skye, too. Judging by the uncomfortable look on Noah's face, his sister-in-law was going to get to him, too.

Obviously, he couldn't stand to see any woman in his family upset or sad.

It was his one weakness, and the family was playing it for all it was worth. It might be a shitty thing to do, but we were all desperate to get Noah away from his work.

Nobody could work as much as he did and stay sane.

We'd all been worried about him for a long time.

Now, no dirty tricks were off-limits if it would get Noah to relax and take a break.

Maybe if we truly believed that working like he did made him happy, we'd leave him alone. But he *wasn't* happy. Lines of stress were starting to show on his face, and he had lost some weight because he forgot to eat. I knew he worked out when he remembered. But this crazy work shit was starting to affect his health.

"Please, Noah," Brooke whimpered pathetically. "We really wanted to do this for you."

Jade sniffed. "We wanted you to have a vacation so badly."

"Come take a walk with me," I whispered into Riley's ear. "I think Brooke and Jade have all this under control."

There was so much family crammed into the living room that nobody even acknowledged our exit.

Riley smiled as we left, and I hauled her toward the beach. "Was all of that just a setup?" she said suspiciously. "Jade was *totally* not herself."

I grinned down at her as we walked. "A complete sham. The girls planned it themselves, and they're doing a pretty damn good job. I'd say Noah will relent within a couple of minutes. Crying females are his only weakness. We're desperate to get him to take a break. He needs it. He's lost some weight, and he's showing signs of stress."

She nodded. "I get that. I just wish he didn't have to be tricked."

"He won't go otherwise."

"It was a pretty good show," she mused. "Where are we going?"

It was a really nice day. Warm without a cloud in the sky. So I just walked the two of us down the beach.

"Somewhere that we can be alone," I said vaguely.

"We're alone at home all the time," she pointed out.

We were at *my home* nearly all the time now. So it felt pretty damn good to hear her talk like it was *ours*.

"I guess I just wanted to get outside," I answered noncommittally.

I threaded our fingers together as we walked, unwilling to admit that I was actually nervous.

What in the hell was I going to do if she said *no?*

Problem was, I couldn't wait anymore. I had to make Riley mine before I completely lost my shit.

I'd gone a couple of weeks beyond the day that she'd told me about her pregnancy scare. I'd wanted to cement our relationship, make her see that we could work out any problem together.

Now, I was pretty sure she realized that. I'd seen no hesitation from her regarding our relationship, or any desire to run away.

She was as solid as a rock.

She finally trusts me completely.

"Is everything okay?" she asked, her voice concerned.

"Okay?" I asked as we finally reached the old dock on the property that was going to become a wildlife sanctuary. "Baby, it's damn near perfect."

We strolled down the wooden structure, and she plopped down on her ass when we reached the very end. "I love it here," she said. "Can we just sit here for a while?"

I sat right in front of her. "That was the plan," I admitted.

I'd wanted to find a destination that she loved. I was pretty certain that this place, the location that would always be a sanctuary for the endangered least terns, was exactly where we belonged.

She took my hand. "You're quiet today. Anything you want to talk about?"

My fucking chest felt tight as I looked at her. I had her total attention because she was convinced that something wasn't right with me.

With her fiery hair being lifted gently by the wind, and her gorgeous hazel eyes fixated on me, it was hard to keep my head straight.

"Actually, yeah," I answered. "There's been something on my mind all damn day."

I fished into the pocket of my jeans with my free hand and pulled out the item that had been solidly in my pocket since I'd made the purchase.

I popped it open with no fanfare. "I've been trying to figure out how to ask you to marry me without being worried that you'd say *no*."

Her face looked stunned as she stared from me to the diamond ring inside the box.

The ring was only a few carats, but the diamond was flawless. I'd been tempted to get an enormous rock that nobody could miss, but that wouldn't have been Riley. I would have done it because I wanted everyone to know she was mine.

"Oh, my God. Seth," she said as she reached out to gingerly touch the diamond. "It's beautiful."

I didn't like the way she was just admiring the piece of jewelry like it wasn't hers. "For fuck's sake, say *yes,* Riley. You're killing me here," I said tightly.

She looked at me with tears in her eyes. "Did you, for even one moment, think that I'd say *no?* I told you that you were stuck with me. So, yes. *Yes. Yes. Yes.*"

Riley threw herself into my lap and wrapped her arms around my neck with so much enthusiasm that I nearly dropped her ring over the side of the dock.

I grabbed it and tossed the box aside. "Let me put it on."

When she put her hand out, it was visibly shaking. "You're nervous," I said unhappily as I pushed the ring onto her finger.

She shook her head hard. "Not nervous. Excited. Touched. Happy. Right now, I feel like the luckiest woman in the world."

I kissed the ring on her finger and then her gorgeous lips.

I lost track of how much time we stayed like that, entwined together, touching, kissing. I didn't give a shit. I was determined to celebrate the fact that Riley, the only woman I'd ever loved, was finally fucking *mine*.

She was willing to take me on *for life*. I was sure that I was a hell of a lot more ecstatic than she was at the moment.

"I was hoping you'd ask me," she murmured into my ear. "I guess I just didn't expect it so soon."

"Baby, I've had this ring in my pocket for weeks."

"Why didn't you say something?"

"I wanted to make sure it was the right time. I didn't want to push. You needed to trust me before you could agree to marry me," I said huskily.

"I did. I do." Her voice was hushed and serious. "Any of those trust issues I had were about me, not about you, Seth."

"All gone now?" I asked hoarsely.

She nodded. "Since the day I realized that I was hurting you."

I was over that. Had been since she'd explained

why she was running away. "Don't make me wait long for the ceremony."

"I'm ready whenever you are," she answered as she beamed at me, her entire face lit up with excitement and happiness.

"Today?" I said hopefully.

She laughed, a sound I knew I'd never get tired of hearing.

"I love you," she said breathlessly. "We'll do it as soon as humanly possible. I'd like a small, private ceremony."

"I love you, too, baby. Whatever you want," I agreed happily as I tightened my arms around her deliciously curvy body.

I didn't give a damn how she wanted to seal the deal. I just wanted to make sure she was mine.

"January?" I asked.

"Seth, that's next month. We can't possibly get things together that fast, and it's the holidays. March or April?"

"February," I insisted.

Riley dropped a kiss on my forehead. "We'll see. I'll talk to Skye and Jade to see if they can help. But it might not be possible."

I grinned at her, but I didn't say anything else.

It would be February. No matter what my siblings said, I'd *make it happen*.

Maybe this was one of those times when being stubborn was actually a very good asset.

EPILOGUE
Riley

A few months later . . .

I was a February bride.

Once Seth had decided when the ceremony was going to happen, his family had all fallen in line to help him.

My wedding was small, but incredibly romantic and beautiful.

Hudson had offered to walk me down the aisle, but I'd decided to take that joyful stroll alone.

I'd known exactly what I was doing, and I didn't have an ounce of hesitation.

It hadn't been necessary for anyone to give me away since my heart *already* belonged to Seth.

I looked down at my left hand, smiling as I saw the thin band that Seth had placed on my hand just an hour or so ago. He'd pushed it right next to my beautiful engagement ring.

I lifted my head to look around the ballroom that we'd rented from the Citrus Beach Country Club.

The ceremony had been small, but Seth had insisted on inviting *a lot more* people to the reception.

The Sinclairs had grown up here in Citrus

Beach, and there were plenty of people he'd wanted to include in the festivities.

The large room was steadily filling up, and I smiled when Jade, Brooke, and Skye pushed their way through the people entering the venue to stand beside me.

"Oh, my God. You look so beautiful, Riley," Jade said, like she hadn't seen me earlier, before the ceremony.

The three women, my bridesmaids, looked pretty amazing themselves.

I'd settled on a chiffon, A-line, scoop-neck wedding gown with a minimal amount of beading so the dress wasn't incredibly fussy.

Jade, Brooke, and Skye looked gorgeous in their slate-blue gowns that we'd chosen. They were formal without too much fluff.

Because I was a woman who loved color, I'd carried a large bouquet with a huge assortment of flowers.

"Thank you all," I said sincerely as I hugged each one of them. "There's no way I could have pulled this together without you."

"I kind of think Seth would have single-handedly arranged it if we hadn't," Jade said teasingly.

I smiled at her. "You might be right." My new husband had been adamant about getting married in February.

He'd wanted the first Saturday in February.

I'd pushed until he agreed to make it the last week of the month.

"You have to love the fact that he was that eager to officially make you a Sinclair," Skye said with a sigh.

Riley Sinclair. It might take some time to get used to my new name, but it had a nice ring to it.

"I'm kind of glad he got his way," I confessed. "I'm more than ready to start our life together. Not that we haven't done that already, but it's nice to have it official."

"Are you excited about your honeymoon?" Skye asked.

"Three weeks in Costa Rica? Definitely," I answered with a sigh.

Seth and I would have twenty-one days in Playa Hermosa, a location we could explore together since neither one of us had ever been there before.

"I'm glad all the family could make it," Brooke said earnestly.

"Me, too," I agreed. "Although getting all their names right is a challenge."

Jade grinned. "Having all of us together is a little overwhelming."

I'd been excited to meet Seth's extended family, his half-siblings and cousins from Amesport, Maine. But having that much family *was* a little mind boggling.

My brothers seemed to like all the Sinclairs, so

everybody got along well. My eyes searched the ballroom and finally landed on my three siblings chatting with Evan and Micah Sinclair. "Maybe the circumstances weren't ideal," I told the women. "But you have an amazing family."

"You inherited us," Brooke said with a laugh. "We're *your* family, too, now."

My heart swelled. I couldn't think of anything better than being part of this big, loud, loving family.

"I'm grateful to be part of this family," I shared with all of them.

Not only did I have Seth, but I had an enormous family who would always be there when I needed them.

No conditions.

No rules.

No etiquette to follow.

Seth's family had just welcomed me with open arms.

I wished they knew how rare that experience was, and how special they all were.

"Hey, gorgeous," Seth said huskily into my ear as he came up behind me. "I wondered where you went. I was hoping you weren't going to be my runaway bride."

I turned around and threw my arms around his neck. "Not going to happen, handsome," I said with a laugh.

I'd stepped away to find the restroom and to

take a quick breather. I just hadn't found my way back to him yet.

I should have known that he'd find me.

He always did.

"I think everybody is waiting for us to open up the dance floor," he told me as his arms wrapped around my waist.

"We're going to find our dance partners," Skye informed us as the women walked away in search of their husbands.

"Alone at last," Seth said in a sexy baritone close to my ear.

"We're in a room full of people," I reminded him.

"I haven't seen anyone else but you," he answered.

"Did I tell you that you look breathtakingly handsome today?" I asked.

As usual, Seth was gorgeous in formal wear. But it had been the intensity in his eyes that had captured me inside a beautiful bubble of happiness at the ceremony.

He'd repeated his vows like they truly were a promise to me, and I answered the same way, knowing that neither one of us would ever hurt the other intentionally . . . *as long as we both shall live.*

"You did tell me that," he finally responded. "And as I told you earlier, you captivate me every single time I look at you."

He had told me that more than once. And not just today. Seth reminded me that he thought I was the most beautiful woman on earth each and every day.

"Come dance with me, Riley Sinclair," he said persuasively.

I took his hand, and we walked together to the dance floor amid a round of applause.

I had a fleeting moment of hesitation, a brief second where I was uncomfortable with so much attention in the middle of a fancy ballroom. I had to remind myself that this was an event with family and friends. My wedding day. And it was enchanting.

I didn't have to fear large, fancy events anymore. Not when there was so much love in one very big space.

Every single person in the room was happy for us.

Seth took me into his arms, and I sighed.

Once I looked into his eyes, no one else in the room even existed anymore.

I followed his lead, mesmerized by the look of devotion in his gaze.

"Happy?" he asked.

I nodded. "I've never been happier. You?"

"I'm fucking elated." He grinned. "You're finally officially mine."

Out of the corner of my eye, I saw other couples taking to the floor, so Seth and I weren't in a fishbowl anymore, much to my relief.

I stroked the hair at the nape of his neck. "I've got news for you, handsome. I've always been yours. And you've always been mine."

Today was our wedding day, which was undeniably special, but Seth and I had grown so close during the lead-up to the ceremony that I'd discovered another thing to love about him every single day.

Maybe he'd always be just a little bit possessive and overly protective, but I'd learned that I could be the same way.

I was sure neither one of us would ever let those emotions run rampant until they were out of control, but those instincts would always be there.

He held me closer, and I let my head rest on his shoulder as he growled, "Jesus! I love you so damn much, Riley."

My heart started to race, just like it did every time he said those words. "I love you, too," I said without hesitation.

"I can't wait to get you out of here and out of that dress," he said huskily.

I smiled. "We're the bride and groom. We can't exactly run out of our own reception. Not yet."

"I wouldn't," he admitted. "Maybe I'd like to, but I want to enjoy this day with you, too. I don't want to miss a minute of it. So my dick will just have to wait."

I nodded because I had a huge lump in my throat. "Later," I said, finally getting the word out of my mouth.

Maybe Seth and I did lust after each other, but he was constantly proving to me that we were so much more to each other than just lovers.

We were confidants.

We were best friends.

We were soulmates.

We laughed.

And we loved.

It didn't get much better than that.

"Maybe I'd be willing to let you grope my ass," I contemplated jokingly.

"Still wanting to keep breaking that contract?" he teased as his hand moved down my back.

"Maybe," I said mischievously.

"Even though I appreciate the offer," he said as his hand stopped at my lower back, "I'd rather feel you up when we're alone. I'd prefer not to have an audience, gorgeous."

One more thing to love about him.

Seth never wanted to treat me with anything less than respect in public. He was insatiable in private, but he made damn sure he never embarrassed me when we were out.

I lifted my head. "Then kiss me," I insisted.

He grinned. "I can definitely do that."

I sighed as his lips touched mine, knowing that

my days of feeling completely alone were gone forever.

Seth had filled all of those dark places inside me with light, until my past didn't matter anymore.

He was my present, and my future.

I wound my arms around his neck and kissed him back.

The man I loved grinned at me as he lifted his head, and I smiled back at him, grateful that I had the rest of my life to show him just how happy he made me.

I'd been lost when I'd moved to Citrus Beach, but Seth Sinclair had found me.

For a woman who had never fit in, it was pure bliss to finally know *exactly* where I belonged.

A NOTE ABOUT VICTIMS OF CHILD ABUSE

Every year, over seven million children come to the attention of Child Protective Services. Many other victims of abuse are never reported.

What happens to kids during childhood really does affect their lives as adults. It takes a lot to undo the damage that was done.

I think every adult should be a protector of every child. Please, if you suspect a child is being abused, maltreated, or neglected, report it. You can remain anonymous, and you could change a child's present *and* future.

AUTHOR'S NOTE

Although this is a work of fiction, the plight of least terns is real. The birds have lost most of their natural habitat due to human development in their nesting areas along the California coastline. The least terns were one of the first animals to land on the federal endangered-species list, and they still remain there today. Their numbers recovered somewhat during the first three decades on the list, but they are in decline once again. Warming seawater is driving the anchovies they feed on farther out into the ocean, and their nests are often trampled by beachgoers or dogs who invade their nesting spots on the sand, unaware that the bird nests even exist. It's getting critical to preserve this species before they're gone. To learn more about how the loss of these birds will affect the ecosystem, you can check out the information on least terns on the Audubon California website.

ACKNOWLEDGMENTS

Here we are, already on Book Three of the Accidental Billionaires! This series has gone so quickly for me, maybe because I love this family. I can't wait to write Noah's book!

As always, I'd like to thank my senior editor, Maria Gomez, and the entire team at Montlake Romance for supporting this series.

Many thanks to my own KA team, and my reader group, Jan's Gems, who are always encouraging me on every single title.

Finally, thank you to all of my amazing readers who make it possible for me to continue a career that I absolutely love.

I couldn't do what I do without all of you.

((((Hugs!))))

xxxxxx Jan

ABOUT THE AUTHOR

J.S. "Jan" Scott is the *New York Times* and *USA Today* bestselling author of numerous contemporary and paranormal romances, including The Sinclairs and The Accidental Billionaires series. She's an avid reader of all types of books and literature, but romance has always been her genre of choice—so she writes what she loves to read: stories that are almost always steamy, generally feature an alpha male, and have a happily ever after, because she just can't seem to write them any other way! Jan loves to connect with readers. Visit her website at www.authorjsscott.com.

Books are produced in the United States using U.S.-based materials

Books are printed using a revolutionary new process called THINKtech™ that lowers energy usage by 70% and increases overall quality

Books are durable and flexible because of Smyth-sewing

Paper is sourced using environmentally responsible foresting methods and the paper is acid-free

Center Point Large Print
600 Brooks Road / PO Box 1
Thorndike, ME 04986-0001 USA

(207) 568-3717

US & Canada:
1 800 929-9108
www.centerpointlargeprint.com